ABOUT THE AU

Elizabeth O'Roark spent many years as a medical writer before publishing her first novel in 2013. She holds two bachelor's degrees from the University of Texas, and a master's degree from Notre Dame. She lives in Washington, D.C. with her three children. Join her book group, Elizabeth O'Roark Books, on Facebook for updates, book talk and lots of complaints about her children.

ALSO BY ELIZABETH O'ROARK

THE SUMMER I FIRST SAW YOU

ELIZABETH O'ROARK

PIATKUS

PIATKUS

First published in Great Britain in 2024 by Piatkus

1 3 5 7 9 10 8 6 4 2

A CIP catalogue record for this book
is available from the British Library.

ISBN: 978-0-349-44081-1

Printed and bound in Great Britain by Clays Ltd, Elcograf S.p.A.

Papers used by Piatkus are from well-managed forests
and other responsible sources.

MIX
Paper | Supporting
responsible forestry
FSC® C104740

Piatkus
An imprint of
Little, Brown Book Group
Carmelite House
50 Victoria Embankment
London EC4Y 0DZ

An Hachette UK Company
www.hachette.co.uk

www.littlebrown.co.uk

THE SUMMER I FIRST
SAW YOU

1

DAISY

It was a mistake to come home.

I probably already knew this, but I know it with certainty once my mom pulls out her wedding video. Whenever Bridget Doherty starts in some way fetishizing the glorious start of her marriage, shit always goes downhill. I just arrived in California yesterday—my car's death rattle warning me I'd need another way to get back to DC in August—and it's already clear I came here for nothing.

I keep it all to myself since we've got company. I try, these days, to be subtle in expressing my hatred for Scott, my stepfather. As the video is about to prove, however, I wasn't always this chill.

"Ave Maria" plays as my mother and I—the only bridesmaid—walk down the aisle.

I throw a pillow at my Uncle Liam, who's now laughing. "Fuck off."

"That's *you*?" gasps Emerson, the woman he is clearly sleeping with but who he's introduced as a *colleague*. Her shock makes sense. While *I* am your basic California girl—blonde, blue-eyed, tan—the girl angrily stomping toward the altar is pale and hollow-eyed. She also has hair dyed black and cut short with kitchen scissors, a look crafted the night before the wedding.

I did not pull it off.

"It was a phase," I reply.

Liam snorts. "A long phase."

The video continues and I do my best to ignore it. Scott's up at the altar—smug, self-satisfied, overconfident—saying, *"Bridget, you grow more beautiful to me each day."* That should have been my mom's first red flag right there: when a dude starts your life together by lauding you for your increasing beauty, a feat that would *defy the laws of nature if you pulled it off*, you're already fighting a losing battle.

If I ever get married—highly doubtful—I hope the groom simply says, "Your beauty will wither a little more each day until you are unrecognizable, but even then, I won't go fuck the neighbor's au pair like Scott did."

An awkward thing to address in the middle of the wedding, I realize, but at least it's *achievable*.

I stop watching but am soon clued into my reappearance on the screen by Liam's laughter. That hair of mine is the gift that never stops giving.

We are now at the reception. I stand against a wall, shoulders hunched over to make myself concave. The breasts that seemed to appear overnight and swelled way past anything I'd considered reasonable were the envy of all my friends and the worst thing that had ever happened to me—or so I'd thought.

"There she is," says a voice. It goes down like caramelized sugar, gritty and smooth and sweet all at once. "Goth Wedding Barbie."

Even now, all these years later, butterflies don't take flight in my stomach—they freaking *explode*.

Harrison Reid appears on the screen, and through the living room, there's a collective intake of breath followed by a low, wistful exhale. It's the sound made when multiple women's ovaries go into overdrive simultaneously.

Harrison's been inspiring it for most of my life.

He's in a suit, of course, because it's a wedding, but he somehow makes the suit look like *more*: feral, filthy, expensive, testosterone-laced. His dark hair gleams, that hint of five o'clock shadow roughening up the prettiness of his face just enough.

His smile is a devastating promise of things to come. A smile that says, "*Turn off the camera so I can fuck you into the next century.*"

It's pretty easy to imagine him wanting to leave the camera *on*, too.

"Mmmm. Wouldn't kick him out of bed for eating crackers," says Jackie, my mother's best friend. "And he's single now too, right?"

We all look at Liam expectantly, though I'm not sure why. If we want to know who Harrison drafted in Fantasy Football anytime over the last decade, Liam's got us covered, but he's useless where anything relevant is concerned.

Why did Harrison and Audrey split up? Liam doesn't know. He figures they grew apart.

Is Harrison upset? Liam never asked but assumes not.

"You missed your shot, Jackie," Liam replies. "Harrison's got a girlfriend."

My head whips toward him as if it's been punched in his direction. It figures that when Liam finally has information, it's information I'd rather not have.

"Already?" My voice is unreasonably high. "*Who?*"

Liam shrugs. "Some girl in LA. None of us have met her, but it seems pretty serious. I don't know anything more."

Even if Harrison will never see me as anything but Liam's bratty niece, those words—*it seems pretty serious*—make my stomach drop hard.

"He moved on awfully fast," my mom says. "You're sure he didn't start dating this girl *before* his marriage fell apart?"

Liam rolls his eyes. "Come on, Bridget. Harrison wouldn't do that."

I sigh. Jackie sighs. Even my mother sighs. That's why Harrison's the ultimate man: he saves all that feral, filthy, testosterone-laced perfection for one girl.

A girl who will never be me.

DAISY

One day, you're simply lusting after a guy. Six days later, you're breaking into his home.

To be fair, though, I've been lusting after Harrison for most of my life and waiting *decades* to break into your crush's house is slightly more reasonable. Also, I'm not actually breaking in. I'm just sleeping on his deck while he's out of town, and though this is probably still against the law, I don't think Harrison would mind.

Okay, he might mind, because he'd be horrified by the idea of having such limited resources, horrified by the idea of little *Lazy Daisy* going through life without a trust fund to cushion her through life's semi-homeless moments. I guarantee that his ex has never once been forced to sleep outdoors because she had nowhere else to go, but then again, Audrey does not have a mother like mine, one who claims she's going through a divorce and begs you to return for the summer only to announce five days after you've arrived that the divorce isn't happening and your odious stepfather is on his way home.

What she really said was "*Scott's coming over to talk, and we'll see what happens*" but I know exactly what *we'll see* means, because we've done this dance before. She might as well have put that wedding ring back on her finger. *We'll see* means Scott's moving in, and if my mother's managed to save a penny over the past month, he'll have convinced her to blow it on some stupid shit only *he* benefits from—a golf membership somewhere, a bacon-of-the-month club, an investment opportunity he claims will "pay off big."

We'll see means I gave up everything in DC for nothing and have nowhere to stay until August—a thought that makes my breath come fast and my eyes sting.

A thought that also led to the current break-in plan. It takes about thirty minutes to reach Santa Cruz from Elliott Springs, and another ten minutes to find the eye-popping vacation home Harrison and Audrey bought, which sits high atop a cliff, only separated from the ocean by a quiet two-lane road.

I still don't get why they bought it—Audrey was the sort who'd only enjoy a beach if it came with a butler and cocktails —but I guarantee there's a nice chaise on their deck just made for sleeping, probably with some artfully arranged Hermès blanket that's never been used. And in the morning, when I'm not exhausted and distressed and my world isn't caving in, the day will begin anew. I'll do my morning exercises, borrow his outdoor shower, and go see if Liam's "colleague"-who's-clearly-his-girlfriend is gone so I can crash there. No, that won't fix the utter trainwreck that is my life, but at least it'll occur without me ~~breaking into~~...er...*borrowing* someone's home.

It's late and silent. This makes me feel more criminal than I already did as I climb up the cement steps with one of my two suitcases, sagging with exhaustion, ready to sink into a soft chair.

Except there is no soft chair.

The only seating is modern and uncomfortable, without a single pillow or blanket. And it's ice cold. Sure, there's glass surrounding the deck, but the ocean breeze is still nippy tonight. I'll freeze to death before anyone even gets the chance to arrest me.

"Fuck, Daisy," I say with a sigh as I drop into a chair and press my head into my hands. "What now?" I'm too damn tired to drive back to Liam's even if I was *willing* to ruin his fun, which means I'm sleeping in my car. I hate how much that sounds like something my father would do, but there's no choice unless—

Unless...

I turn to the sliding glass door. I'm certain Harrison would have locked it. He's not the type to make a careless mistake of any kind. But maybe, just maybe—made reckless by lust for the LA girlfriend—he didn't.

I'd prefer he *not* have a girlfriend who makes him reckless with lust, but an unlocked door would be a decent consolation prize.

I rise and place my palm around the handle.

When it slides, I stare in shock, wanting to weep at my good fortune, but I was already about to weep at my *bad* fortune, so the desire is both happy and sad at once.

I grab my bag and hit a light switch as I step inside. The house has an open floor plan—a large living area with a kitchen/dining area at its far end. The décor, however, is as spare and cold as Audrey: hard, uncomfortable furniture that only looks good to people who don't have to use it. Cement floors.

If this room was a person, it would say things like "*I can't imagine flying in coach*" or "*I don't understand people who eat bread*." I've heard Audrey say both.

Before I can think of more ways I hate this room, and also hate Harrison's ex-wife, there's a *clink* somewhere ahead of me —a noise that is distinctly, unnervingly human, and probably attached to the shadow now moving my way with heavy steps.

In true Daisy fashion, I remain frozen solid.

I'm not a dumb girl. Yes, I guess I'm dumb enough to enter a house that's unlocked without questioning *why* it's unlocked, but not so dumb that I don't know I should run for my life.

I just *can't*. My limbs are impossibly heavy. I'm not even sure I can breathe.

"Don't know who the fuck you are," the monster's voice slurs, "but you'd better get the fuck out of my home cuz I'm not in the mood."

Oh, God. It would be just like me to have broken into the wrong house. I manage to take a step toward the door just as the monster emerges into the light.

"Harrison?" I whisper.

I'm not sure why I ask. *Obviously* it's Harrison. No one else is this tall, this broad-shouldered. No one else has that angelic bone structure and the most bitable lips God ever created. Except the square-jawed, endlessly responsible Harrison I remember would *never* sway drunkenly, clad only in boxer shorts, while gripping a fifth of bourbon.

And this one is doing all of the above.

"Who the fuck are you?" he demands, grabbing the back of a chair to stay upright.

My jaw falls. Because no matter how drunk he is and no matter how long it's been since I saw him last, Harrison should still know who I am. "Jesus, Harrison, you've known me since I was a newborn. How much have you had to drink?"

His eyes narrow. "Daisy? Little Lazy Daisy?"

God, I hate that nickname, though I guess it's better than *Goth Wedding Barbie* or the other variants he came up with. "Took you long enough," I sigh, setting my bag down.

His gaze roams from my face down to my T-shirt and shorts before it jerks away. "You grew up."

He says it the way someone else might say *you've got a gun*— as if this fact makes me a danger. He apparently thought I'd be stuck as a pouting teenager forever. "Right. It's a thing that happens to humans over time, Harrison."

Normally this would make him laugh, or smile, or say something funny in response. But I don't even *know* this version of him, the one acting as if my presence is the worst thing that could possibly happen to him.

"Why are you here?" he demands.

I release the death grip I had on my keys and perch on the edge of the sofa. "Why are *you* here?" I counter. When Liam spoke to him this afternoon, Harrison claimed he was already in LA. He was *"clearly preoccupied,"* according to Liam, which forced me to envision Harrison having sex with someone who wasn't me. "You're supposed to be out of town."

Harrison's eyes darken. His scowl grows. "Something came up." He collapses into the leather chair to his left. "I'm not sure why I'm explaining while you're the one here committing a felony."

I set my keys on the coffee table. "I got in a fight with my mom, and Liam's got his new girlfriend over. I thought I could crash on your deck, but the door was open."

"You thought wrong," he says. "You're lucky I wasn't armed."

I laugh quietly. "You're too drunk right now to aim successfully. I think I'd have been okay."

Which is weird. Since when does Harrison get drunk? He's the guy who stays sober just in case the designated driver fails to. He's the guy telling Liam to *take it down a notch*, the guy who says *everyone needs to settle the fuck down* when a fight's about to start.

He remains endlessly in control when no one else is. For him to be drunk at all, much less so drunk he can barely stay upright, means something must have gone dramatically wrong.

I kick off my shoes and sink back into the uncomfortable couch, curling my legs beneath me. "What happened with the girl in LA?"

He's a lawyer and being quick on his feet is one of his greatest skills, yet he freezes at this very simple question. And why did he tell Liam he was already *there*?

"There *is* no girl in LA," I blurt loudly, my surprise echoing against the cement floors.

"What?" he asks. He looks around him, as if he's seeking a way to distract me, which is exactly how a liar would respond. If someone suggests that you've fabricated your *real* girlfriend, you don't look around for help.

It was mostly a guess on my end, but this pretty much confirms it. Honest, ever-responsible Harrison has told everyone that he doesn't care about the end of his marriage and that he's so busy with work and his new girlfriend that he can't make time for them, and some of that is a lie. Maybe even all of it.

"I'm not sure *why* you're lying, but either there was never a girl in LA or there's no *longer* a girl in LA and—I'm spit-balling here, but I assume it's because you were trying to get the guys off your back or didn't want to admit to two failed relationships."

He looks so crushed that I wish I'd kept the theory to myself. I wish I'd pretended it makes perfect sense that he's sitting here drinking in his boxers when he's supposed to be six hours south.

"Congratulations," he says quietly, raising the bottle to his lips. "Now leave."

I ignore him, and it's really not out of self-interest. Yeah, I'm not eager to sleep in my car, but what really worries me is that he is the most wonderful of Liam's friends, and I have no idea who he's become.

He clearly hasn't been eating. He looks like he could use a year of sleep and possibly a stomach pump if I knew how to operate one. It hasn't diminished his loveliness one bit—he

remains a 1950s Cary Grant/Gregory Peck lookalike come to life
—but this just isn't *him*.

"Look, I don't know what's going on, but..." In an unusual
show of self-restraint, I manage to rein in my summation of
how he's fallen apart. "You seem exhausted. Maybe you should
go to bed."

His eyes narrow. "I was on my way to bed when you broke
into my goddamned house."

My gaze veers to the bottle in his hand. If Harrison's now a
guy who'd go to bed with a fifth of bourbon, the situation is
even more dire than I thought.

"Let's get you upstairs," I say, rising.

He pushes to his feet, scowling as he lumbers toward the
tall cement staircase, swaying as he climbs. I follow, calculating
the odds of us both dying if he falls backward. At least I'd go
out with him on top of me. *The second silver lining of the evening.*

He turns toward me when we reach the second floor. I
expect him to reluctantly offer me a room, but instead, his brow
furrows, and there's something in his gaze. A spark of interest—
a passing thought.

Men don't see an aimless twenty-one-year-old when they
look at me. They see curves and an overly wide mouth—
features they associate with blow jobs and porn and whatever
their most graphic fantasies entail—but until this moment,
Harrison did not. He saw me as Lazy Daisy or Bridget's bratty
kid or Liam's rebellious niece, eleven years younger than he is.

But he's not looking at me as if I'm any of those things right
now, and I can taste the impulse in the air. I can already feel the
soft press of that first kiss, the way his weight would settle atop
mine.

He's drunk. It's something he'd never consider sober, and I
know that even if he propositions me, I can't agree. But I've
spent most of my life waiting for Harrison to give me *that* look,

and he finally is, and I wish I could frame this memory and hang it over my bed forever.

I bet, even drunk, Harrison would obliterate every prior experience. He lurches into his room and slams the door behind him before I can consider all the ways he'd go about obliterating them, however.

I stumble into the nearest room and proceed to fall into a surprisingly comfortable bed, still fully dressed. Sure, Harrison made it pretty clear he wanted me to leave, but Sober Harrison would *never* allow me to sleep in my car. Sober Harrison would, in fact, give me a stern lecture about the dangers of sleeping in a car and make me swear I'd never do it again.

But...what the hell happened here? How is it possible that Harrison—suave, confident, accomplished Harrison—is now a guy who wanders through an empty house in his boxers, drinking straight off a fifth of bourbon? And how is it possible that I still find him so attractive anyway?

When I close my eyes, I'm no longer seeing Hot Married Lawyer Harrison. I'm seeing Half-Naked, Unrestrained Harrison in Need of a Shave.

I want the new version just as badly as I want the old one.

That vow of celibacy I just took already feels optimistic.

3

HARRISON

Each day begins in exactly the same way—with a dull throbbing in my head and a blissful ten seconds during which I don't entirely remember what's gone wrong. When I still believe I have my house, my flourishing career, my wife, and the respect of my peers.

And then I realize I've lost most of those things, and the day truly begins.

I wander downstairs for painkillers, bracing myself resentfully for the view I've paid so much money for. The sun is out, but I prefer the days when the weather and my mood are perfectly aligned, when it's storming and I don't have to watch all these assholes biking past, or the couples walking hand-in-hand.

The trucks lining the road won't improve my mood, either. When I bought this place a year ago, I pictured a future in which I'd get up to surf each morning before work. I imagined taking my future children on bike rides along the path, teaching them to catch the more manageable waves down by the wharf. Except Audrey wasn't picturing any of those things when she moved to London a year ago, and now every goddamn one of them is off the table.

But when I turn, expecting cheerful couples and the endless blue of the Pacific, I'm instead staring at a woman's ass in baby blue yoga pants. Bending over like an invitation.

On *my* deck.

I ignore the way my gut tightens at the sight. I don't care how lush an ass it is—this is private property and its owner shouldn't be here. I ignore my pounding head and march toward her, fully prepared to let her have it...just as she rises and turns.

Daisy.

Daisy, Liam's niece, is on my deck. I feel like I should know why. I think maybe I dreamed about her last night, but I sure as hell wouldn't have dreamed of this very adult iteration of her. Because holy *fucking* shit...the curves on this girl. The curve of her pouty little mouth, her cheeks, her tits barely covered by a sports bra, her tiny waist flaring out to her hips.

My body reacts before I can stop it, and her gaze drops.

"Wow, *one* part of you is wide awake," she says with a grin. "And impressive. I'd offer to take care of it, but you smell like a distillery even from here."

Hearing her suggest she'd be willing to *take care of it*, even in jest, should horrify me, but instead I'm about to burst out of my boxers.

I roll my eyes as I place a discreet hand in front of my junk. "Before you get too flattered, let me make it clear that it has nothing to do with you because I didn't know I'd be finding you on my fucking deck, now did I? Why are you here?"

Her mouth falls open. "Harrison, we had a lengthy conversation last night. Are you really saying you don't remember any of it?"

I pinch the bridge of my nose between two fingers and squeeze my eyes shut. Do I remember? There was something about a really hot girl bickering with me. I thought it was a dream.

A car passes on the street below us, and my head throbs in time with the *thump, thump, thump* of the bass. I'm exhausted and I can't think right now. I turn on my heel and go to the kitchen, where I swallow down twice the recommended number of painkillers with a swig of bourbon. She follows, pulling her blonde hair out of her ponytail as she takes a seat at the counter.

I should have told her to stay outside.

I love Daisy—she's practically family—but I want solitude. I want to sleep for the rest of the day. I don't want to have to be polite to anyone. Most of all, I need to keep my current situation to myself.

"Look," she says, "I showed up last night because I fought with my mom and couldn't stay at Liam's, but—"

"I have no idea why I said you could stay," I cut in, "but you need to go."

Her eyes widen and I get that...Even I'm surprised I was so rude, so abrupt. But she really does need to go. And I wish she'd put on a goddamn shirt in the meantime.

Her arms cross. "No, I don't think so."

I press my index fingers to my temples. "Daisy, you're no longer the adorable toddler who can just say *no* to a request and be indulged."

"Right," she says with a smile. "I'm the adorable *adult* who knows you've been lying to your friends for six months about the girlfriend you made up—you admitted it last night."

Fuck. This incredibly bad situation just got infinitely worse. I'm too hungover to even talk my way out of it, but I've got to try. "That's not what I was doing."

"Cool." She picks up her phone and starts to type. "Let me just text Liam and tell him you're around this weekend, despite claiming you were in LA with your fabricated girlfriend. He'd love to see you."

I exhale heavily. If she texts Liam, the next thing you know he'll be descending on me, mad that I lied yet determined to fix this situation in a thousand ways that won't help. It's the last thing I need right now, though his niece is proving to be a close second.

"Stop," I croak. "I wasn't avoiding them, okay? I'm just trying to sort my shit out on my own, without dragging them into it."

She sets the phone down. "Interesting. When *I* have to sort my shit out, I don't normally do it by getting blackout drunk alone and half-naked."

I groan. Today was hardly shaping up to be an ideal Saturday—I just wanted to take some aspirin and sleep off my hangover. I'd had no idea things could get so much worse. "Look, I've had a really long week. I tried to take the edge off and went a little far."

She laughs. "I just watched you wash down painkillers with bourbon. It's ten in the morning."

I start the coffeemaker and turn toward her. "That was to deal with the pain of your presence here, Goth Barbie."

She runs her thumb over the lip of her water bottle. "Harrison, I'm not leaving until I've seen some proof that *this*"—she waves a hand at me—"isn't your normal state."

I'm in hell right now. How am I going to get rid of her? I either admit what's gone wrong to all my friends or spend the next week living with Bridget's indecently hot *child* while proving my life is together.

"What's it going to take, Daisy?" I growl. "I'll write you a check. You're a student, right? Students usually need money."

She takes another long sip of her water, and I look away quickly. This is how the human race survives: no matter how hungover or heartbroken a man is, he can still get an erection from the mere sight of a woman swallowing.

"I don't want your money," she says. There's a flash of hurt in her eyes. "But I would like you to stop being such an asshole. Tell your friends the truth or get ready to do everything I say."

She walks back outside and bends over again. I bury the desire to watch her as deep as it'll go and head upstairs.

What a really inopportune—and deeply *inappropriate*—time for my libido to make a reappearance.

I changed her fucking diapers.

4

DAISY

Harrison's door is still shut the next morning. There was no sign of him again after our conversation yesterday. Is he eating? Is he drinking alone under a bridge? I don't know, and it's a situation far beyond my pay grade. I've set myself up to be the heroine of this story—the little Mary Poppins who saves the day with a spoonful of sugar and a couple quotes about resilience—when I need saving most of all.

I put on leggings and a sports bra and go downstairs to the deck. The air is crisp, the ocean coated in a thin glaze of sunlight, and the road is lined with guys climbing out of cars and pickups in wetsuits.

There must be a surf break across the street. A *good* surf break. You don't buy a board like the Vissla currently being unloaded if you're just fucking around.

Liam says Harrison never surfs anymore, but I still understand why he wanted this house. The ocean makes you feel a little more alive just by being *near* it.

Which reminds me why I came down here in the first place. I turn away and begin my morning routine, the thing that has kept me sane of late. Once I've stretched, I follow the same sequence of burpees and lunges and squats and pushups and planks I've completed every morning without fail for weeks, a sequence I find strangely comforting. When I start to spiral, I cling to the thought that no matter how bad I feel, no matter how dire the future appears, in the morning I'll be moving through this same routine, and that life might not be better by then but it probably can't get worse.

Not until August, anyway.

In August, it could definitely get worse.

When I'm done, I collapse in one of Harrison's uncomfortable chairs, hoping he might appear in boxers again, because that erection of his was a visual delight.

His attempt to block it from view was ridiculous...and required two hands.

A guy across the street starts the laborious process of pulling on a wetsuit. And as much as I hated getting into and out of a wetsuit...I miss it. I miss the elation of surfing, the exhaustion. I miss wanting something, *anything*, as much as I used to want that. I've slowly shut out *all* the things that make me happy over the past few years, but that's the one I miss most.

Harrison used to love to surf too—I can still remember him as a sunburned teenager, attempting to surf backward—but the boards I saw leaning against his garage wall yesterday when I carried my wetsuit inside had cobwebs on it. I bet he's never gone out here once.

He and I are in different places in our lives—wealthy lawyer with oceanfront mansion versus homeless, blackmailing drifter —but we're on the same trajectory: a steep downward spiral, with our best selves behind us.

And in order to reverse his trajectory, maybe I've got to reverse my own first.

I probably shouldn't try to resume surfing *here*, but

suddenly I want this too much to tell myself *no*. I move fast before I can chicken out—a bikini from my room, followed by the wetsuit I left hanging in the garage—fighting a nervous pulse of excitement the entire way.

It's like riding a bike, right? A bike you ride at high speed toward the face of a cliff, sure, but it will come back to me. At least I hope it will come back to me. I'd prefer not to discover the analogy is false while in the middle of the ocean.

I borrow one of Harrison's many surfboards and wax it quickly, ignoring a queasy hit of fear, and then I swallow hard and cross the street, wincing at the pavement under my bare feet. I have city girl feet now. I wonder if I also have a city girl's ability to gauge the surf, to pop up, to carve.

I wonder if I'm going to plow straight into the face of a cliff because any one of those things, or all of them, is true.

A sign at the top of the stairs says, "Welcome to Horseshoe Point. Proceed at your own risk."

I hiss quietly under my breath, not at the warning, but because I recognize the name.

I've heard of this place. People refer to *the Horseshoe* in the same hushed tones reserved for Mavericks. Based on the cliff, I assume the break is much like Steamer Lane—one where you've got to pop up fast and angle to the side immediately to avoid smashing into the rocks. Technical, challenging surfing. Incredible when it works out and fatal when it doesn't.

I have no business surfing here after so long out of the water, but if I back out now, I'll keep backing out. When's the next time I'll be in a house thirty yards from a fucking surf break?

I descend the steep staircase and wrap my leash tight around my ankle at the bottom. It's best to jump in just as the tide starts to go back out—that way the water's doing some of the work for you. But the water sweeps in and recedes, and I stay in place with my heart in my throat.

I look like an idiot, standing here, not jumping, as one wave after another sloshes against the stairs. I'm not sure if my fear is about surfing or something bigger, but I know that I'm really fucking tired of feeling scared.

Another wave comes in, and this time I jump. The water is ice cold, of course, but it's not the kind of thing you dwell on when you're at risk of smashing into the rocks. I scramble atop my board and begin to paddle. I don't have the arm and shoulder strength I once did, but I fall into a rhythm, turtle rolling beneath the incoming wave without even thinking and then continuing on.

I really hope the rest of it comes back to me too.

I reach the break, ignoring the guys down at the good end of the wave. I'm sure I'm a curiosity—the lone female, one who doesn't appear to know what she's doing.

A small wave approaches and I have to *force* myself to turn my board toward the shore for the first time in years and start to paddle. When I don't catch it in time, it's more out of fear than lack of skill.

I close my eyes, wishing Harrison was here. When I was a kid and the terror inside me was visible, Liam used to say, "*Shit or get off the pot,*" which usually had the wrong effect. Harrison was kinder. "*Just push up, Daisy,*" he'd say with quiet certainty. "*The rest will take care of itself.*"

And he was always right. Surfing isn't complex—it's a sequence, and you only need the courage to let that sequence begin. You push up your chest, and your body takes over.

Two of the guys are getting ready for the next wave and I do the same, maneuvering myself to face the shore, paddling slow, then hard.

Just push up, Daisy.

With my heart hammering, I push up my chest, planting my back foot while I swing my left leg forward and...I'm on my feet.

The water beneath the board vibrates like a freight train,

and that old joy hits me square in the chest, a sort of euphoria I've experienced nowhere else.

I don't have to carve to avoid the cliff but I do it anyway, simply for the rush. It's as effortless as it ever was, and when I finally dive off the side of the board, I'm smiling for the first time in weeks.

Today, the water just handed a small piece of me back.

5

HARRISON

It's not a great sign that my first thought when I wake is "*I need a drink*." And today is worse. Now I've got Daisy here, a disturbingly *adult* version of Daisy who is all curves and pouty lips, bending over on my deck just in case I'd missed the fact that she has the most perfect ass God ever created.

I've got to get rid of her. The obvious solution, of course, is just to come clean to my friends, but that would mean admitting that I've been blatantly lying to them for months, and dealing with their less-than-helpful reactions—pity from Caleb and Beck; Liam pushing me to *get back on the horse*. All I want in the entire world is to be left alone, and if I came clean, I'd be guaranteeing the opposite for weeks or months to come.

I throw on sweatpants and a T-shirt. I resent that I'm forced to wear clothes in my own goddamned house—the one good thing about my divorce was the solitude, that I could wander around in boxers without an acerbic comment from Audrey—but I don't need a repeat of yesterday's erection incident.

To my vast relief, she doesn't appear to be around when I get downstairs. I make a cup of coffee, add a splash of bourbon to it, and slump into a chair on the deck as I stare blankly at the view.

Across the street, one of those fucking surfers emerges from the staircase with his insanely hot girlfriend behind him—long blonde hair dripping down her back, hourglass figure barely encased by a wetsuit. Not looking at women other than my wife once came easily. After she stopped sleeping with me it got harder, and I guess there's no reason to feel guilty about it now. I guess it's perfectly fine that I'm checking out this lucky prick's girlfriend as if my life depends on it.

He goes to a truck parked twenty yards from the staircase while she leans her board against the railing and unzips her wetsuit, leaving it hanging off her waist. The bikini she's got on is barely up to the job of covering her lush curves. There's an awful lot of smooth, tan skin on display.

And nipples. She's shivering in her bikini, and I can make out those tight nipples from here. I take a swig of my coffee as if it's bourbon and scald my tongue. *Jesus Christ. It's been a really long time.* My envy of this guy has grown exponentially in seconds.

But when she picks up her board, she doesn't walk to him. Instead, she crosses the street, and something sinks in my stomach. Because she's in my driveway now and...

Oh, shit. The girl in question is *Daisy*.

Daisy, the toddler who used to follow us around. The kid in pigtails we taught to surf. The teenage brat doing her best to ruin her mom's wedding.

She's been gone for years, but in my head there was always a wall there, a wall that meant *no matter how old she gets, you will never look at this kid the way you'd look at grown women.*

I've now looked at her that way *twice.* And if she sticks around, it'll undoubtedly happen again.

She disappears beneath the house, and a few minutes later she comes out to the deck with a towel around her waist and another around her shoulders, radiating the sort of contentment I haven't felt in ages.

I remember it, though—that ecstatic exhaustion after a few hours of surfing, your skin tight from the saltwater, warming in the sun as you mentally relive your best ride. For a half second, I hunger for it. That feeling. My lost youth. I want it all back.

"You should have been out there," she says, throwing her wetsuit over the rail.

"You *shouldn't* have been out there," I growl. "Especially not alone."

She rolls her eyes. "A, I'm twenty-one, not twelve, and"—she gestures to the trucks lining the road—"B, I obviously wasn't alone. There were a bunch of guys down there."

I don't like that either. The Horseshoe is too dangerous for her, and so are the guys who surf it. I'm responsible for Daisy if she's in my home. I don't need her taking off with some douchebag whose slight heroin habit she'll only discover after she's trapped in his unmarked van.

One more reason to get her out of here as soon as possible, though not the most important one. "So, how long are you planning to stay anyway?" I ask.

She looks over at me. "How long are you planning to put bourbon in your coffee?"

"As long as I please," I reply, "because I'm thirty-two, this is my fucking house, and I'm off work."

"Well, that sounds entirely healthy. Clearly, my work here is done."

This entire situation is rich. I could fill a piece of college-ruled paper listing the various ways Daisy's not been *healthy* over the last decade, and I'd only be hitting the high points. "Daisy, you stole a golf cart and crashed it into a ravine because your mom wasn't paying enough attention to you, and you nearly burned down her house a month later. Do you really think I'd be inclined to take *your* advice?"

Her tongue sweeps over her upper lip. "Wow, is that the best you can do? Reproaching me for things that happened when I was *fourteen*? Even Mother Teresa was crashing golf carts when she was fourteen."

If I wasn't hungover, I'd probably laugh. Instead, the pounding in my head worsens. "Look, you can stay for a few days until this thing with your mom blows over. But I'm going to do exactly what I fucking want to, and you're going to stay out of the ocean and also out of my hair as much as possible until that happens."

"You seem to be forgetting something," she says with a saccharine smile. "I've got you by the balls."

"Excuse me?"

She picks up her phone and pretends to dial a number. "Hey, Liam? Yeah, I'm with Harrison, and I'm super worried. He's not eating, he's drunk all the time, and he's been lying to you guys about this supposed girlfriend in LA. Get everyone down here, and tell Audrey too."

My eyes narrow. She's hit upon the *ultimate* last thing I want: Audrey learning I'm here in a cocoon of self-pity. Audrey feeling vindicated by the way she's come out on top while I'm barely surviving.

"I already said you could stay," I bark. "What more do you want?"

Her smile grows delighted, in a deeply evil sort of way. "I'm still figuring that out. All I know is it's going to be super fun. Get all the drinking out of your system because you're cut off after today."

My head jerks toward her. "What?"

"You heard me. Drink all the booze you've got. But I want the old, sober Harrison back tomorrow, ready to do my bidding."

The towel has slipped off her shoulders. I get a flash of

ample cleavage just as she says the words *ready to do my bidding* in that husky voice of hers.

Fuck my life.

"You can never tell Liam you stayed with me," I say.

Her eyes roll. "Well, I thought that was obvious. I mean, I couldn't explain how I blackmailed you without ruining everything."

"Yeah, I just—" I search for a way to say this delicately. "If it came out, it would look really bad."

Because everyone would think we were sleeping together. And now her gaze is meeting mine, and we're both thinking about it too, simultaneously. *Fuck.*

"Everyone would think you were the luckiest man in the world," she says.

Yeah, probably. I'm not touching that one. "Your uncle wouldn't. Neither would your mom."

Her mouth curves into a smile. Maybe she's noticed that I didn't actually deny what she said, but how the fuck could I? I mean, look at her—

Stop, Harrison.

For the love of God, stop looking at her and stop thinking about how she's changed.

I will walk away—as soon as I'm able. And then I'm going to avoid her until I've figured out how to get her the fuck out of my home.

6

DAISY

My muscles hurt. My ligaments hurt. I'm pretty sure even my blood hurts. I'd forgotten that surfing is the kind of sport you're supposed to work up to. I'd forgotten that it's been four years since paddling as if my life depended on it and popping up were daily occurrences. But it's a good kind of pain—the kind that reminds me I'm alive instead of making me wish I wasn't. That other pain is still inside me, not entirely healed, and I resent that it's there. My ex doesn't deserve to be something that continues to hurt me now.

Once upon a time, I was this pitcher of joy, a pitcher men drank from in small sips and long gulps. But Christian...he emptied it. He emptied it and then smashed that pitcher to make sure it couldn't hold anything again.

I attempt to rise from bed and groan. "Harrison," I call, "my blood hurts."

I'm met with silence, which I mostly expected. He's gone by the time I get downstairs. Only a coffee cup in the sink indicates he's even been here since we spoke yesterday.

I shuffle toward the deck and proceed through my exercises. The push-ups are excruciating and when I jump up after each burpee, I barely get an inch of air, but they must be done. Without this, who knows what I'll give up next? Maybe I'll stop getting out of bed again, maybe I'll stop showering, maybe I'll spin a web of lies about my life every time my mother calls— though I suppose I'm already doing the last bit. I lied to her all year, and now I'm going to have to juggle those lies while I throw in a few more.

When I'm done with the exercises, I wander into the kitchen and grab one of the protein bars I brought with me. Did Harrison even eat? There's no food in the house, and in the two days I've been here, I haven't seen him consume a single thing but coffee and bourbon.

Most women wouldn't complain. This diet of booze and irritation he's on has starved him down to *Versace underwear model* hot, but I prefer the more substantial version of him, the one I used to imagine pinning me to a bed, immobilizing me with his weight. Of course, he's still well over six feet, so he could immobilize me now easily too.

I imagine it wouldn't even be an effort for him.

I google the nearest store and walk there, continuing to imagine it.

I don't know how Audrey possibly could have given him up. Did she somehow forget that she'd married the hottest man who ever breathed air, that she didn't *have* to move to London? Hell, she didn't even need to *work*. She could have just surfed and sat in the hot tub reading books all day, waiting for Harrison to come home and fuck her senseless, which is what I'd have done.

I imagine Harrison fucking me senseless for the second half of my walk and arrive at The Hillside Market having imagined only two of the four positions through which he would accomplish this. I should have chosen a store farther from his house, and only partly so I could have continued fantasizing.

My first clue that The Hillside Market is way out of my

price range is the display of local honey right inside the door—rich people don't mind paying three times the cost for artisanal honey because it makes them feel virtuous, supporting a local business. They don't mind the risk of getting salmonella from this locally grown and perhaps unvetted beekeeper because even getting salmonella is easier for the rich—they can afford two weeks off work with a bout of food poisoning. Their doctors will go the extra mile to make sure they don't die, the same doctors who'd send the rest of us off with some ibuprofen and a warning about making better food choices.

I walk through the aisles, unsurprised to find that it's every bit as ridiculous as I'd expected. No middle-class breadcrumbs for this set—you've got to buy panko in a tiny box that costs thirteen bucks.

I bet Audrey shopped here, though I doubt it was ever in order to make a meal for Harrison. She bought herself kombucha and fish oil harvested from baby salmon in the Arctic, and walked right back out, panicked she might have accidentally inhaled calories when she cut through the bakery. Later, she'd come back and buy a few jars of that locally grown honey and give it to friends, secure in the knowledge that even after a long bout with salmonella, none of those friends would be quite as thin as she was.

Maybe I'm being unfair. Everyone but me believed they were the perfect couple, and I guess on paper they were. They were both gorgeous and smart and possessed that mysterious reserve that says *I was raised with loads of money and you were not.*

But to me, Harrison's reserve has always screamed of repressed sexual hunger while Audrey's screamed, *"I wonder if the waitress washed her hands"* and *"My wine was not served at the correct temperature."*

Regardless, Audrey would definitely be better at shopping

here, at coming up with the ingredients for a rich person dinner than I am. I'm not even sure what that would be—beluga caviar, perhaps? Even if I could afford it, I'd have no clue how it was served—on a Triscuit? In a ramekin, eaten with a tiny cocaine spoon?

It's the kind of question that would have made Christian laugh when we'd first started dating but would have exasperated him toward the end.

It's funny, the way a girl's naivete is no longer hot once you've fucked her behind your girlfriend's back enough times.

HARRISON GETS HOME late and blinks at me in surprise, as if he'd forgotten I was even here, tugging at his tie as he throws his keys on the counter.

Why do I find it so hot, the way he pulls at his tie? Why is it an aphrodisiac for me that it only takes him a matter of hours to acquire the scruffy jawline of a lumberjack?

"I made dinner," I announce. "And before you suggest that offering you lukewarm chicken parm isn't really a quid pro quo for staying in your palace for free, allow me to counter that as I'm blackmailing you, I didn't technically *have* to cook anything."

His mouth turns up at the corner, but he successfully fights it back down. "Thanks."

He fills a glass with ice and pours bourbon to the top before taking a long sip. There's something erotic about the relief on his face. Maybe it's just that I see something erotic in everything he does. I could probably get off to a film of him clipping his nails.

He sets the glass down and rolls up his shirtsleeves before he reaches into the fridge for the chicken. He has such nice forearms—broad, but not too broad. All tendon-y and lightly dusted with dark hair. Long fingers. *How are you so perfect, Harrison? Couldn't you have one flaw, aside from your apparent alcoholism?*

"Since you're still here," he says as he places the chicken in the microwave, "I assume that means you and your mother haven't made up. So what's it about *this* time?"

It annoys me, the way he says *this time*, as if he's already certain it's my fault. As if he's already taken my mother's side.

"If I tell you, are you just going to give me some big fucking lecture about how much she sacrificed on my behalf?"

"I don't know. That depends on what the fight was about. She *did* sacrifice a lot on your behalf." Harrison's mom abandoned him when he was four to return to France, leaving him with a workaholic dad who was never around. I can see why he'd think what my mother did was extraordinary, but I've been reminded at least once a week since I was born that every bad thing that's happened to my mom can be traced back to the decisions she made at age seventeen, and I'm over it.

"Do you know how tiresome it gets being reminded that your mom didn't plan to have you and could easily have chosen not to?" I demand. "And I'm not sure why people think it's a valid point to make...*Anyone's* mother could have chosen not to have them. Choosing to have a kid when it's inconvenient isn't some get-out-of-jail-free card. It doesn't mean you don't get held accountable for *anything*."

Harrison pulls the chicken from the microwave, laughing to himself. "I find it suspicious that you're having such a hard time admitting what the fight was about."

I stare at the counter, at my hand pressed flat to its surface. No one will ever entirely understand my beef with Scott. They simply think I was a petulant teen who wanted her mom to herself, and I've allowed them to think it for my mother's sake and my own.

"My mom kicked Scott out two weeks ago and *begged* me to come home for moral support. I gave up my job and sublet my room for less than what I'm paying in rent, and drove my piece-of-shit car across the country—and not one week in, not a single week in, she's already let him come home."

Harrison glances up at me from his plate, his gaze more serious than it was a moment prior. There's a glimmer of the old Harrison there—worried, responsible, determined to fix things. "I'm sorry, Daisy. But your mom loves you, and you've been gone for years. Even if Scott annoys you, can't you just suck it up when he's around and give your mom the summer she wants?"

If I had a dollar for every time someone told me to *suck it up* while understanding absolutely nothing about my situation, I'd be nearly as wealthy as Harrison.

I hop off the stool and walk to the refrigerator. "I'm not sure why I'd go to that much trouble when I've got this amazing house at my disposal."

"My house *isn't* at your disposal," he growls.

"You clearly need me," I reply, filling my water bottle. "There was nothing in here but orange juice and some Chinese food. You're going to get sick if you keep ordering in for every meal."

"I've been eating like this for a decade without issue, and given that I used to have to tell you not to eat *sand*, it's hard to take any nutritional advice you offer me seriously."

I ignore the way he's throwing my childhood in my face so I can focus on the more interesting issue. Because even though he and Audrey had been unhappy for a while, I did picture them as the type of lame couple who'd stay in making boring but complicated meals, which they'd then eat by candlelight while discussing their stock portfolio.

"You and Audrey didn't cook?" I ask.

He glances up, and his dark eyes empty as he closes himself

off to me. He grabs the bourbon and his plate. "Thanks for dinner." He walks upstairs without another word.

Which is a pretty severe reaction when their split was theoretically mutual.

Harrison lied about the girlfriend in LA.

Maybe he lied about other things too.

7

HARRISON

I wake, hoping to escape running into Daisy if at all possible.

And then I arrive downstairs to discover her naked on my balcony. "I do not need this shit," I mutter to myself, and even after she stands up and I realize she's not nude—she simply appears to be, thanks to taupe leggings and a matching bra—I remain pissed off.

I bet every goddamn surfer outside is doing a double take and then a third. I'm surprised car crashes haven't occurred, bikers haven't collided, small aircraft haven't fallen from the sky. Seriously...it's just a matter of time.

She walks in before I can demand it of her, thank God. "Good morning, sunshine," she sings, taking a seat at the counter. Apparently, she's cold quite often. I can once again see her nipples clear as day.

I grunt something unintelligible in response, trying not to look at her as I make my coffee. "Start wearing more clothes when you're doing yoga. I don't need people asking questions about the naked woman on my balcony."

She rolls her eyes. "First of all, I'm not naked. Secondly, I'm not doing yoga. Third, if the neighbors *did* notice they'd obviously think this was some kind of monetary situation, and I sort of like being thought of as a sugar baby."

I set my mug down on the counter slightly too hard. I'm irritated and also...something else I don't want to put words to. There shouldn't be this stirring in my gut when she suggests whatever's going on here is sexual. "This might come as a surprise, Daisy, but I don't want to be thought of as a man who has to *pay* for female companionship, especially from someone who's barely legal."

She laughs. "I was kidding, obviously. No one is going to think *you'd* need to pay for it. You could get laid ten ways from Sunday anytime you wanted with anyone you wanted." She starts walking toward the stairs. "But I'm not interested in wearing more clothes, so learn to live with it."

I can't even come up with a response.

Mostly because I'm still stuck on her saying I could get laid by *anyone* I want.

Jesus fucking Christ. I absolutely have to get her out of my home.

WORK HAS BEEN awkward since I returned. Daisy's presence in my life makes it the closest thing I've got to a comfort zone, but it's still uncomfortable as fuck.

Six months ago, I was the golden boy—the youngest partner and the top-earning one—and then I put half of our stuff in storage and shipped the rest overseas, sold our house, and quit my job, all to save a failing marriage. The office threw me a London-themed goodbye party, complete with tea cakes and tiny flags, and off I flew, halfway across the world.

Daisy's carping about a few drinks when she has no clue how hard it was to get where I am now. To return to my old firm with my tail between my legs admitting I'd failed, after I'd already handed off every client to someone else. It doesn't matter what excuse I gave about why I'm back: all anyone can see is that I fucked up. It's all I can see too.

I know she means well—even as a little kid, Daisy had a big heart. She'd weep over the three-legged dog that came to the beach. She'd hand her lunch to the first homeless guy she saw at the wharf. But the one thing she can do to improve my situation is to leave me alone, and I can't keep waiting for her to realize it.

> I've been giving it some thought, and while I appreciate what you're trying to do, I also really value my privacy. You need to go back to your mom's house. Things with Scott will work out.

DAISY

> Hmmm…let me think.

> Okay, I've thought. And I'm staying.

> If you need a place to stay, I'll help you find something. I'll even pay for it.

> Will it be an oceanfront home looking over the Horseshoe? Because I'm kind of liking it right where I am.

> Look, I work from home in the evening, and that information is privileged. I can't make calls if you're there listening. You need to leave.

> I'll go on the balcony while you make your calls *if* you're actually making calls, which I doubt.

> My calls can take hours. You're not going to want to sit out there for hours.

> Sure I will. Wearing my most revealing
> clothing. If the neighbors ask why I'm there, I'll
> tell them you make me stand outside when
> I've been a bad, bad girl. They'll understand.

And there it is, once again—my muscles tensing, a thrill up my spine, all the blood in my body flowing south, exactly where I don't want it, over someone it shouldn't flow *for* at all.

I snarl as I shut down my phone and return to working on behalf of the handful of clients I've gotten back since I returned to the office. The work is dull, but then again...it was always dull. The most exciting client I've got at present is a guy who wants his neighbor's tree house torn down. And it's still preferable to dealing with Daisy, but eventually, I've got to go home.

She's curled up on the couch under a blanket, watching TV, but pauses her show when I walk in. "You're home late," she says.

I look at my watch. "It's only *nine*."

"You left at seven-thirty, Harrison. You can't possibly think that's a reasonable number of hours to work."

I throw my keys on the counter. "I can see where that might seem excessive to someone currently working *zero* hours." I grab a glass and uncap the bourbon, which she watches with a brow raised.

I exhale wearily. "Don't start. You yourself pointed out what a long day I had. I need this to decompress, or I'll never fall asleep."

I take a long sip, relishing the heat as it flows through my chest. Already I'm better, more level.

"Some people would argue that if you need to slam bourbon at nine at night to decompress, there are other things about your life that need changing."

My tongue prods my cheek. "Some people would argue that no twenty-one-year-old should be as uptight and judgmental as you are. How has some lucky guy not locked you down yet?"

She turns away, but not before something flashes across her face. I can't begin to imagine why that hurt her. She isn't even old enough to be locked down.

I take another long sip. "It was a joke, Daisy."

"I know," she replies, but she's more subdued than she was before.

Guilt squeezes my chest, and again—this is bullshit. I don't need to feel excessive guilt about an innocuous statement made to the woman who's *blackmailing* me.

"Did you eat?" she asks. "There's chicken tikka in the fridge. Doesn't that make you glad I'm staying here?"

I sigh. Jesus Christ...why won't she let this go? "No. And I need you out of here by tomorrow."

"I need a million dollars and a breast reduction," she replies. "And those aren't likely to happen either."

I flinch, wishing I'd never even noticed she has breasts, but since I have...why the fuck would she want a reduction? Her breasts are a gift from God, a gift millions of women would pay good money for, and it would be a tragedy to—

Stop, Harrison. Stop thinking about her breasts, in any capacity.

I get the chicken out of the fridge, and a minute later, when I've pulled it from the microwave and the whole kitchen is redolent with the smell of tomatoes and garam masala, I'm suddenly famished. I unknot my tie, roll up my shirtsleeves, and groan as I take my first bite.

"Thanks," I grunt as she walks over to the counter. "But you don't *have* to cook, you know."

She bites down on a smile. "I thought it would help convince you not to make me sit on the balcony for hours while you take your work calls."

"You're fully dressed, for once, so apparently I wasn't the only one bluffing."

She rises, pulling her sweatshirt off and standing in front of me in nothing but leggings and a bra—blue again. "Not bluffing at all."

She sashays outside, her hips swaying, and leans suggestively over the railing of the deck as she calls to someone out on the street.

I grab my phone, the chicken, and my bourbon, and walk quickly to my room. I swear to God that I will not think about her bent over in those pants. I definitely won't think about those pants pulled down to her knees.

But if it did happen, it would be nothing I could stand to admit, even to myself.

8

DAISY

I never wanted to major in English. My mother insisted it was a good degree to get before applying to law school, and though I'd never necessarily wanted to go to law school either, she'd been talking about it for so long it was hard for me to even imagine what I'd do in its place.

I walked into Dr. Cooper's creative writing class the first day of the term with my stomach in knots, knots that tightened when I realized there were only twelve desks in the room, arranged in a circle—and that my ex-boyfriend was already in one of them, fresh off a summer in Greece with the model he dumped me for.

I'd spent an entire summer tortured by our breakup. Tortured by the way he'd said he was looking for "more," and the way I'd secretly agreed when he'd said I was too aimless and unambitious. And now I was going to spend an entire semester across from him, failing at this, too, proving he'd made the right decision.

Dr. Cooper entered the room without looking at any of us, as dickish as I'd expect of a guy who'd just had a book optioned by HBO. Already, I foresaw an entire semester of him scoffing at my writing in front of the others, confirming every ugly thought my boyfriend ever had about me.

"Give me a paragraph or two about a favorite childhood memory," he announced without preamble. "You've got five minutes beginning now."

There was a moment of panic as we scrambled to open our laptops and start typing. The pressure to create something fast made the task nearly impossible—pressure that got worse when I discovered he was reading over our shoulders as we typed.

I managed only five lines—about the elation of catching my first wave without needing Liam to push me—before he called time and asked for volunteers.

My ex went first. He'd written about walking on stage when his dad won his first senate race, and the reminder chafed. No wonder he'd wanted more. His dad was a fucking senator and his mom was a lobbyist, while my mom was a receptionist and my dad was homeless, living somewhere on the streets of San Francisco.

The next student described sailing through the British Virgin Islands. A third volunteer wrote about getting a pony for Christmas. I sank lower and lower in my seat as the hour came to a close.

"What's interesting," said Dr. Cooper just before he dismissed us, "is that the very best writers are the ones who weren't certain enough of their work to read it aloud." And then he turned to me. "Be a little braver next time, Miss Doherty. Yours was the only one that deserved to be heard."

God, I'd been so shocked. So thrilled. And when I glanced at my ex, something had changed in his expression. It was as if there was something more to me and he'd missed it, which was exactly what I wanted—to be *enough* to someone.

I wanted it so badly I'd have believed anything. And I did.

In that moment, I really believed it was possible there was more to me.

The problem with amazing moments like that one is that they're simply waves. A temporary high. You forget that the bigger and better a wave is, the harder it will eventually crash. The wave I took last fall...it crashed harder than most. Nine months have passed, and I'm still trying to take a full breath.

I push myself out of bed. The first hints of the sunrise are appearing over the horizon, lighting up the sky in swaths of gray and violet. Soon the sun will be a bright orange haze across the water, and I want to be out there when it happens. I want it to erase the memory of school, of all my failures.

I pass Harrison's closed door and keep walking to the garage.

I give the board a quick wax and cross the street, fighting the same nerves that hit me over the weekend. I dread the cold water. I dread the possibility of getting hurt. But what mostly scares me is how much I have riding on this.

I came back Sunday, exuberant and hopeful for the first time in ages. What if that doesn't happen today? I got a piece of myself back, but it was a shard. A sliver. There are so many more pieces to go. I'm scared the men in my past have managed to keep the rest for themselves.

I reach the bottom of the stairs, secure my leash, and jump without hesitation this time, paddling to the lineup, ignoring the guys on the better end of the break.

I take one conservative wave after another, noting the errors I make occasionally and the errors I make consistently. What I love about surfing is that you know what you've done wrong and can fix your mistakes, as opposed to real life, where you think everything's fine until you find yourself dumped unceremoniously by the boyfriend who won't tell you why.

Except if I'm ever going to get to the point where I can surf directly in front of the cliff face, I need to be less conservative, and a monster wave is forming, one that will peak closer to me than it will the rest of the guys in the lineup. But that voice in my head says, *I'm not ready yet.*

Maybe that voice is wise. Maybe that voice understands my limitations. Or maybe I've just spent so much time letting men tell me I'm worthless that I no longer know what I am or what I can do.

"Fuck it," I whisper, and I start paddling hard. The power of the wave under my board is unnerving and thrilling at once. *It was a bad idea, and I'm not ready and—*

"*Just push up, Daisy,*" Harrison says in my head. "*The rest will take care of itself.*"

And so I do. I push up and let nature take over...back foot, front foot, ass tucked in, arms forward, eyes on the horizon.

Back in the lineup, someone cheers.

The sun is on my face, the breeze is blowing, and the water has washed me clean. All the shit I woke up thinking no longer matters.

"Fuck you, Christian!" I shout.

I've said *fuck you* to him often since last winter, but this is the first time I've said it *triumphantly.* He's three thousand miles away, but I hope some part of him felt that.

I'm grinning as I dive off my board and paddle in, weak-legged with exhaustion as I finally climb from the water, pulling my board with me.

"You're good," shouts a guy coming in behind me. "I didn't expect it."

I scoot out of his way. "I'm not sure if I'm flattered or insulted."

He laughs, shaking his hair from his face as he rips off his leash. "Definitely be flattered. We don't get a lot of girls out here and you're new—that's all I meant. You're staying with the rich guy, right? Big house across the street?"

I bristle. I know what I look like, but I resent that it's the only thing men see in me, and though I suggested to Harrison that I didn't mind people thinking I was an escort or a sugar baby, I do care a little.

"He's, like, my uncle," I say, my voice more defensive than it should be.

He raises a brow. I guess saying Harrison's, *like,* my uncle doesn't sound all that much better than saying he's, *like,* paying me to blow him every night.

"No, seriously. He's one of my uncle's best friends. It's not like that."

We walk up the stairs together. "A bunch of us go down to this bar near Pleasure Point if you want to meet up," he says. "I mean...if you're free, and it wouldn't piss off your *uncle's friend* or whatever."

I laugh over my shoulder at him as I reach the sidewalk. "I swear I'm not a prostitute and he's not some jealous boyfriend—"

But the words fall away when I look across the street. Harrison is in the driveway, glaring at me.

"What the fuck are you doing?" he demands.

He sure as hell sounds like a jealous boyfriend.

9

HARRISON

I woke hoping Daisy was still asleep, so I could sneak out of the house without seeing her. And sure, I wanted to avoid some ridiculous harassment about my work schedule or my drinking or whatever bullshit a twenty-one-year-old freeloader who's blackmailing me deems *problematic*, but mostly, I didn't want to face her after the dream I had last night, a dream which began with her doing yoga on the deck and ended with her naked on all fours, swearing no one could see us because my balcony was made of bulletproof glass.

My balcony is not made of bulletproof glass and I doubt it would help much with transparency even if it was, but you can't control what your subconscious comes up with. And you shouldn't have to feel guilty about a dream you couldn't have controlled in the first place...but you probably should feel guilty about what you did once you woke up from it.

I was so hard that it hurt when I reached into my boxers. Three hard tugs and I was spilling over my hand, with her name hissed from my lips.

It was an intense relief, under the circumstances, not to find her downstairs, bent in half on my deck. I was safe from another uncomfortable interaction, safe from the guilt of seeing her blinking up at me all blue-eyed and flushed and innocent, knowing how very *un-innocent* she'd looked in my head a few hours before, begging me to fuck her harder.

Even if I resented having to flee my own home to get away from her, I was grateful it was even an option. Gratitude that ended the moment I realized one of the goddamn surfboards was no longer leaning against the wall.

After I'd asked so very little of her, she'd gone across the street to surf anyway. And I am going to drag her ass out of that water in a goddamn suit and tie if I have to.

I'm marching down the driveway like an irate father when she appears—radiant, with long hair dripping over her shoulders, surfboard under one arm, yukking it up with the guy walking behind her. Her happiness pisses me off. *His* happiness pisses me off. The way they both stop short when they see me, as if I'm a cop here to bust up their underage party, pisses me off most.

I've never had the urge to spank someone before, but I sure have one now.

"What the fuck are you doing?" I demand.

Daisy gives the guy a shrug and crosses the street toward me.

"Well done, my dude," she says. "I was just trying to convince that guy that I'm not an escort, and you come out here looking like a sexy but jealous customer."

Sexy?

Not the point, Harrison.

"What you're seeing, Daisy, is *irritation*. We had a whole conversation the other day about the fact that I don't want you surfing out there, one I *know* you understood, yet here we are."

She walks ahead of me to the garage and leans her board against the wall.

"You didn't say I *couldn't* surf," she argues, grabbing a towel from the stack kept by the outdoor shower and pressing it to her face. "You said it wasn't advisable and I disagreed. I've surfed down there twice without incident, so maybe you were wrong."

"Or maybe it's an accident waiting to happen," I snap. "Just because you surfed there twice doesn't make it safe. You know we had a friend die in college in a surf accident, right? You know what happened to your dad? Shit goes wrong."

She tugs at the zipper of her wetsuit. "You bought a house here for a reason. Because at some point, you thought you'd want to surf across the street. So why the hell can't *I* surf there?"

There's a whole lot of cleavage on display while she struggles to get her arms free of the wetsuit. I look away. "Because I grew up surfing, and I did it a lot longer than you did."

"Harrison, I grew up surfing too. And just because you left for college and didn't *see* me surfing as a teenager doesn't mean it didn't happen. Or were you under the impression that I just ceased to exist once I was out of sight?"

The accusation hits a little close to home. "*I don't think he even remembers he has a wife when he leaves for the day*," Audrey once said in couples counseling. I argued with her about it. I promised to change. And a month later, I called a realtor and told her I wanted this house before it ever even occurred to me that I should mention it to my wife.

"You've lived in DC for the past four years," I counter. "Even if you surfed in high school, you haven't been doing much of it since. If you're going to surf, and especially if you're going to surf alone, go down by the wharf."

Her eyes darken. "The *wharf*? Are you shitting me? The waves there are a foot high. Do me a favor and stop commenting on what I'm capable of until you've witnessed it firsthand. I surf as well as you do."

I'm entirely certain that's not true, but I know from experience that arguing with Daisy is pointless. As a toddler she'd

demand one particular food—a hot dog or Goldfish or candy—
and refuse to eat anything until she'd received it. She once went
thirty-six hours without so much as a bite until Bridget broke
down and gave her a lollipop. Beneath that all-too-adult body,
she's still the exact same kid who'd go three days without food
until she got what she wanted.

"Well, until I've witnessed it, you're not going back out there
—are we clear? You benefit from this blackmail situation a lot
more than I do. I'll blow the whole thing up if I think you're
taking your life in your hands."

There's an angry glimmer in her eyes, but her mouth is
curving upward. "Fine. Come out tomorrow then."

*How shocking that the little freeloader has forgotten about this
thing known as 'work'.* "*I* actually have a job. We'll go down to the
wharf on Saturday and see how you do."

"The wharf? For fuck's sake, Harrison. That's where you
teach a five-year-old. We'll go across the street Friday."

She finally gets her other arm out of the wetsuit and pulls it
down to her waist, revealing yet another bikini that is barely
containing her assets and through which it is amply apparent
she is cold—very, very cold. Jesus Christ, I'd give up all of my
limbs to remove that bikini entirely and—

Stop, Harrison. For the love of God, stop.

"Saturday," I repeat firmly.

"For someone who negotiates for a living," she says, shim-
mying the wetsuit around her hips, "you're spectacularly bad
at it."

"That's because I'm not fucking negotiating with you. I can't
spend an hour surfing at the crack of dawn and then go put in a
full day."

"Fine, we can wait until Saturday, but if I surf well
enough, you have to go for a run with me on Sunday
morning."

"And if *I'm* right, you leave, no questions asked."

She bends down to peel the wetsuit off her legs. The bikini bottoms are wedged in the crack of her ass.

"Jesus Christ, Daisy," I say hoarsely, turning toward my car, "buy a one-piece. I just got a view of your cleavage *and* your ass that no one but your husband should ever get. Maybe not even him."

"Maybe you should stop looking, then."

"That's why I need you out of my house," I reply under my breath.

10

DAISY

I shiver with pleasure as I step into the outdoor shower and the warm water hits my icy skin. I'd forgotten how much I love this. I forgot how much I love the ocean breeze against my shins as the water hits me, how much I love my shampoo, the one that smells like roses, and the body gel that smells like suntan lotion. I forgot how amplified everything is after a few hours in the water, that foam is decadent and the silkiness of my legs post-shave is a seduction all on its own.

What scares me about that dark time last winter is that I forgot that I could love things at all. I knew I'd been a girl who once loved her life, who wanted to inhale and devour her days, but last winter I was so empty that it felt like a trick, a false memory. As if maybe I'd just been too dumb and naïve to see how hollow real life is.

And now I'm remembering, and it isn't a trick. There aren't enough hours to do all the things I want to do.

I want to don a clean bikini and bask in the morning sun on Harrison's deck, where the glass surrounding it will shield me from the cool breeze. I want to sip a soda and read a filthy romance and let my skin sizzle. I don't care, today, that the sun causes cancer, that soda causes diabetes, that I should probably be reading some book that won a Pulitzer Prize.

I spent months and months last winter longing to be absent from the world, thinking there was nothing left to relish, but these things make me feel alive. They make me *want* again. This tiny trickle of joy in my chest? It's the start of something infinite. Something hungry and *happy*. It's worth any cost.

Of course, Harrison has far more to do with that trickle of joy than he should.

That's why I need you out of my house, he said.

It wasn't meant for my ears. Fortunately for one of us, I have excellent hearing.

He finally admitted—albeit unwillingly—that he knows I'm female. He's looking, and he's bothered by what he sees, and even if nothing in the world has worked in my favor in the past year, that righted the balance a bit.

Sure, I should probably be more worried about the bet we just made—one that could theoretically see me out on my ass Saturday—but we really didn't define the terms anyway: do I simply need to be good enough to surf at the Horseshoe or do I need to be better at surfing than *him*? Only one of those is a possibility, but I'm not sure why he thinks a girl who's willing to blackmail him would honor a bet she loses in the first place.

Blackmail alone won't pay all my bills, however, so once I'm dressed, I drive downtown to fill out job applications. I park by the wharf and glance toward the beach as I climb out of the car. The tourists practice pop-ups under a stormy sky and the ocean is so placid it's practically a lake. I still can't believe Harrison suggested I surf here. For all his sexy "*that's why I need you out of my house*" grumbling, he continues to believe I'm a kid.

"There's way better surfing at Steamer's or the Horseshoe," says a guy tying his board on the car beside mine.

I stifle my eye roll as I turn toward him. For every five male surfers who are super-cool, there's always one who assumes you need his guidance simply because you're a girl. "Then why are *you* surfing here?" I ask. It comes out bitchier than I'd intended. I force a polite smile to soften it.

"It's close to the office," he says with a grin, using his thumb to point at a restaurant just off the wharf. "Shift starts soon, and there wasn't time to surf somewhere else."

I glance from the restaurant to him. I could spend the whole day turning in applications when I've got no experience, but it would be a lot easier to meet someone who has the inside track. "Are you guys hiring, by chance?"

He hitches a shoulder. "I don't know, but the manager's chill. Walk over with me and I'll introduce you."

He tells me his name is Alex. He's already graduated from college and is just in Santa Cruz "figuring things out," which is something I bet a lot of the guys here say.

We cross the street together to Wharf Seafood, one of those old places that should have been renovated decades ago, but instead tries to hide its age under accumulated junk: fisherman's netting, funny signs, origami parrots, and a mannequin dressed as a pirate.

Alex nods at a guy behind the bar. "Hey, Mike, this is Daisy. She's looking for a summer job. Daisy, this is Mike, our manager."

Mike tips his chin toward me. He looks young but old at the same time—a lot of guys who grew up on the water do. His skin is a little leathery and there are laugh lines around his eyes. "You waited tables before?"

Well, this is off to an excellent start. "Um, I was a hostess for a while?"

In other words, no, I have never waited tables.

He glances at me, though he's mostly looking below my neck, and shrugs. "You'll figure it out."

In other words, I have things that matter more to him than experience. Two things.

Perhaps it should bother me that this is what I've been reduced to, but I'm simply relieved we're on the same page. I'm not certain I bring anything other than D cups to the table and neither is he. At least he's being honest about it.

He tells me to come back Monday—weekends are too busy to have me underfoot—and I walk outside.

Two months ago, I'd have sworn I'd lost everything, but here I am, employed, living in an oceanfront mansion, surfing again, and getting brief glimpses of Harrison's lovely, brooding face.

It's been a year full of endings, but suddenly, it's as if something is beginning instead.

By the time I reach my car, the clouds have completely disappeared.

11

I 'm a grown man, yet my first impulse when I see Liam on Main Street is to dive into the nearest store like a kid who's about to get caught cutting school.

Liam's smile is easy, guilt-free. "Hey, stranger. What are you doing down this way?"

"Just meeting a client." I'm not normally so terse, but this situation is a disaster in the making. Everything I'd normally be inclined to ask Liam is something I shouldn't know about: *I hear you're sleeping with that girl you're doing work for; I hear Bridget and Scott are back together.*

Worse yet, there are the truths I can barely admit to myself, truths he'd punch me in the face over, like the way I can't stop thinking about his niece. And the things I'm thinking when I do.

Punching me would be entirely fair. I want to punch myself too.

"How's it going with the girl in LA?" he asks.

"Good," I say, then change the topic before I'm forced to make up a bunch of facts about my pretend girlfriend, facts I'm unlikely to remember later. "What's new with you?"

"Not much. Daisy's home for the summer. Applying to law school—can you believe it?"

No, actually, I can't. She hasn't mentioned law school once.

And the entire conversation feels like a trick. If I act as if I'm unaware that Daisy's here, it'll turn out she told him she saw me. If I say I've heard she's home, he'll ask who told me, and a whole new set of lies will be necessary. Fabricated mutual friends, a chance run-in at a restaurant when I've been telling him I'm too busy to go out.

He shakes his head. "It's weird, man. It's like Daisy grew up while I wasn't looking."

Yes, I know. *God*, do I know.

"Tell her I said *hi*," I say, glancing at my watch. "Hey, I've got to get to a meeting. Let's catch up soon, yeah?"

He nods, but it's impossible to miss that he's hurt. He's been one of my best friends for most of my life, and I can't even give him five minutes of my time.

But the truth would hurt him a lot more.

I WORK LATE WEDNESDAY NIGHT, mostly to avoid her. When I get home on Thursday, she's sitting at the kitchen counter eating lasagna. I'd sworn I was going straight to my room—I mostly skip dinner these days—but the smell has me salivating.

"I know you want some," she says, smirking. "It's in the fridge."

I don't want to give her the satisfaction. I don't want her thinking it's okay that she's here.

I'll go back to making a point tomorrow when I'm well-fed and less tired.

"So what did you do all day?" I ask. "I mean, aside from blackmailing me?"

"Blackmailing you takes up a surprising amount of my

waking hours." She licks her fingers. My eyes catch on the motion. "But actually, I got a job yesterday. The seafood place down on the pier. I start Monday."

I set the lasagna in the microwave. "That won't be very convenient for you once you're back at your mom's."

She laughs. "Nothing you've done has given me the impression that I'll be back at my mom's."

I pour myself a drink. Even the sound of the ice crackling as the bourbon flows over it is a hit of dopamine now, a sign that relief is on the way.

"Oh, is it that time already?" She pulls a bottle of Malibu from the chair beside her. "Sweet."

"I'm not sure what you're doing there." I lift the glass to my mouth. "Are you even old enough to drink?"

She rolls her eyes as she twists the top off. "It's so flattering, how little you remember about me. And what we're doing is drinking *together*. Every sip you take, I'll take one too."

I pause. "I'm twice your weight. You realize you'll be under the table by the time I've finished this lasagna, yes?"

Her eyes twinkle. "Why yes, Harrison. I *do* realize that."

Ah, clever. She thinks my conscience will keep me from getting her drunk, and it probably would under normal circumstances, but I'm not playing this game with her.

I take a nice long drink of my bourbon, holding her eye the entire time.

She chugs straight from her bottle of Malibu, holding mine.

I go to the microwave for the lasagna. I'm so hungry that I take a bite before it's cooled off and scald my tongue, which I then soothe with a nice long sip of bourbon.

Her shoulders sag. She takes another drink of her rum. This is getting tedious.

"I could just take this to my room, you know," I tell her.

"If you take that bottle to your room, I'll take this one to mine and finish it," she replies, satisfied with herself.

She'd do it too. If she could go without food for days as a toddler to prove a point, drinking an entire bottle of Malibu as an adult would be a walk in the park.

"How's the lasagna?" she asks.

"Good, and the bourbon gives it a little extra kick. I'll probably have more."

Her nostrils flare, and she heaves a sigh. "Excellent. I'll have more too."

We're at a standoff, and already she's turned drinking into a chore, something I wish I didn't have to do. *Goddammit, Daisy.*

I finish the first piece of lasagna. I finish most of the bourbon and refill it. She matches me sip for sip.

I heat up a second piece and carry it to the table. She follows, setting the Malibu down on the table with a heavy thud.

"So what happened with you and Audrey?" she asks as I raise the fork to my mouth, and every muscle in my stomach tightens.

"We split up," I reply coolly. "I figured you knew, given it's how you've maliciously inserted yourself into my life."

She shakes her head. "No. I mean, what *really* happened? Because you wouldn't be lying to everyone about a girlfriend if it went the way you said. You'd be out at a bar telling Liam how much those two months in London sucked and that it was time to pull the cord."

"You sure seem to know a lot about relationships. Have you ever even had one?"

Her smile fades. She takes an extra sip of the rum though I didn't sip off mine. "I have, actually. And you're trying to change the topic. So what really happened?"

I'm starting to lose my appetite. I'd just go to my room but I know she'll keep on asking every day she's here until I've managed to kick her out.

I take a long swig of the bourbon. "There's no secret story,

Daisy, and if there were, do you really think I'd share it with someone already blackmailing me with the one secret she's privy to?"

She drinks from the bottle of Malibu and stares at me, still waiting for the fucking answer. "I won't blackmail you with it. I mean, I will if it's *juicy*. If it turns out you want to be diapered like a baby or are into coprophilia, it would be really hard not to blackmail you a *little*."

"What the hell is coprophilia?"

She grins. "Ah, now, who's the innocent one? It's when someone wants to take a dump on your face."

"I don't even want to know how you know that. And my marriage failed. That's sufficiently embarrassing, I think."

"Half of all marriages end in divorce, dude." She's already slurring a little. "There's nothing embarrassing about it. So, I'm forced to assume the issue was coprophilia. Or, God...is it *worse*? I can only think of two things that are worse, and they're both illegal. No, wait, I can think of three things. They're all sexual, by the way. Nope, just came up with a fourth. Four things. Wow, I'm seeing you in a whole new light."

I'm torn between laughing and walking out of the room.

"I'm scared to even ask what those four things are," I begin and raise my hand when her mouth opens. "That wasn't an invitation for you to tell me. And no, there was no sexual deviance underlying my divorce. What's embarrassing is that I quit my job and sold my house and went halfway around the world only to pack it in after two months." It's partly true. Which, by definition, means it's also partly false. And I'm not sure why I'm even replying to her, but the bourbon has loosened my tongue, and now that she's clearly wondering if I'm a pedophile or human trafficker, the truth seems like less of a big deal than it did.

She laughs. "Poor Harrison. Failing at a relationship is a

regular day on the job for most people. You were just too accus-
tomed to being good at everything."

She's missing a lot of the nuance here, but she isn't entirely
wrong: I *was* used to excelling at life. There was a time when I
had every fucking thing and couldn't get through a day without
someone mentioning how lucky I was. I had family money. I
graduated at the top of my class and married a woman who was
beautiful and brilliant and loved me enough to follow me
across the country. Work came easily, winning came easily, and
I assumed, soon enough, that parenting would come easily too.

And suddenly it was all gone, and nothing was coming at
all, easily or otherwise.

"When I left, I was the top-grossing partner at my firm. Now
I'm starting from scratch at thirty-two and everyone's looking at
me like I'm a clown for doing it, which I am."

Her unfocused eyes meet mine. "Why didn't you just go to a
different firm?"

I considered it. I should have. I probably should have
moved someplace else entirely, and I'm still not sure why I
didn't. "There's not a lot in Elliott Springs in the first place, and
certainly nobody who was going to bring me in as a partner. I
guess I didn't want to go even farther backward than I have."

I drink and so does she, though it's really fucking clear she
needs to stop. I also want to take the focus off myself. "Go to
bed, Daisy. I'm just going to sit on the deck and finish this
bourbon and I'm done for the night."

She laughs, rising when I do. "Oh, no, my friend. I'm
sticking it out as long as you're here. And I'm a college student.
Nine isn't bedtime for me...I'm just getting started."

I remember those days well, except I had a lot more fun
during my summers than she's having. I was working, sure, but
my nights were full. I'd surf until dark and then sit around a
bonfire with my friends, and there weren't enough minutes in
the day for me to fit it all in—I couldn't wait to be done with

school so that the hours would become my own, but then they became my own and I wound up filling them with none of those things at all.

"You *should* be getting started," I reply. "You're too young to be spending every summer night sitting inside with me."

It's true. I don't know why it's a hard thing to say to her, though—perhaps because then I'll have to worry about heroin addicts in unmarked vans.

I leave my plate where it is and walk out to the deck. Aside from the distant lights of Santa Cruz, the night is pitch black and peaceful. I can't see the ocean, but I like knowing it's there, the roar of waves attacking the Horseshoe's jagged cliff face.

Daisy drops into the seat across from mine, that bottle of Malibu looking less heavy than it did before. "I love it here," she says with a happy sigh. "I missed this so much in DC."

Two decades ago she was a tan, blonde toddler who refused to wear shoes and always had sand in her hair. I suspect, beneath the curves and the pout and the porn voice, she's still that same kid.

"I was surprised you left," I admit. "I always thought you'd stay out here."

The glance that flickers my way is wary, tinged with unhappiness. "It was easier than dealing with Scott all the time. And I wanted to give my mom the whole experience."

"Experience?"

She laughs. "She's a little obsessed with the idea of college, but not real college. I'm talking, like, college the way it appears in old movies. Buildings covered in ivy, tea with the dean. But anyway...I wanted to give her that. I wanted her to live vicariously through me since she never got it for herself."

Daisy's always been such a mix of contrasts. Ridiculously rebellious one moment—refusing to get out of the water as a kid, or dying her hair black before Bridget's wedding—but endlessly sweet at the same time, like this. Moving across the country to ease an awkward situation with her stepfather. Going to an old East Coast school to suit her mom rather than herself.

Blackmailing me, but making me dinner each night while she does it and trying to force me to clean up my shit. What would Audrey have done in her shoes? If we were still together and she'd discovered me drinking in my boxer shorts, lying to all my friends...

I guess it's fair to say she wouldn't have done a goddamned thing. Or that she'd have been too busy cheating on me to notice.

"I guess you're not as terrible a daughter as I thought," I say with a grin, and she swings her leg out and kicks me before curling up in her chair, pulling the oversized sweatshirt around her knees for warmth. The bottle of Malibu is now clutched to her chest like a beloved toy.

"I'm the only kid she's got," she says with a shrug. "Speaking of other kids, do you see your stepsiblings much?"

I give her a half-hearted smile. "Seeing them would be a full-time job at the rate my father's going." I now have four half-sisters in various countries and a fifth on the way. "I was supposed to see Oliver and Matthew in France this summer, but—"

I run a hand over my head. That was a plan made when I'd thought I'd be reaching them via a two-hour train ride rather than a thirteen-hour flight. "Oliver will be in LA for work in a few weeks. I'll probably try to see him then."

"Oliver," she muses. "Was he the hot one?"

There's...a twinge. A tiny pinch of irritation where there should be none.

"This might come as a shock to you, Daisy, but I don't think of my brothers in terms of *hotness*. He's the one who looks like me." There's an iciness to my voice that shouldn't be there. Why should I give a shit if Daisy was ever attracted to one of my brothers? "And he's too old for you, so I'm not sure why that would be relevant anyway."

She laughs. "Too old? When he came to visit you, he was fifteen and I was nine. Unless time works differently in France, that only makes him six years older than me."

"There's a world of difference between twenty-one and twenty-seven," I argue. "The years after college change everything."

And, more to the point, I just can't stand the idea of her with my brother.

When she looks at me over her bottle of Malibu, I'm disturbed by how amused she is and by how very *adult* her amusement appears to be. "Harrison, you went to school at eighteen with two wealthy parents to pay your way and what was, I'm sure, a very generous trust fund. I went at seventeen on loans and part-time jobs and have been scraping by ever since. You probably never had to support yourself until you left law school, right? Which means that you've only had one more year of independence than I've had. A six-year age gap isn't the deal-breaker you think it should be."

She's right, and it changes nothing. Because I don't think what really bothers me is the idea of Daisy with someone older, or with one of my siblings. It's the idea of her with anyone at all.

"You should still be dating guys your own age," I insist.

She smiles. "Like the surfers across the street?"

My eyes narrow. "No. Not the surfers across the street."

She stretches out her legs and wiggles her toes. "You've got an awfully dim view of surfers for someone who used to be one."

"That's *why* I have such a dim view of them," I growl. I distinctly remember being a college-aged douchebag who wanted to fuck every cute girl he saw in a bikini and *did* fuck more than his share. The idea of Daisy falling prey to one of them makes my jaw grind.

"Why did you buy a place here, then?" she asks. "Audrey didn't surf, you clearly don't surf much, if at all, and you already had that mansion in Elliott Springs."

I rattle the ice in my glass. "My dad sold his beach house and I thought we might just move out this way, eventually. It seemed like a nice place to raise a family."

I think I was trying to salvage something then—our marriage, maybe, or the dreams I'd once had for adulthood. I just didn't know it. I've always said it was an accident, the way I forgot to tell Audrey, but I'm not sure it really was. I was just fucking desperate to acquire something I knew I needed. You don't grow old in a single step—it's a long, quiet descent. It begins with saying you can't take a week off to surf in Hawaii. Then you can't spare a weekend, then two hours on a Saturday. Suddenly you're old, and all the things you loved the most are behind you, out of reach. I'd been making that slow descent for a while, and I wanted to stop it somehow.

"I made the offer before I'd ever even mentioned it to Audrey," I admit quietly. "She was pissed, and she had every right to be. I should have known it wasn't going to work."

"Why wouldn't it work?"

I sigh. "Audrey hates the beach."

Daisy laughs as if I'm joking, but then her eyes widen when she realizes I wasn't. "What kind of monster doesn't like the beach?"

It's the exact question I'd expect of a kid who used to throw herself down and *howl* when we told her it was time to leave for the day. "It was something about not liking the feel of the sand."

Daisy snorts. "Are you serious right now?"

I shrug. Yes, Audrey hated sand. She flinched every time she felt it underfoot. And God forbid if there was sand in the sheets. "Yeah. She needed to shower ten times a day if she came out here, and I was *careful*. I can't imagine how much worse it would have been if we'd had kids."

Daisy sips off the bottle. "Man, she must've been a blast in bed. If she didn't like the feel of sand, what was her take on having you come all over her tits?"

I choke on the bourbon I'm swallowing. "*What?*"

"You heard me."

Yeah, I did. And those fucking words tripped off Daisy's tongue far too easily, with a smirk on her full, pink lips as if letting a guy paint her with his cum was an everyday event.

"Jesus." I'm on my feet and walking back inside with that bottle of bourbon in front of my crotch before I've even thought it through. "Daisy, the shit that comes out of your mouth sometimes..."

She laughs behind me. "You don't have to run away! I already know that made you hard."

And she is correct. It did.

It should not have.

WHEN I WAKE in the morning, Daisy's door is already open. I go downstairs but see none of the typical signs of her presence. There's no coffee cup in the sink, no perfect ass bent over on my deck. And the bottle of Malibu isn't here either.

"Goddammit, Daisy," I hiss. "Tell me you didn't actually go drink in your room."

Of course she did, and I'm a fucking idiot for thinking she *wouldn't*.

I march back up the stairs to find her sprawled face-down in bed. The covers are on the floor, her T-shirt is bunched around her waist, and her little red panties have ridden up until they're basically a thong.

Now *there's* an image I didn't fucking need.

I pick up the covers and place them over her. From beneath all the hair covering her face, she moans. "Sick," she whispers.

I lift the Malibu. There's some in there still but not a lot. "Yeah, I bet you are."

"Shit," she hisses before she leaps from the bed and runs to the bathroom, followed by the sound of retching.

She's brought all of this on herself, and guilt tweaks me anyway. I walk to the threshold of the bathroom, where she's curled up on the floor, her face pressed to the tile.

"Daisy, go back to bed," I say softly.

"Just leave me behind!" she cries as if this is a war movie. "Save yourself!"

I laugh. "I'm pretty sure what you have isn't contagious. Come on." I scoop her up. She feels tiny, fragile, in my arms. "Let's get you into bed."

"Yeah, you'd like that, wouldn't you?" she mumbles.

I grin as I set her on the mattress. "Have you looked in the mirror today? You're not exactly the height of seduction at present. And you smell like vomit."

She buries her head into her pillow. "Let me brush my teeth. You'll change your tune."

"Absolutely," I reply. "That's all it would take. I'm getting you aspirin. Stay put."

I go downstairs, deeply annoyed that she's done this to herself on my behalf, but warmed by it at the same time. Daisy and her ridiculously big heart. Apparently, I'm the three-legged dog she's going to cry over all summer, and I guess I need to resign myself to that fact.

When I get back to the room, she's half asleep and has to be forced into swallowing the pills before she collapses on her pillow.

I push her hair back from her face.

Christ. When did she turn so beautiful? When did she develop those cheekbones? That pout? Even now, sweating and pale, she's so pretty she's hard to look away from and hard to look at all at the same time.

Liam warned us off his sister. He never felt he needed to warn us away from his niece.

I hate that it was apparently necessary.

12

DAISY

God, I hate DC.

From November until April and sometimes May, the air is cold, the trees are mostly bare, and the sunlight is weak if it's present at all. There are no waves here, no endless vistas, no gentle breezes.

There are cars. A lot of fucking cars. Not a night goes by when I'm not woken by the sound of sirens, or honking, or drunks yelling as they stumble down the sidewalk outside. Sometimes I want to weep with the desire for fresh air, sunlight, crashing waves.

The phone rings. It's my mom, and I'm not sure I can summon the energy to talk to her, but it's her second call, and by not answering, I'm digging a bigger and bigger hole, one that will require better lies, more good cheer.

I push my arm from my comforter, cringing at the apartment's chill as I reach for the phone.

"Hi, Mom," I say.

"You sound like you were asleep," she frets. "Didn't you have class this morning?"

My eyes fall closed. It's getting harder to keep all my lies straight. "Our prof cancelled. She's sick. Covid, I think."

It's best to give her more information than she's requested—it keeps her from coming up with questions of her own.

"But it's going well?"

My hand curls into a fist to keep the crack out of my voice. "Yeah. Just tired of winter."

I want to pull my arm back inside this unwashed comforter and sleep until it's over, though I'm starting to wonder if that will ever happen.

There's a beat of awkward silence, her waiting for me to fill in the gaps. My poor mother, wanting so much for me and being consistently disappointed with the outcome. "Do you know when they'll send details about graduation?" *she asks.* "I want to book plane tickets before it gets expensive."

Fuck. I knew this was coming. I just thought I had time, though I'm not sure what I thought time would accomplish. Maybe I hoped I'd have grown a pair by now, but that was always unlikely.

"I think I'm going to need an extra semester, actually," *I tell her.*

"Extra? Why?"

The dismay in her voice is like a sharp poke. Needing a few extra classes is nothing compared to the truth, so God only knows how she'd react to that. "I wasn't able to get into everything I needed to graduate," *I tell her.* "It's not a big deal. It's pretty common to take more than four years these days."

"You do realize all those extra classes you take cost money, right?" *she chides.* "Money you'll have to pay back."

My jaw grinds. Yes, Mom. I'm aware that I, alone, will be paying back those loans. I'm the one who's here, remember? I'm the one who acquired them. "Yeah, I know. I'd better get going. I have a five o'clock lab."

"Daisy…" *she begins, and then she's quiet.* "I'm so proud of you. We'll talk later, okay? I love you."

"Love you too," *I say, ending the call and pulling my arm beneath the comforter.*

I just want to go back to sleep and stay asleep so I never have to face the mess I've made of everything.

When my eyes open, it's a relief to see the stark lines of Harrison's sunlit guest room instead of my grim apartment in DC, to discover this churning in my stomach is half a bottle of Malibu as opposed to guilt and helplessness.

Though I guess some guilt remains. I've still made a mess of things. I'm still lying to everyone about it.

Steps echo down the hall and I look toward the door. Harrison stands there, still in his oxford but with the jacket off and the tie loosened. Based on the light, it's going on noon. He should have left hours ago.

"You didn't go into work?" I rasp, pushing up onto my elbows to get a better view of him.

He sits at the foot of the bed. "I stuck around in case EMS had to be let in. It's an expensive door. I didn't want them breaking it down."

"Ha, ha."

He twists the cap off the Gatorade he's carrying and hands it to me. "Drink up, sunshine. You need to replenish some fluids."

I take a long chug from the bottle. Nothing in the history of the world has ever tasted better than this neon-green ambrosia. "You can go to work. I'm fine."

He hesitates. "You're sure?"

I nod quickly. "Positive. The only thing that hurts right now is how badly my plan backfired."

He laughs. "It wasn't your best."

"I've got a better one," I reply, though I do not. I don't actually have any plan at all. If he's willing to watch me poison myself to prove he won't be bullied and I can't keep threatening to tell his friends, what else is left? What's he more scared of than my death—which he clearly wasn't that worried about—or Liam's involvement?

He pats my leg and rises, though I wish he'd stay. "Hopefully, it's less likely to end with a fatality than this one was."

"Maybe I'll remove a piece of clothing every time you drink."

His laughter is low and dismissive. "Given the way you dress, your threat doesn't have much of a shelf life."

I guess he's got a point.

He leaves, and I flop back onto the pillows with a groan.

All I've got left is tomorrow morning, and I really hope it works.

MY ALARM GOES OFF JUST BEFORE seven the next day. The road in front of the house is already lined with trucks, and there's no time to waste.

I don my bikini and knock on Harrison's door. When he doesn't answer, I try the handle.

Yes, this is something I've thought of doing many times before, but never for the reason I'm doing it now.

He's sound asleep under a tangled mess of covers, deliciously scruffy and full-lipped and unconscious. I'm pretty sure I see the start of some morning wood, too. I picture sliding under the covers from the bottom of the bed and—

Bad, Daisy. Not why we're here.

"Harrison, wake up. It's time to surf."

He doesn't blink. He doesn't even budge. I shake his shoulder and he rolls away from me, mumbling something in his sleep about a bilateral agreement, which makes it even weirder that he's got an erection.

So I do climb on the bed, though in a far less sexy way than I'd previously imagined.

I'm standing.

And jumping.

"Wake up, wake up, wake up," I chant, and though this is certainly not going to convince him that I'm an adult, it's effective.

He rolls onto his stomach. "Daisy, get the fuck out of my room."

"We're surfing," I say, continuing to jump, making the bed roll beneath him. "And it's high tide right now. That's why I told you to be up by seven."

He covers his head with a pillow. "Daisy, get the fuck out of my room. *Now*."

Shit. I've looked forward to this all week, and he's clearly not going to budge. I jump on the floor and land with a thud. "Awesome." My voice is flat, barely disguising the ache of disappointment in my chest. "Then I guess we're agreeing I can stay and surf *wherever* I want."

I walk out, slamming the door behind me, but there's a lump in my throat as I head down the stairs. I really saw him going along with it. I saw more than that, too. I pictured him getting out in the water, riding a wave or two, and remembering how good it was. I imagined us as a team. Like, not a professional surf team, but just...buddies. Buddies who'd wake up every morning at daybreak to surf, who'd get out there in the afternoons. I thought he'd remember who he used to be and allow me to be there beside him when he discovered it, and I was so fucking excited about it, wasn't I? Which is pathetic. The guy doesn't even want me in his home, so he wasn't about to suddenly turn into my best friend.

I go to the garage and pull on my wetsuit, fighting tears. I hate him for ruining this, for making me go out there alone when—

The door from the house opens and he marches out, already in his wetsuit. He walks past me and grabs his board off the opposite wall. "Let's get this over with," he barks, heading for the driveway.

My tears dry as I scramble to get my board too, fighting a smile. "Don't you want to wax it first?"

"I doubt we'll be out there long enough for it to matter," he replies without stopping.

Dickish of him. I decide to let it go.

He crosses the street and heads down the stairs as if he's going into battle—I'm not sure why he's acting like this is such a chore unless Audrey actually *did* manage to change him into some trust-fund douche who'd rather spend a Saturday morning having brunch at the country club than surfing.

His shoulders hunch when he reaches the water, his jaw locked and his brow furrowed. He takes in the rocks, the cliff, the dark and dangerous waves, the eddies swirling nearby, and when he glances back at me, I know exactly what he's going to do. He's scared—not for himself, but for me, and I refuse to be the reason he doesn't get in this morning.

"Daisy," he begins, "I think this is a bad—"

I jump.

"If you want to puss out, be my guest," I call, floating on my back while I tie the leash around my ankle. "But I've waited since Wednesday, and I'm not waiting another minute."

I pretend that I don't hear him cursing behind me and start to paddle. He catches me easily—of course he does with those delightful shoulders of his—and mumbles something about me being a brat, which I choose not to respond to.

"Do *not* go over in front of the cliff," he snarls.

I glare over my shoulder. "I've managed to keep myself alive for the past five years without any adult guidance, so I'm not sure why you think I need you to leap in now."

"Yes, you've proven to be a model of responsible behavior with the way you're forcing yourself on me."

"Oh, Harrison," I say silkily, "I haven't even *begun* to force myself on you. Believe me, you'll know when I do."

He sighs. "You're too young to make every word out of your mouth sound so dirty."

I straddle my board, waiting for the next set to come in. "You realize I've had sex, right? I've had a lot of sex, actually."

"More than I needed to know," he mutters.

I grin. Why is his discomfort so much fun for me? "So, so much sex. Do you want to hear about my first time? I was fourteen. He was eighteen and in a band."

"Continue describing this situation, which is considered statutory rape in California, and I'll have a legal duty to report it."

He's probably bluffing. But he might not be. And the next set is coming in. I get flat on my board and turn to face the shore.

"Not this one," he snaps. "It's too big."

I roll my eyes. It's not that big. If he'd seen the wave I took Wednesday, the one the guys cheered for, he'd have had a heart attack. I start to paddle, trying to ignore my nerves. It *isn't* a huge wave, but I'm so anxious about messing up in front of him that I might very well do something dumb.

"*Just push up, Daisy,*" Harrison says in my head. The old, sweet version who wanted to see me fly. The version I know is still inside him somewhere.

My chest lifts and all the other steps fall into place—I plant my back leg and then my front, and when I glance over my shoulder, he's right behind me, carving into the wave. For a moment, our eyes catch. I don't miss his reluctant grin before I turn away.

It's a perfect ride, and I feel more free and more *complete* during the seconds it lasts than I've felt in a very long time.

When the wave dies out, I jump off the board and he does the same. Our heads surface at the same moment, and I'm on the cusp of giving him the finger, but the sheer joy on his face makes it impossible to do anything but smile.

"Have anything you'd like to say to me?" I shout, paddling his way.

"Your forefoot wasn't quite centered," he replies.

So I do give him the finger.

"Fine, I was wrong," he admits. "I shouldn't have told you where you could surf."

His gaze meets mine and he smiles again, happier than I've seen him in a very long time.

That smile of his presses right to the center of my chest like a thumbprint.

I want to hold it there forever.

AFTER AN HOUR IN THE WATER, we walk back to the house together and shower—the showering is done separately, of course, though I could easily be persuaded to go about it another way.

I go to the kitchen after I get dressed, put on music, and start making myself a peanut butter and jelly sandwich with this gross, healthy bread and super-oily peanut butter from the rich people store. I've got no clue why rich people like bread that's full of grains. Someone should introduce them to the white bread I grew up on, the kind that melts in your mouth and doesn't go bad for weeks. They'd never go back.

Liam texts while I'm attempting to make the gross rich-people peanut butter mix together. We've played phone tag all week, and even though he's preoccupied with his new girl-friend, I feel bad anyway.

LIAM

> There's this old James Bond movie playing at
> the new theater in town. You want to go?

I love James Bond. But if I see Liam, he's going to ask where

I'm staying, and he'll pursue details he wouldn't pursue normally because he's actually asking on my mother's behalf. He'll ask which friend I'm staying with, where she lives, how I know her, why he doesn't remember her.

Eventually it'll come out that I'm in Santa Cruz. And he'll say, *"We should meet Harrison down there,"* and I'll somehow wind up telling him that Harrison's not dating anyone in LA. Oh, and that I'm living with him and he gets erections a *lot*, shockingly large ones, and I might even have been responsible for one or two of them.

If I know my uncle at all, that will not go over well.

Harrison walks into the kitchen, his gaze sweeping over me. "I'd forgotten about that," he says.

"Forgotten what?"

He nudges me out of the way to make himself a sandwich. "The way you dance around the kitchen when you're cooking."

I roll my eyes. "Great. One more way you've remembered my childhood."

"There isn't anything childish about it *now*," he grunts. Something in that grunt makes my stomach tighten deliciously.

Two months ago, it seemed like an easy decision to give up on men and sex and the roller coaster of it all. Harrison has obliterated that ease with a single low noise in his throat. If he suddenly turned around and said, *"Hop up on this counter. I've decided to fuck you,"* I'd knock dishes off in my haste.

I set my sandwich down. "Hey, clearly you lost our bet, but I'll let you out of running tomorrow if you agree to go to the movies with Liam instead."

He raises a brow as he spreads jelly on the bread. "This deal seems a little too good to be true. Why don't *you* want to go?"

I shrug. "Because I'm not a good liar—you probably wouldn't expect that given how good I am at blackmailing—but I'm worried I'll tell him the truth."

"Yeah," he says, dropping the knife in the sink, "I'm a little worried about that too."

"Cool, so you'll go? He wants to see some old Bond movie playing downtown."

"*Bond*?" he asks. "No." He was completely on board and now his voice is hard—a voice I normally wouldn't even bother to argue with.

"It's exactly the kind of male-centered drivel I'd expect you to love."

"The last thing I need is to sit in a theater listening to some pompous British asshole," he mutters, and he's *angry*, as if James Bond personally hurt him at some point in their mutual past.

Which makes no sense. Not only because James Bond is fictional, but because Harrison loves the UK. He spent a semester there in college. He chose to *move* there last winter, for God's sake.

The only way it would make sense is if...

"This is about Audrey, isn't it?" I blurt out, my voice running ahead of my brain. "She met someone else."

He swallows, jaw grinding as if he's about to mount an argument. "I'm not discussing this with you," he says instead, walking out to the deck.

13

HARRISON

I slump into a chair outside, sinking into one of my least happy memories.

When I landed in London, I hadn't seen my wife in four months.

We'd *intended* to see each other—she was supposed to come to California in November but ran into an issue at work, and my trip planned for the holidays got canceled because I'd had to prep for a trial. And the second the trial was over, I had to pack up our house and leave my job, and there wasn't a second to spare.

I texted her as I walked toward customs to say I'd caught an earlier flight. I saw the three swirling dots of her reply, but nothing came, and I knew what that meant—that she was flustered, rushing to get to the flat and irritated that I'd changed the plan. Resentment began stirring in my chest over her *imagined* irritation. Marriage is like an old country road that gets a little more banged up with each passing year. You start expecting the holes and the bumps before you've even hit them. You feel the resentment before it's even been earned. Audrey and I hadn't been married all that long, but there were already a lot of holes and bumps. Too many, according to my friends.

"Cut it out," I'd told myself. "This is a fresh start."

Sure, it wasn't a fresh start I'd necessarily wanted, but what was I supposed to do? She'd moved to California with me after law school and she'd always hated it. It was time to try things her way instead.

When I reached customs, my passport wouldn't scan and I was sent into a long line with other weary passengers to wait for an agent. And Audrey still hadn't replied.

*You're sleep deprived, Harrison. Don't read into this, and don't see it all as a bad omen. You're about to get laid for the first time in...*I couldn't even remember how long it had been. Not since the summer before, at the earliest, when we'd had too much to drink and she became the girl I'd fallen for in law school— giggly, relaxed, flirtatious. Which is the second problem with marriage. You fall in love with someone, and when that version of them disappears...do you wait? Do you try to love the new version instead? Is it your fault she disappeared in the first place?

"Visiting?" the customs agent asked.

"No, actually. My wife is working here now. We're moving."

He glanced from the passport to me. "Do you have a job, then?"

"Not yet." Lots of American firms had a London office, but it was uncomfortable, admitting that I was now unemployed for the first time in my adult life. I'd given up every client, though I'd been earning twice what Audrey was in California, and I wasn't quite sure what I was getting in exchange. Not if she couldn't even reply to a fucking text.

My passport was stamped. "Enjoy your visit," he said, as if he was already certain I wouldn't be staying.

I took the express train to Paddington Station. A group of school children ran past in uniform, laughing as they clutched sketchbooks to their chests. That was what Audrey wanted for the family we were about to start working on—an urban upbringing full of art classes and museums on weekends. I'd always pictured my kids living a childhood like mine—weekends surfing or out at the lake—but it was too late for doing it my way. I was here, and so was she. Unwillingly, I moved toward the line for High Street—and she finally texted.

AUDREY

I left you a phone message. Didn't you get it?

No. What's up? I just got off the express train.

Oh God. Please go listen to the message.

I swiped over the screen of my phone until I found the voicemail. I hadn't even listened yet, and I was already tired.

"Hi," she began, her voice choking on a sob. "Hi. God, Harrison, I can't believe I'm doing this, but…I don't think you should come. I know you're probably on your way to the airport right now, but this just isn't going to work." She made this high-pitched noise I'd never heard from her before, but it was the man's voice behind her, murmuring reassurance, that rang the first warning bell. "This is so hard to say, and I know the timing is terrible, but David? My boss?"

A piece of me, something darker and wiser, knew what she was going to say. Even as I was telling myself not to jump to conclusions, I knew exactly what she was about to fucking say.

It was something I didn't want to discuss with anyone then, and now, six months later, I still don't want to discuss it.

"I'm not going to ask," Daisy says, taking the seat beside mine. "I shouldn't have suggested it."

I stare out at the ocean. I guess it doesn't matter at this point —she's mostly figured it out. "Audrey's engaged. To her boss. She was sleeping with him pretty much the whole goddamn time I was here selling our house and packing our stuff."

"Oh," she whispers. "God. I'm so sorry."

I laugh, a trifle bitterly. "He's got a title. She's going to be *Lady* Audrey, apparently."

Daisy blows out a breath. "She sucked, Harrison. And I'm not saying that because of what she did. I'm saying that because she *always* sucked. She was stuck up and miserable."

"She wasn't always." It's less about defending Audrey than it is about defending myself, defending what were, in retrospect, several really poor choices on my end—marrying her, agreeing to move. I'm no longer sure I even did it because I wanted our marriage to work. I think I was just unwilling to fail at something.

"She changed after her brother died. And I think she blamed me. She didn't want to leave the East Coast in the first place."

Daisy shakes her head. "You married a girl who hates the *beach*. Someone like that was never going to make you happy. She was like...all the worst parts of you."

I turn her way. "Worst parts?"

"The super high-charged, *willing to work 'til all hours to get ahead* side. You should have taken some time off after London." She frowns. "Wait. If you knew she was with someone else, why'd you stay there for two *months*?"

I release a slow exhale. I could lie, but why bother? She'll probably divine the truth about that too, eventually.

"I didn't." My head falls to the top of the chair. "I sat here for two months pretending I was still in London before I told anyone I was back. It would have been too obvious what happened if they knew I flew home the very next day. Please don't repeat any of this."

The whole situation was so fucking embarrassing. But it's more embarrassing that I sat here in silence for two months, lying to my friends and my family.

She reaches out and squeezes my hand. "I understand that better than you think."

I can't imagine she actually understands much. She's twenty-one. What could possibly have happened in her life that would compare?

"And I won't tell anyone. I was never going to tell anyone about the girlfriend thing anyway," she adds. "I'm still making you run tomorrow, though."

I laugh. I like that she's not treating me like a kicked puppy. "Yeah," I tell her. "I knew that too."

There's something adult in the smile she gives me as she squeezes my hand and walks away.

She's mature for her age.

Of course, that's the same bullshit every man tells himself to justify a very bad decision, isn't it? It's a slippery slope from *tempted* to *villain*.

I'm worried I've already begun to slide.

14

DAISY

Audrey, you crazy fucking bitch.

I have no idea who this titled asshole is that she's moved onto, but if she wasn't smart enough to see what she already had in Harrison, and decent enough to honor the commitment she'd made, she didn't deserve him in the first place.

And I'd already suspected that anyway.

I leave Harrison alone after his revelation, mostly because I think he prefers to be left alone, and because he isn't the type of guy who'd want to hear me trash-talk his ex, no matter how badly she deserves it.

Also because I don't think I could stop myself from trash-talking his ex, no matter how badly I tried.

I walk down to the backyard and sink into Harrison's delicious hot tub with a sigh, thinking about what an amazing life Audrey could have had if she hadn't blown it up, living in this oceanfront mansion with a weekly cleaning lady I've only seen in passing.

She could have learned to surf. She could have climbed into this hot tub after a long day or simply dragged Harrison to bed a few hours early. She always seemed so intimidatingly smart. Now I think she's the dumbest human who's ever lived.

The wind picks up, and the temperature starts to drop. It's too cozy to climb out of the hot tub, much like it was too cozy to shirk off my comforter last winter when my life was imploding. The difference is that I'm happy now. I'm not in here because I'm trying to vacate my life but simply because this is one more way to enjoy it.

Sometimes it's hard to distinguish between those things. I had to figure it out at my own pace, and maybe Harrison does too. I've got no business telling him how to live anyway. We both torpedoed our lives, but at least *he's* made some progress toward fixing his.

I doze off and am woken by his hand on my shoulder. "Hey," he says quietly. "I just heard thunder."

My eyes open. His gaze is on me in that way it often is, as if I'm simultaneously something he wants to see and something he wishes would disappear forever.

I climb from the hot tub. He keeps his gaze averted until I'm wrapped in a towel. "I'm gonna run to the store before it gets bad," I tell him. "Do you want anything?"

His mouth presses flat. "You don't have to do this shit, you know. Shop, cook, all that. We can just order pizza tonight."

I give a small shrug. "I like it." What I really mean is "*I like taking care of* you." Generations of hardworking Doherty women toiled away over hot stoves and ironing boards on behalf of men who took them for granted, all so I could...toil away on behalf of a man who doesn't want me around in the first place.

I guess at least the blackmail aspect gives it a modern, independent twist.

"Then take my credit card. I don't want you paying for it."

I smile. "You don't want to offer me that. I'll just come back with locally grown honey."

A single brow lifts. "*Honey?*"

I nod. "We'll get salmonella, but I'll be the only one of us to die from it because you can afford decent health care."

He grins, reaching for his wallet. "In that case, buy several."

I MAKE baked potato soup for dinner, an old family recipe and the perfect food for tonight, with rain lashing the windows and the temperature dropping so fast that I begged Harrison to turn on the fireplace.

"I remember you making this for us when you were a kid," Harrison says as he sits down to join me. "You were always cooking when you stayed at the beach house."

I grin. "That's because my mom wasn't around then. Anytime she saw me do something domestic she got scared I wasn't going to fulfill all her big plans."

He laughs quietly under his breath. "I remember that. She tried to convince us all that you should become an artist because you were so good at drawing in preschool, and then she showed us one of these supposedly amazing works of art..."

I already know exactly where this story is going—the same direction these stories always went with my mom. I'd learn a smattering of Spanish from Harrison's dad's staff and she'd decide I would one day be a translator for the United Nations. I'd try to rescue a wounded animal and suddenly, I was destined to be a vet, and if I built a decent sandcastle, I was born to be an architect.

Except I didn't want to be a translator or an architect or a vet. My dreams were smaller: I wanted a home at the beach, a kitchen counter lined with sandy, sunburned kids, and a husband who couldn't wait to join us. I dreamed of making them potato soup and tucking them into bed.

There's a throb in my chest for the things my mom and I

will never have. My mother's efforts to make me into something big have gone nowhere and my silenced dreams of a quieter life will probably go nowhere as well.

He blows on a spoonful of soup. "Have you talked to her?"

"Not really. She's texted a few times to apologize and I told her it's fine." I shrug. "I guess it makes sense that she'd choose him over me...He's the one who'll still be here in three months."

He winces. "Daisy, I'm an outsider here, but...I've known your mom most of my life. I've known her as *your* mom since the day you were born. I can't imagine her ever choosing anyone over you."

"I know." I've backed myself into a corner and this corner is where I'll stay—missing the mother I adore; looking like a petulant child to everyone on the outside. There's no point in discussing it when I always end up in the same place.

He leans back in his chair. "Are you ever going to tell me why you hate Scott so much?"

I hitch a shoulder. "You've met him. He's a dick."

His gaze bites into mine, peeling back layers whether I want him to or not. "I've been an unbelievable dick to you all week. You've put up with it like a champ."

I frown. "I thought we'd agreed that you were going to stop trying to get rid of me."

"I'm not. I swear. I suppose I don't mind having you around. I'm just thinking of your mom."

I grin. "Really? So you *love* having me live with you?"

He raises a brow. "Let's not get ahead of ourselves. But you're not the worst roommate I've ever had."

"Come on," I argue, glancing at my chest. "I mean, look at these puppies. Lots of men would want me living with them. I'm at least in your top five."

He does not look at *these puppies*, as requested, but instead rolls his eyes. "You could potentially be in the top five if you'd stop referencing your tits so often."

"Just admit that if you were forty years younger, you'd totally want to date me."

"If I was forty years younger, I wouldn't even be born yet. You'd be sixty when I was nineteen."

"I'm going to be incredibly hot when I'm sixty," I reply. "You'd be dying to fuck me even then."

"You just dropped back into the bottom five roommates," he says.

But I notice he didn't deny anything I said either.

15

HARRISON

"I'm going to be incredibly hot when I'm sixty," she said. "You'd be dying to fuck me even then."

And I thought, *yes, yes I would, and you'd still be too goddamned young.*

I go to my room once we've cleaned up dinner, making a concerted effort to not think about Daisy. To not think about her surfing, to not think about her pulling off a wetsuit, or climbing out of the hot tub, or saying *I'd offer to take care of it* as she stared at my dick.

I put on movies—first a documentary about Ted Bundy, but the way he inserted himself into his victims' lives with a combination of charm and good looks reminds me a little too much of my houseguest.

I try a sci-fi movie next. That fails too. When you're getting hard watching an alien crawl toward its human prey, it's probably time to just give up. Eventually, I go into the shower, which is the only form of privacy you've got when said houseguest is walking back and forth outside of your room and is likely to pick your lock if she wants to chat.

I grip myself, trying to think about someone else. *Anyone*

else. My first high school girlfriend. The woman on the news who found a baby alligator in her toilet. Even Audrey would be preferable.

But as I spill all over my hand, biting my lip to keep in my gasp, I am definitely imagining it's all over Daisy, bent in half on my deck.

I wake the next morning, ashamed of myself and slightly hungover, and go downstairs for aspirin, fully intending to go back to bed. Daisy's on the deck doing her exercise, which is the last fucking thing I want to see. I wince, hoping to escape to my room before she spies me.

"That outfit doesn't work," she says, walking in, continuing to stretch. Her bra rides up perilously high as she reaches overhead. I see a flash of under boob.

I reach for the aspirin and swallow more than I'm supposed to take. "If we're instituting a dress code, I've got some notes for you too."

"If you go running in those sweatpants, through which I can *already* see your dick, you'll be giving all the little kids outside quite the anatomy show. And probably set them on a course for future disappointment, because from what I could tell last weekend, you're packing an excessive amount in there."

For a moment my eyes lock with hers. It's automatic. Involuntary. When one of the most stunning women you've ever laid eyes on is talking about your dick, you consider where you could take the conversation. Reminding yourself she's practically family comes a moment later and is accompanied by suffocating guilt.

"Fuck that. I'm not going running."

"*Au contraire*, Harrison. You are indeed going running. We had a bet."

"Right," I grouse, "like you'd have kept the bet if you'd lost."

She smiles. "*Obviously* I wasn't going to keep my end of the bargain, but we both expect more from you. You're one of the few guys I know who lives up to his promises."

My mouth is dry; my head is pounding. I want to ignore her. And yet...I like the idea of being among the few men who haven't disappointed her.

"I need coffee first," I say with a sigh. "And you're a pain in the ass."

"It's my best quality," she chirps.

"It's far from your best quality."

"I have a number of amazing qualities," she replies. "Which one is your favorite?"

My gaze drops to the jogging bra that barely contains her breasts before I can stop it, and I wince for the third time this morning. "I'm still struggling to come up with one I even find bearable."

I begrudgingly head to my room and put on boxer briefs and shorts for our run. She, naturally, does not change *her* clothes. We cross the street to the path and start running south toward Steamer Lane and the wharf. I've always considered myself to be a reasonably fit guy, but between the soreness from surfing yesterday and the hangover, this run is pretty fucking miserable.

My chest hurts. My knees hurt. I want to stop, and we've barely run a mile. "This sucks."

"Your hips are too tight," she says. "You need yoga."

I roll my eyes. "My hips are fine, Daisy. And I'm not doing yoga, because the last time anyone checked, I still had a dick. And, actually, the person checking was you, and you implied it was excessive."

"It was *adequate*," she counters. "And lots of men do yoga. I mean, maybe back in your day they didn't, but they do now."

"Back in *my* day? How old, exactly, do you think I am?"

She grins. "Based on your chronological age or your outdated thoughts on gender norms?"

I drop behind her, worried I might get sick, but this means I'm looking at her ass. I console myself with the reminder that she doesn't know it's happening, but quickly realize that's perhaps even worse. I wish there was one goddamn line of thought I could have regarding Daisy that didn't wind up with *me* being the guilty party.

I run alongside her to end the mental debate.

"Finally caught up, did you?" she asks with a grin. I want to die, whereas she is positively glowing. "I assumed you were just back there, enjoying the view."

"I don't need to run behind you for that. You're offering that view freely every goddamn time I walk downstairs."

She stops when we reach the wharf, pointing to a restaurant off to the left. "That's where I'll be working, though I can't guarantee the job will last since I've got no experience."

There's already a waitress outside setting up tables and wearing a very tight T-shirt that says, "*I got lei'd at The Wharf.*"

I have a good idea why Daisy got hired. "I'm not sure I like—"

She isn't listening. She's already walking farther down the wharf when we should be turning back for the house.

"Daisy, where the hell are you going?"

She smiles over her shoulder as she continues to walk, her hips swaying. "It's time for your reward," she purrs.

My jaw grinds. "I thought we discussed you not making every word out of your mouth sound dirty."

"I was talking about *ice cream*, perv," she replies. "And it only sounded dirty to you."

I beg to differ, Daisy. There's not a grown man in the world who wouldn't hear sex dripping out of half the things she says, especially when she's purring, "*It's time for your reward*" over her shoulder.

"Why the hell would you get ice cream now?" I argue. "It's not even lunch."

She's practically skipping there. "Because I want one."

I'd like to continue objecting, but she's so fucking excited about it that I don't have the heart to shut her down. As I recall, this is how she got her way with me as a kid, too. It shouldn't still be working.

There's no line yet at the ice cream stand, which isn't surprising, given that most reasonable people are just waking up.

"You remember we still have to run home, yes?" I ask, as we take a seat at the nearest table.

"It'll give me energy," she argues. "And besides, what's the point of doing all this stuff to lead a long life if I'm not going to enjoy it?"

There was a time when I'd have agreed with her, back in those days when I surfed every morning in front of my dad's house and surfed every afternoon at Long Point. The world was like a candy store back then—endlessly colorful, the options nearly infinite. There was so much to choose from I didn't know where to look first.

Now I don't even enter the store, but Daisy's in the thick of it. She's reaching for one experience after another, and she's licking that soft serve like she's never had ice cream in her life.

Which leaves me wanting to lick a thing or two as well.

She swipes her tongue obscenely along its length. She's being intentionally lascivious, but...it's been a very long time, and the way she really seems to be *enjoying* that cone hits me in a way it should not. Beneath the table, I adjust myself.

She grins. "Is it so sexy, watching me eat this?"

"Yes, almost as sexy as it'll be when you're throwing it up in someone's bushes on the way home."

She licks down the sides again, and I sigh heavily to disguise this thing in my gut that is not exasperation at all.

"How about now?" She deep throats it, shoving the entire cone in her mouth and pulling it back out. "*Now* is it sexy?"

I've had it with this. I'd walk away entirely if I *could* walk away. I adjust myself again. "Just for the record, this is what I mean when I accuse you of making everything sound dirty."

She laughs. "You love it."

Do I? Perhaps. Much like my love for jalapeños, however, it causes me far more pain than pleasure. And at least I don't have to feel guilty about the jalapeños.

My phone vibrates and I flip it over to find a text from Oliver, telling me he's flying into LA on the tenth and wants to hang out in Malibu for the weekend. It's been the plan for a while. I'm not sure why, but when I look at Daisy—still going after that ice cream cone with a skill porn stars only *wish* they had—I find myself reluctant to agree to the trip.

She throws out the rest of her cone, presumably because she's had enough and probably because she was just tired of getting no reaction from me, and we start walking back toward West Cliff. And as much as I did not want to go on this run, there's now a strange part of me that's actually eager to stretch myself and take a nice hot shower when it's done. To watch her dance around the kitchen as she makes lunch and sit across from her over dinner.

I'd never admit it to her, but I'm happy she came. And I sort of don't want her to leave.

16

DAISY

I t's weird how many people look at a menu full of options and then request something else. Wharf Seafood has mahi-mahi, shrimp, trout, and salmon, but there have already been two assholes who perused the entire menu and asked for different fish, as if this is some Michelin-starred restaurant saving the more *exotic* products for those customers savvy enough to ask.

"You don't have lobster?" asks the woman in front of us, fretting as she feeds her infant bits of a buttered roll while her glum husband stares at the menu. "Johnny loves lobster."

"I'm so sorry, we don't," says Mia, the waitress I'm shadowing. She actually sounds sincere. I'm not sure I'd manage it myself.

"Okay, can you at least put truffles on his smiley fries?"

That is when I realize Johnny is the *baby*. She wanted us to procure a special, off-the-menu item for her one-year-old. And put truffles on his fries.

Mia apologizes once more. "Sorry. We don't have shaved truffles either."

Of course we don't. We have gross fried fish and a drink

called The Purple Nurple, which is the equivalent of ten shots of liquor served in an oversized baby bottle—this is not where you go for fucking truffles.

The woman asks her still-glum husband if he's sure he wants to eat here before we walk away.

"The rich are not like you and I," says Mia once we're out of hearing distance.

I laugh, though I think if they were *actually* rich they'd realize a restaurant decorated with fisherman's netting wasn't likely to offer much beyond coronary artery disease and a hangover.

I'm sent home following the lunch shift. I earned nothing at all since I'm only shadowing, and it costs fifteen dollars to get my car out of the lot—so far, gainful employment is less rewarding than I'd hoped.

I go straight to Harrison's outdoor shower to wash the smell of fried food from my hair. I'm emerging with one towel around my head and one around my chest when Harrison's Range Rover pulls into the garage.

His sunglasses are still on, but I don't miss the way his gaze travels over me as he climbs out of the car.

I adjust the towel atop my head. "You're home when it's still light out? Has someone died?"

His mouth quirks up on one side. "I was falsely hoping it might be the one time of day you'd wear sufficient clothing."

I laugh as I open the door to walk inside. "You should know better than to ever hope I'd wear sufficient clothing." I glance over my shoulder at him as I climb the stairs and catch him checking out my ass.

He blinks away guiltily. "I assumed you'd have gotten fired and would be in need of moral support."

I turn as I reach the main floor, holding my towel in place with one hand. "You seriously assumed I'd be fired on my first day?"

"How many customers did you mouth off to, Daisy?" he asks, eyes twinkling.

"Not a single one, for your information. To be completely transparent, however, I wasn't allowed to speak to any of the customers, so my opportunities were limited."

He laughs. "I guess that explains it."

I glance toward the ocean. "Tide's coming in."

"I guess you wouldn't want to surf, since you just showered."

I run my tongue across my lip. "Of course I want to surf. Unlike Audrey, I don't mind the feeling of *sand* one bit."

His gaze meets mine. He's thinking of my comment from last week and so am I.

I don't mind the feeling of a lot of things, Harrison.

"Only you could make the word *sand* sound filthy," he grumbles, heading to his room.

Ten minutes later, we're in wetsuits, crossing the street quickly, eager to make the most of the remaining sun.

I follow him to the lineup, closer to the heart of the break, though still a fair distance from the other guys already out here. "Apparently, I've graduated."

"Don't make me regret it."

"I'll probably make you regret it."

He laughs. "I know."

I take the first decent wave, and he takes the second. My gut tightens, watching him. He's so fucking big, so sure of himself, so focused.

Is he like that in bed too? Would he look at me as if nothing else mattered, as if the world could be ending and he'd never even notice?

Perhaps. But that doesn't mean there wouldn't come a day when he *stopped* doing it. When his eyes would remain shut because he was pretending I was someone else—someone smarter, someone special in all the ways he'd finally seen I wasn't.

We each take another handful of waves and return to the lineup at the same time. The sun is now an orange ball on the horizon, painting streaks of gold in his dark hair, lighting up his face.

"This is more like the rich guy adulthood I always imagined you'd have," I tell him.

He shoots me a lazy smile. "How exactly does a rich guy spend his day? In case I've forgotten."

"Well, you start by counting your money, obviously."

"Obviously. Gold coins in a vault. I did that first. Then what?"

"Then you demand something unreasonable for breakfast, and lash out when you get that thing because you now want something else."

He nods. "Well, it *is* frustrating to discover you've chosen poorly."

"Then you fire an employee—perhaps someone on parole or in witness protection so he or she will be too scared to sue for wrongful termination."

"That *is* easiest, yes. And then?"

I hitch a shoulder. "Really, the sky's the limit. Talk to other rich people about how rich you are. Go hunt poor people for sport. Impregnate supermodels—the ones your dad hasn't impregnated first, that is."

A laugh rumbles in his chest. "What a fascinating place your mind is. I'd like to peel it back to see all the rest."

"I'm sure you'd love to peel back my mind, but you're not getting rid of me *that* easily."

"I don't want to get rid of you," he replies, and something flutters in my chest again. Not lust, this time. It's sweeter.

If I were already head over heels in love with him, I'm guessing it would feel a lot like this.

I SPEND my next shift in the dreary restaurant, thinking about my grandmother, oddly enough—how she used to tell me I was just like my dad, and how much I hated it.

He could never stand to be indoors either, she'd say when I'd visit them, always with this combination of pride and wistfulness, as if it were a good thing.

The official story, according to my grandparents, is that my father got held under too long at Mavericks and had a reaction to the meds he was put on afterward for depression.

My mother says they don't want to acknowledge he was ill all along—that all those qualities in him that seemed quirky and wild and offbeat, like risking your life to surf Mavericks when it's clear you're not ready for it, were simply the early signs. I think she's probably right, which is what made my grandmother's words so hard to hear. I don't want to be anything like him, and I suspect I am.

The last time I saw my father, when I was twelve, he was living in a residential center for the mentally ill. Even medicated, most of what he said didn't make sense, but what scared me was that a little of it did. He insisted they were poisoning him with all the fluorescent light at the exact moment I was thinking the lights were making me tired. He told me he'd rather be dead than be kept indoors all day, and it was a thought I'd had a thousand times. I'd said it to Liam whenever he was blowing off work to catch the winter swell while sending *me* to school.

People told my mom she put too much pressure on me to become something extraordinary, but I put that same pressure on myself. It felt as if the only other option might be...him.

I look toward the water longingly—there's a voice in my head as I go to fulfill Mia's drink orders, saying *just walk out, Daisy. Get some sun. Go surfing.* Maybe my dad heard that voice too. Maybe at heart, I'm someone who can't be inside, can't suck it up and function at a normal job, skilled or unskilled.

I bus Mia's tables. A guy stops me to ask if our fish is ethically sourced, and it's all I can do not to point at our drink menu, which features a cocktail called *"Bitch Had it Coming,"* and ask if he's serious.

Another of her customers is drawing a picture, glancing my way every three seconds as he sketches. I can tell that it's me, though he's got me in some weird dominatrix outfit and the boobs are impossibly big. He hands it to me when he's done, and I thank him because I'm not sure what to say. As I walk away, I think about that day in creative writing when I was invited to join the writing group that was mostly for grad students...and no one else was. Oh, the look on my ex's face when I was invited and he was not. The *speed* with which he raced after me when class ended to beg me to take him back, claiming it was "pretty much over" with the model, which is what men say when they are very much in a relationship but want to fuck you anyway.

I made the wrong decision that day and then proceeded to make worse ones, all because I wanted to be more, because I wanted to be special, because I needed to believe that the reason I hadn't found my place in the world was because I was *extraordinary* rather than defective.

And now I'm sucking at waiting tables and thanking people for pornographic drawings, and I'm probably not getting back into school, and I can't stand the way my life is narrowing, is turning me into my father no matter how hard I've tried not to become him.

I don't take a single deep breath until my shift ends and I'm back outside.

17

HARRISON

After months of not having enough to do, on Tuesday afternoon, I'm swamped and resentful.

I stare at the dying sun, picturing Daisy out on the water, telling me how rich people live. I want to surf. I want to talk to her as we straddle our boards, the water rolling beneath us. I want to take a hot shower afterward and watch her pad around the kitchen with wet hair, humming as she cooks.

I'd forgotten this hunger for things, the way I once couldn't fucking wait to leave work to surf with my friends. And maybe this hunger is about more than surfing, but that point is best left unexplored.

I don't get home 'til late. She's on the couch, curled up with a book, her bare feet peeking out of the end of the blanket. I fight the urge to cover them, tugging at my tie instead. I can't reconcile these two sides of her—the cute little kid I babied for years and the grown woman who is seductive even when she's wrapped in a blanket, reading.

"There's some shrimp and pasta in the fridge," she says.

I ate at work, but I heat some of it up anyway, just in case she made it for me.

She comes to the counter, yawning as she scrapes her hair back into a ponytail. "Hey, can I borrow one of the bikes in the garage? I'm not being paid yet, and the lot I'm parking in costs fifteen bucks a day."

"What do you mean they're not paying you?" I demand. "By law, they have to pay you."

She waves her hand. "The restaurant is the least of my problems, believe me."

I shut the microwave door and turn toward her. Under Daisy's perpetually sunny outlook I've sensed something, and it was something I mostly wanted to ignore. Things are too complicated between us already. I want to take care of her the way I always did, and at the same time, we'd both be better off if I stayed away. But is she lonely? When I was her age, I was only at home to sleep, nothing more, while she doesn't go out at all.

"I know I was a dick about letting you stay here, but you're allowed to have friends." I have to force the next words out. "You're allowed to have a social life. Or date."

I picture some idiot showing up at the front door to get her. I wish I could retract the offer.

She forces another smile. "I'm good. I'm not looking to date, and I've just been pretty content with the way things are."

Is that why I was so reluctant to meet Oliver in Malibu? Because I've been kind of content with her too?

"I'll come home in time to surf tomorrow," I tell her. It's a promise I really can't make because God knows what will come up at work, but I'm making it anyway. "We'll surf until the last minute and order a pizza for dinner."

Her smile is not forced. It lights up the room like the starriest night of the fucking year.

~

WE GET a solid two hours of surfing in the next afternoon. Between sets she tells me she hates the new job and the one customer she waited on "sucked," but she doesn't elaborate. Being in the water seems to take care of whatever it is that ails her, however. By the time we're done, her shoulders have lowered, and her eyes are peaceful again.

She takes one of her beloved outdoor showers. I'm carrying the pizza into the kitchen when she shows up, her hair damp, her face flushed. She appears to be wearing nothing but an oversized sweatshirt—all I see are tan, muscular thighs running all the way up to its hem. I glance away fast and carry the pizza to the table, suddenly famished.

My appetite has been entirely absent for a full year. It's reemerged with a vengeance since she arrived. A lot of appetites have.

"Pizza is one of those foods," she says, groaning as she swallows her first bite. "I thought you were so lucky to have a housekeeper-slash-cook growing up, but nothing beats a standard delivery pizza."

Pizza, sunshine, surfing, a shower outdoors or the smell of her body wash—these things all thrill her, and she tells me about every single one of them. I don't think I've ever known anyone who relishes life quite the way Daisy does.

"I thought you guys were the lucky ones," I reply, already reaching for a second slice. The Dohertys' tiny house was crowded and chaotic—Bridget, Liam, their parents, and then Daisy—but it was full of life. There was always noise and laughter, always something cooking and someone yelling, while my father's homes seemed empty. The staff knew they'd better be silent whether he was there or not and scurried out of any room I entered.

She rolls her eyes. "In what possible way were *we* lucky?"

"Your house was lively and you guys had *fun*. You'd have been too little to remember it, but your mom took you and Liam on this trip down through Big Sur once. You rented some kind of log cabin and saw a waterfall emptying into the ocean."

Her mouth curves. "Dude, you realize you can reach Big Sur in ninety minutes, right?"

I laugh. "I know. But it sounded very cool when I was twelve. Anyway, we can order in pizza or whatever you want going forward. You don't have to cook."

She blushes. "I like cooking for you. I know I'm not supposed to, and I'm sure Audrey thinks women like me are putting feminism back a hundred years, but there you have it."

My gaze drops to her bare legs. "I think Audrey would be more troubled by the fact that it looks like you've got nothing on under that sweatshirt."

"Maybe if Audrey had wandered around in nothing but a sweatshirt more often, you'd have seemed a little happier when you were stuck with her."

"So you're saying that my marital problems could have been solved by a slight wardrobe change? And here I thought our issues ran deeper than that."

Her smile is knowing, *adult*. "I'm saying that if you were married to a woman who was wearing nothing but a sweatshirt when you got home, she'd probably welcome you back by climbing into your lap and showing you how much she'd missed you. And that would solve a problem or two right there."

My jaw locks, and my eyes fall closed. I can't help but picture Daisy straddling me on the couch, pulling one of my hands between her thighs to show me how fucking eager she'd been for my arrival.

"Yeah," I croak. "That might have solved a few problems."

Right now, though, it's only creating them.

18

DAISY

I'm alone on Friday and making dinner when my mom calls.

I used to love talking to my mom, but for the last year, I've lied so much that I cringe every time her name lights up my phone. This summer, of course, it's only gotten worse. If I tell her I'm working in Santa Cruz, she'll ask if I've seen Harrison and then she'll probably *call* Harrison and ask him to check on me. I've resorted to a very childish stance of "it's none of your business" solely to keep this house of cards from caving in.

"Hi, baby!" she cries, clearly excited I'm actually answering. "How are things? What are you doing?"

"Trying to get super greens into a protein shake without it tasting like ass. Oh, and attempting to make tartiflette—I saw it on a cooking show and it looked amazing."

"You shouldn't be messing around in the kitchen," she scolds. "You should be studying for the LSAT."

I sigh. She'd have been the perfect mom for someone like Harrison, someone driven. Instead, she wound up with me. "I enjoy messing around in the kitchen."

"Daisy, this matters. I wish you'd just come home. You could study full-time."

"Mom." My voice takes on a hard edge, the one that warns her to drop it. "I'm happy with the way things are."

"I don't know what's gotten into you," she says, but there's despair in her voice rather than irritation. "I'm just trying to help, but I feel like I can't say the right thing anymore."

My heart squeezes. She wants so much for me, more than I've ever wanted for myself, and I don't know how to tell her to stop wanting it. "I'm sorry," I reply. "I just...don't need the pressure right now, okay?"

"You're right." She forces a laugh. "What would I know about law school? Everything I've ever heard is secondhand. Anyway, I miss you. Can we get dinner?"

I wonder when Harrison's leaving for LA. I don't want to voluntarily give up a single hour by his side before I return to DC.

"Sure, let me check my schedule at work, okay?"

"I can make that pasta you like, with the feta and tomatoes?" she asks. "Or maybe chicken Kiev?"

I stiffen. "I sort of thought we'd meet at a restaurant."

"Wouldn't you prefer a home-cooked meal?"

"What I'd prefer is to not eat dinner with Scott," I snap. Why is it so fucking hard for her to understand this? Is there any possible way I could have made it more clear? Doubtful.

She's still scrambling to get her fairy tale ending—the loving husband, the accomplished daughter—while I'm here with Harrison pretending I've already got mine.

And we're both going to wind up empty-handed.

IT'S BARELY dawn when Harrison knocks on my door. "Let's go, Daisy," he calls. "Tide's coming in."

I rush out of bed, brush my teeth, and race down to the garage while trying to tie my bikini on. He's already in his wetsuit by the time I reach him. I tug on mine while he waxes our boards.

As much as I loved surfing with him and Liam and their friends as a kid, this is better. I always felt like the fifth wheel back then, but here, when it's just the two of us...it's like being a vital part of a team. I love my uncle and I love his friends, but it wouldn't be the same if any of them were here.

We get to the water and dive in. It's a bit calmer than normal, which makes it easier to paddle out, but we have to wait a while for a decent set.

"How was work last night?" I ask, straddling my board. I'm surprised he woke before me—he got in late, long after I'd gone to bed.

He leans forward, resting on his palms. "As scintillating as ever." The sarcasm in his voice would be impossible to miss. I know he had a few interesting clients before he left for London, clients who made up for what was otherwise a tedious job. But he transferred them. So why is he still there?

I throw out my hands. "Why are you torturing yourself at a job that makes you miserable when we both know you're rich as hell? Take a year off. Find the job of your dreams. Everything's online now anyway. I bet some law firm would let you do the work you want from here if you refuse to move."

"I'm not rich, Daisy—I'm comfortable. My father has money. I just have a decent job."

I laugh. "Yes, I see the way you're barely scraping by here."

He shrugs a shoulder. "I make a good living and yeah, I started off with some money I inherited, but that still doesn't make me rich."

Which sounds exactly like the kind of thing a rich person would say.

"Speaking of *work*," he adds with a brow raised, "Liam said you're spending the summer studying for the LSAT, yet I haven't seen you do anything vaguely academic even once."

Shit. "I was studying all week. Didn't you see me reading?"

He gives me a lopsided grin. "Funny, I don't recall reading *Diary of a Rock Star Groupie* before law school myself."

"The heroine has to sign a nondisclosure agreement, so it's legal in nature," I reply, but I can tell he's still waiting for a real answer, dammit. I sigh heavily. "I'm not actually sure about law school. It's another of my mom's plans."

"You can't get an expensive three-year degree just to make your mom happy."

Oh, can't I? Because I just undertook an expensive four-year degree to make her happy—not that it has.

"I know. This professor told me I was a good writer last year and suggested I consider an MFA, and I was excited simply because it seemed like a way *out* of law school."

"Are you interested in getting an MFA?"

"No. Not at all." I've been grasping at straws just as recklessly as my mother has, trying to find a way to make her proud. I wanted to become someone for her more than I wanted to actually grow into a better version of myself.

The board rolls beneath me as a small wave approaches. "I just don't know how to tell her. Because if I'm not going to law school, she's just going to come up with a different plan, some new way for me to be special when I need her to understand that I'm just...not. I'm not special."

"Of *course* you're special," he insists, sounding almost angry on my behalf.

I laugh, but it's a sad sound. "You had to say that. But I'm really not. My mother was a great student, and she loved school. I'm just okay at everything, at best, and I hate school." I tip my head toward the wave ahead of us, but he ignores it.

"There are other ways to be special—"

I shake my head as I start to turn my board. "Not ways that matter. Not to her. And I'm not really sure what to do with myself in the meantime."

"I think you start by considering that maybe you don't have to do *anything* with yourself," he says as we paddle, and once again he sounds angry, as if he's defending me from myself. "You're perfect just the way you are."

I smile, unwillingly.

There are a hundred people in the world who could detail my failures. It's hard to care when Harrison, the best of them, likes me regardless.

WHEN WE GET HOME, I take an extra-long, extra-hot shower, and then open all the doors and blast music while I make us acai bowls. He playfully carps about the mess I've made and eats every bite.

We both sit out on the deck together afterward. He reads the paper and does some work. I finish reading *Diary of a Rock Star Groupie* and am disappointed to discover there's only one sex scene between the main character and the rest of the band.

In the evening, he grills us steaks while I make potatoes and salad. I hum as I cook, and it hits me that I'm happy, just like this. That if I really didn't have to make something of myself, if I could simply *exist*, this is the precise existence I'd choose. I'd cook, and I'd surf, and I'd take care of someone, and it would be more than enough, as long as he was the one I was caring for.

It would be *everything*.

"You want to watch a movie?" I ask as we clean up dinner.

He hesitates. Most nights he goes to his room and watches something on his laptop, and it's pretty clear he'd prefer to do that tonight too.

"Not if it's some Teen Disney bullshit," he finally says. "The two times I babysat you, you made me watch *both* of the *Camp Rock* movies."

I groan. "Harrison, I was what...seven? What did you want to watch when you were seven, and do you *still* want to watch it?"

"*Star Wars*," he replies. "And yes. But I see your point."

We pick an older movie, one that has a little something for both of us—violence for him, Ryan Gosling for me.

He positions himself on one end of the couch and I curl up on the other, though soon I'm stretched out, taking up most of the space. My toes brush his thigh, and he scrapes a nail along the sole of my foot, which makes me laugh.

The movie is slightly too violent for my liking and slightly too romantic for Harrison's. Every time Ryan Gosling starts flirting with the heroine, Harrison mutters, "Give me a break," which I ignore because it's the best part of the movie.

No matter how committed I am to remaining single, I want what Ryan Gosling and that girl on screen have, though it's clearly not going to turn out well for either of them. When Ryan Gosling kisses her, I release a wistful sigh. I want that too.

Harrison smirks. "He just bludgeoned someone to death, yet you're still swooning over him."

"I'm not swooning over *him*. I'm swooning over the way he kissed her. It's romantic—the way he did it. The way he grabbed her face and held it."

"You just made the case for him to be tried for assault," Harrison says. "I've never kissed a woman like that in my life."

I shoot him a pointed look, a single brow arched. "Maybe that explains some things. Do not ruin this for me."

He's silent. He's probably creating a list of felonies he'd like to charge Ryan Gosling with.

Or maybe he's hurt.

Did I go too far with my *maybe that explains some things* bullshit? Of course I did. The man just got dumped and is probably still looking for an explanation, which I just provided with my big fucking mouth. "I'm—"

"What makes it romantic?" he asks before I can even get an apology out. His voice is quieter, slightly uncertain. He hits *pause*.

I curl up, tucking my feet beneath me as I face him. "It's... possessive. It's like he'd die before he'd let anyone come between them. You place your hand on a woman's hip when you kiss her and it's sort of like you're just trying something out. You don't know how it will go; you might change your mind; you're not sure about what you want. *That* kiss? With his hands cradling her face? It's committed. He wants her, and he doesn't give a damn if the whole world knows."

"So, is that what you're holding out for?" He nods toward the screen. "Someone who basically assaults you, but it's okay because it shows he *cares?*"

I snatch the remote and turn back toward the TV. "I'm not holding out for anything. I'm done with men."

He raises a brow.

"Before you get all excited, I'm not saying I'm a lesbian either."

He does, in fact, look a bit disappointed.

I shrug. "It's all not worth the effort. Love isn't and sex *definitely* isn't. Why should I risk pregnancy and disease so some idiot who can't even find my clit gets off? I can find it myself in way less time."

His exhale is audible, as if I've punched the air out of him. "Ostensibly," he says, crossing the room to the liquor cabinet, "there's a little more to it than that. And you choose a man who knows what he's doing."

He's nursed one bourbon through the whole movie but now fills his glass to the brim and remains there while he slams it.

When he finally returns, he's carrying the whole bottle with him.

Apparently, I've driven him to drink.

19

HARRISON

I wake with my head pounding. For a moment, I'm puzzled, remembering only a very wholesome evening with Daisy in which we ate dinner together and watched a violent movie.

Oh. Right.

The end of our wholesome evening hits me like a ton of bricks:

Daisy talking about how no one could find her clit.

Daisy saying, "*I can find it myself in way less time.*"

And the raving lunatic inside me who wanted to say, "*I could find your clit. I could make you come so hard you wouldn't be able to form words.*"

Fuck. I probably drank half a bottle of bourbon in the hour after that.

It's ridiculous, of course. There's no way that lush little Daisy with her curves, and her husky voice, and her habit of making everything sound filthy isn't going to find a man who turns her inside out. Everything about her begs you to try.

But it's disgusting how badly I want to be one of the lucky pricks who gives it a shot.

I'M PACKING up my stuff Monday afternoon, eager to get home by high tide, when Aaron Baker, the managing partner, walks in.

"You off to a meeting?" he asks.

He assumes it's a meeting because during all my time here, I never left early to go home. I never once said, *"I feel like surfing"* or *"I want to see my wife."*

"No, actually. I'm just meeting a friend out at the beach. Things are still pretty slow."

He raises a brow. "They aren't going to improve if you're cutting out of work at four-thirty."

My jaw grinds. I worked like a madman for years, but here we are. It's like I'm a fucking associate all over again. "I'm not going to sit here with no work just hoping something comes in, Aaron. My billables are fine."

"You didn't get where you were by doing *fine* before, Harrison. You know that. Look, I've got some contracts I need reviewed. I was going to give them to Zoe, but I'd rather have your eyes on them anyway. I'm heading out, but I'll be back by nine to discuss."

You've got to be fucking kidding me. He's offloading work he was going to give to a junior associate simply to prove a point—that I owe him one for taking me back on.

And I hate reviewing contracts, though it's about ninety percent of my job. How did I end up in this place in my life? I got a law degree because it seemed as if I should. I married Audrey because she seemed like the kind of woman I should marry, stayed with her because I was supposed to, and followed her to London because I couldn't admit I'd fucking failed. It's as if, somewhere along the way, I forgot I was supposed to enjoy my life, not simply win at it.

Normally I'd just shrug it off, but Baker's bullshit means no surfing with Daisy, no dinner with Daisy, no fighting myself *not* to watch her shimmy out of her wetsuit, no coconut breeze as she passes me straight out of the shower.

And if I'm this bothered by missing a night with her, how the hell am I going to stand a weekend away in Malibu?

I can't. I just can't fucking do it.

> Hey—is it okay if I bring someone?

OLIVER

> Someone female I assume? As long as it's not the odious Audrey, the more the merrier.

> Not a girl I'm dating. "Babysitting" is more accurate. You met her ages ago. Liam's niece, Daisy? I don't know if you remember.

> Ah, yes, vaguely. If she's half as attractive as her lovely mother, then she is definitely welcome.

I'd almost forgotten about that. Bridget is cute—blonde and blue-eyed like Daisy—and that alone was enough to make her everyone's first crush. But there's something lush and decadent about Daisy that Bridget never had, something you can't drag your eyes from. I may not see Oliver often, but I know for damn sure it's something he'll want to explore. I think it's why I said I was babysitting—so that he wouldn't get the wrong idea about us, but more importantly, so that he wouldn't get any wrong ideas for *himself*.

> Lovelier. But she's my friend's kid, so any interaction with her needs to be celibate.

OLIVER

> I'll consider myself warned.

The cynic in me—who once watched Oliver *literally* charm

the pants off a woman on the dance floor of a bar in Mykonos —wants to extract further promises but doing that will just prove this is about more than me protecting my friend's kid.

I guess it *is* about more, but as long as I don't act on it, no one ever needs to know.

When I get home, Daisy's curled up on the couch, reading a book, but what grabs my attention is the drawing that sits on the counter.

It's a pencil sketch of her, looking lovely and incredibly fuckable in some weird bondage outfit. "What's this?"

She shrugs. "This guy draws my picture every day. He always leaves me one when he's done."

I'm not sure if cartoon porn is a thing, but this drawing would fit right in with the genre if it was. "What's with the dress?"

"It's some video game he's into. That's what the character wears."

My jaw grinds. This guy is one hundred percent drawing her in even fewer clothes and saving those pictures for himself. I wonder, for perhaps the third time in twenty-four hours, how I can convince her to quit that job.

"You want to come with me to Malibu next weekend?" I ask abruptly. It's *too* abrupt. It sounds like a request I was obligated to make. "Oliver's renting a house."

She rolls her eyes. "Harrison, you don't have to invite me. I'm not going to throw a party or drown, I promise."

I set my keys on the counter and tug at my tie, which is suddenly strangling me. How do I persuade her without making it sound like something I'm doing for myself? "It's not that. I just thought you'd...enjoy it. The place is right on the beach, and it'll be warmer there than it is here. You could surf all day if you wanted."

She eyes me warily, but there's excitement in her gaze too. "I wouldn't be in the way?"

"I haven't spent any significant time with Oliver in years. Matthew was the extrovert of the group, and he isn't coming. If anything, you'll make it less awkward."

Her mouth softens. "Just admit that this is, at least in part, that you're worried I'll drown if you're not looking out for me."

"It is, at least in part, that I'm worried you'll drown if I'm not looking out for you. But I do actually want you to come." Our eyes meet. *Come. I can't think of anything I've wanted this much in years.*

"Then I'll come." Her smile is so wide that I'm stabbed by it, both glad that I asked and regretting it at the same time.

There's no way Oliver's going to leave her alone, and I can hardly blame him.

I'm barely managing to do it myself.

20

DAISY

My ex took me on loads of trips. St. Michael's, New York City, Miami. I'd gladly trade in all of them for two days of surfing with Harrison, even if I suspect he's mostly invited me to make sure I stay alive until Sunday night. Fortunately, I already told Wharf Seafood that I couldn't work weekends, but I'd have quit if it meant not going. I've never been so excited for a trip in my life.

"We should surf on the way," I tell Harrison Tuesday night as he glides up alongside me in the water.

He quirks a brow. The dying light catches on the droplets of water on his unshaved jaw, and my heart quickens. I've never laid eyes on a man who looks better than Harrison on a surfboard.

"Surf on the way *where*? Aren't we surfing now?"

"On the way to Malibu. I was looking at the map last night. We could stop at Asilomar in Monterey, then drive through Big Sur. You could finally see McWay Falls."

"Daisy, it would take us hours longer to travel along the coast, especially if we're stopping. *Especially* if we're surfing."

"Right. That's why we should leave Thursday morning instead and stay in Santa Barbara that night."

He grins. It's that same feral, cocky grin I fell in love with a decade ago, but there's something sweet in his eyes at the same time. I amuse him and irritate him in equal measure. "Thursday? You want me to take *two* days off work?"

"I've got it all plotted out. We spend the first day surfing and driving through Big Sur, like I said." I sit up straight, too excited to be chill about my plans for us. "Then we surf at Rincon on the second day before driving down to Malibu. Come on. When was the last time you took a vacation?"

"Well, there was the two months I spent pretending to be in London."

I lean back on my palms. "That is *not* a vacation."

"You're going to get me fired, Daisy." He says it as if he doesn't really mind, however.

"And then you'll just be a super-rich guy enjoying the final days of his youth while searching for a career he actually enjoys. I can see why you'd be worried." My mouth forms a pout, as if this is indeed a sad state of affairs. His gaze falls for a moment to my lips before he glances away.

"I'm not rich, these are not *the final days* of my youth, and you have an unnerving ability to make ridiculous ideas sound entirely plausible."

"So we're leaving Thursday?"

He laughs. "No, but I can probably take Friday off. Half the office is out with the flu anyway. We can stop at *one* surf break and possibly see McWay Falls."

I guess it's better than nothing, though it does shoot my *"Oh, this hotel only has one bed?"* fantasy to hell.

"Stop pouting," he says. "If I'd agreed to Thursday, you'd have suggested we leave Wednesday to see Carmel too."

"I *do* love Carmel. And there's a good break right at—"

He barks a laugh. "I knew it. You're a bad influence, Daisy."

"I'm the best influence."

"You may be both," he says, smiling.

I WAKE before he does on Friday morning, too excited to stay asleep, and move through my normal cycle of stretches and push-ups and lunges in the early morning sun. When I'm nearly through, I spy Harrison behind me, a cup of coffee in his hand, watching.

He appears guilty, as if he's been caught at something.

I come inside, locking the door behind me. "Were you being extra quiet so I'd let you drink your coffee in peace?"

"Something like that." He can't quite meet my eye, which leaves me wondering. Things are changing with us, whether he's willing to admit it or not. Sure, he's been well aware that I'm female for a while—that erection he was sporting my first morning here is one of my favorite memories—but it's different now. When he looks at me in a certain way, it's as if he's considering the possibilities rather than trying to ignore them.

"Are you ready for this?" I ask.

His gaze meets mine, as if I meant more by the question. Maybe I did.

"Yeah." His smile makes my stomach flutter. "I'm ready."

He drinks his coffee, I take a quick shower and then we are on the road, moving south of Santa Cruz and past farmland—Watsonville, Salinas—that I doubt has changed much since John Steinbeck made it famous.

"It's an amazing state, isn't it?" I ask, staring out the window. "People talk endless shit about California but look at it. We've got everything here."

He glances at me. "You sound like you don't want to leave at the end of August."

There's a small pinch at the center of my chest. It's entirely possible that I've got nothing to go back to in DC, but that still won't mean I get to stay here instead.

"I'm...ooh, pull over!" I cry suddenly. "They've got eight avocados for a dollar at the stand ahead."

"What the hell are we going to do with eight avocados?" he demands. "I'll buy you a thousand avocados if you just agree that we don't have to stop."

"Think of all the money you'll save," I insist.

"I can't reiterate enough that there's never been a time when I needed eight avocados."

"Pull over," I demand.

"What do I get?" he asks, and my head jerks to his. Because *what do I get?* sounds sexual to me.

I raise a brow, letting my gaze drop to his crotch.

He coughs into his hand and turns off the road. "I get to choose the music on the way home."

I guess it's for the best that he answered his own question. I think I'd have had a very different answer. And based on the look in his eyes before he coughed...he had a different one too.

21

HARRISON

We drive through Monterey, then Pacific Point, and reach Asilomar just as dark grey storm clouds slide in from the south.

Daisy's smiling, determined to be out there no matter what Mother Nature throws at us. And I'm unable to tell her no, for some reason. "If we hear thunder, we get out."

"If we see *lightning*. Thunder is meaningless."

"I'm not negotiating with you, Daisy," I warn, parking on the side of the road.

She climbs out of the car and reaches into the back seat for her wetsuit. "What are you going to do? Drag me out of the water?"

We look at each other and start to laugh.

"Fine," she says. "You'd absolutely drag me out of the water."

I untie the boards from the car while trying very hard not to watch her shimmy into her wetsuit. In spite of the weather and the fact that it's nearly lunchtime, the water is full of surfers, people who understand that it's worth everything—blowing off work, risking a lightning strike—for the brief thrill of it.

The water's cold, the sky is gray, and as we paddle to the lineup, her blue eyes are glowing as if she's never been happier. "You love this."

She turns those glowing eyes my way. "It's an adventure. And I don't have to worry about being flung into a cliff, which is surprisingly nice."

I slow my paddle to remain by her side. "Someday, you should go down to southern Costa Rica. Really consistent surf. White, white sand. And the water never gets colder than eighty degrees."

Her eyes fall closed. "God, wouldn't that be amazing? No wetsuits, no shock when you jump in the water..."

If our lives were wildly different, I'd take her there. I'd rent us a cottage right on the beach, where she could surf to her heart's content every day. If our lives were incredibly different, I'd pull that bikini off her the minute we were done.

Leave that thought alone, Harrison.

She's up on the first decent wave that comes in, her focus intense as she carves up then cuts back beautifully.

"That's goals, right there," says a woman near me.

I blink. "Goals?"

"You and her," she says. "My girlfriend and I get along, but she'd never come out here and surf. Like...you guys are clearly super-hot for each other, but you're also *friends*."

"We're not together." I say the words too fast, and there's a hint of guilt in my voice. "She's my friend's daughter."

She raises a brow as if she simultaneously doesn't believe me and is now wondering if I'm a predator. I turn away to watch Daisy paddle back. A dim ray of light breaks through the clouds, highlighting the curves of her face, her long lashes wet and spiky. For a moment, it takes my breath away.

The woman near me was right. A relationship with someone like Daisy would be unbelievable, but it's also completely impossible. And daydreaming about it will only make me less satisfied with the life I end up with instead.

"You look troubled," Daisy says when she reaches me. "Are you thinking I'm wasting my life in college and should join the world surf tour? Because if so, we're on the same page."

I laugh. "Yeah, that's exactly what I was thinking. Is there a two-foot-wave category?"

She flips me off with a smile and then turns to face the shore, ready to go again.

Goals.

If only there was anyone in the world who was just like her, but *not* her. Not Bridget's daughter and Liam's niece, not more than a decade younger, not leaving for DC at the summer's end.

We surf for about forty minutes more, until thunder rumbles. Daisy rolls her eyes at me— for all her supposed responsibility, she'd stay out here until lightning was setting people on fire. To be fair, though, no one else is heading in, so she wouldn't be the only one.

We strip out of our wetsuits beside the car. I do my best to hand her a towel without looking at her, because she's in a bikini that covers next to nothing, and just by the way she's shivering, I bet her nipples are diamond hard.

I've got a long weekend of not noticing ahead. It's in everyone's best interest if I start trying now.

She wraps a towel around her waist then slips off her bikini bottoms and replaces them with sweatpants. "I'd blow anyone who could get me a cup of cocoa in the next five minutes," she says.

Unwillingly, I laugh. I can do my level best to avoid looking at her, but Daisy is still going to be Daisy. "You might want to try *asking* if we can get cocoa before you resort to prostituting yourself for it."

"And you might want to try not looking a gift horse in the

mouth," she replies. "If a girl offers to blow you for cocoa, get her the fucking cocoa and hope she keeps promises."

I'm so hard I have to spend two solid minutes pretending to repack the trunk before I can face her again.

WE GET lunch in Pacific Grove, where she manages to acquire cocoa without having to perform a sex act, and by the time we've gotten onto the stretch of highway leading to Big Sur, the clouds are gone and the sun is out and she's got the windows down, singing along with Jack Harlow.

She opens the sunroof to take pictures of the Bixby Bridge. I play the Jack Harlow song a second time just to watch her dance in her seat, and she laughs when she realizes I know every word.

None of this would have been possible if I'd stayed with Audrey. I wouldn't have surfed today. Audrey would *never* have gone on a road trip. She'd never have allowed the windows down, and she certainly wouldn't be fucking with the sound system to blow up the bass the way Daisy is.

And that's not to say that I wouldn't have enjoyed the things Audrey and I did together. But I wouldn't have enjoyed them like *this*. I wouldn't have loved them so much that there'd be no price worth giving them up.

It takes about an hour to reach McWay Falls. We pay to park in the lot before taking the small, crowded walkway to the viewing deck, patiently waiting our turn while everyone in front of us takes pictures.

"Do you think any of them are really seeing the view?" Daisy asks softly. "Or is it all about how good a shot they're getting and whether or not it's framed right for TikTok?"

I glance at the crowd, and she's right—*no one* is looking at the view. They're looking only at their phones.

I grin at her. "And we'll probably do the same fucking thing."

She's still observing all the people. "You know what it is? The beauty of moments like this is that they can't last. All these people are trying to make them last and in doing so, they're *missing* the moment entirely."

"You're kind of a dark little thing under that perennial *look on the bright side* attitude, aren't you?"

A shadow passes over her face. "Don't say that," she says softly, though I've got no idea why it bothered her.

"It wasn't an insult, Daisy. There's nothing wrong with having a bit of a dark side. I have a rather substantial one, as I'm sure you've noticed."

"Your dark side is hardly as harmless as you'd like to believe," she replies with a half-smile.

We finally get to the observation deck. "Let's not take any photos," she says. "Let's not take a single photo for the entire trip."

I'd wanted to get a photo of *her* as much as the falls. There's something so lovely in her face right now, lovely and calm and brave and sad all at once. It's something I wish I could capture, but I guess that's exactly what she was saying before, isn't it? I'd be trying to take a photo of something so I wouldn't have to lose it. And I'm definitely going to lose it.

I lean against the black metal rail. The spout of water does, indeed, jut mysteriously out of a rock into the deep blue Pacific churning beneath it. "It looks exactly like the pictures."

She nods. "It does."

I don't say anything more, but...it's a little empty, seeing it firsthand when I'd already seen it online.

I prefer the things I wasn't prepared for, the ones that hit out of nowhere like an unexpected gift.

Those are the ones you can't imagine ever leaving behind.

WE ARRIVE in Malibu at sunset, and I steer us to a white oceanfront house that looks like it's straight out of *Architectural Digest.*

"Yet another modest shack, I see," she says as I pull in behind the Porsche my brother is renting.

We climb from the car, and moments later Oliver walks outside, greeting us with a wide smile. His hair is lighter than mine and he's more tan than I am, but we're otherwise pretty similar...aside from my brother's somewhat loose morals, that is. He's me, if I'd been the one raised by a doting mother who made me the center of her world, if I hadn't felt it was necessary to do the right thing all the fucking time, to make up for the fact that neither of my parents would.

He hugs me first. "Babysitting, *mon cul.*"

Babysitting, my ass.

We both glance her way—at her easy smile, her flushed cheeks, her hair wild from our windows-down drive. How did I *ever* think he'd believe me? She is delicious. She is irresistible. And there's not a chance Oliver will even try to resist. She'll fall for his easy French charm because women always do—I've witnessed it firsthand over a hundred summer jaunts with him and Matthew. Santorini, Mallorca, Amsterdam, Lisbon—what do these places have in common? Beautiful women fell like fucking dominos when my brothers turned their way.

I don't know how to stop it, but something seizes up in my chest at the thought of Oliver and Daisy together, and I doubt it has much to do with protecting her virtue.

"Little Daisy, you've changed a bit since the last time I saw you," he says, kissing both her cheeks.

"And you haven't changed at all," she replies. "You're still speaking in French to Harrison when you don't want me to know what you've said."

He laughs. "A bad habit."

"Especially when you have no idea what language I studied in high school and college."

He grins. "You'd have slapped me by now if you spoke French."

Great. We're five seconds into this trip and he's already flirting with her.

He helps us carry our bags upstairs to the living room, where the back wall looks over a wide white beach and waves rolling up in perfect sets under the dying sun. Surfers dot the landscape, straddling boards.

I glance at Daisy and she's already looking at me, eager to be out there. Hungry for it.

That surfer in Asilomar saw in an instant what I should have realized weeks ago: Daisy is *everything* I could ever want in a relationship—someone happy, someone who relishes life and is eager to be a part of it. A woman who will come to my bed with sand in her hair and smile the way Daisy is right now—as if life is an adventure, one she wants to share with me.

"*Mon Dieu*," Oliver says under his breath when she goes to the bathroom to change into a bikini. "You weren't lying before. She blows the mother away, does she not?"

"I meant it, Oliver," I warn. "Don't pursue her."

There's sympathy in his gaze when he glances over. "Yes, I know. You couldn't be making it more clear."

22

DAISY

I t's perfect here. The water is warmer than in Santa Cruz, the sun is bright, and there's nothing to dodge aside from other surfers.

I'd worried that I'd feel like the interloper on this trip, that suddenly Harrison and I would revert to that old routine of *responsible guy saddled with friend's wayward niece*, but the opposite is true.

"What do you think of the house, Daisy?" Oliver asks as we straddle our boards, waiting for the next set to come in. His accent is slight, more in where he places emphasis than in the words themselves.

"Absolutely amazing so far, though I haven't made it past the main floor yet."

I suppose Audrey would have been very sophisticated about the whole thing. She wouldn't have insisted on surfing. She'd have fixed her makeup and opened a bottle of expensive champagne while expressing discontent with some small failing she'd found in the house—"*I really don't love this cabinetry,*" or "*Is there not a wine fridge?*"

I don't think Audrey was happy, and I don't think Harrison was happy with her, but I'd still probably give up everything about myself if it just could make him want me the way he once wanted her.

"I'll give you two the master bedroom on the top floor," Oliver says. "It has its own hot tub, by the way."

My eyes widen as I glance from him to Harrison, who is leveling his brother with the same kind of look Liam has often given me—the one that silently says, "*You are such a pain in the ass.*"

"We are not sharing a room, Oliver," Harrison says. He almost manages to conceal the growl in his voice.

Oliver laughs and reaches for my hand, pressing a gentle kiss to my knuckles. "In that case, Daisy, how do you feel about sharing it with your old friend Oliver? I'm new to your country's strange ways and scared to be alone."

Harrison jerks my board away from Oliver's without explanation. "You're not new to this country," he says, and this time he does *not* conceal his growl, "and she's not staying in your fucking room."

Oliver winks at me, as if this was exactly the outcome he'd hoped for.

The light is nearly gone by the time we get back to the house. There are three master bedrooms, but mine—isolated on the top floor—is the best.

They're beside the kitchen counter chatting amiably in French when I arrive downstairs in a sundress thirty minutes later, my damp hair twisted into a topknot, a touch of red gloss on my mouth.

The conversation comes to a dead stop when they see me and for a moment their expressions are nearly identical. It's as if I'm unexpected, and wondrous—a waterspout, a tidal wave, a sudden snowstorm in the middle of spring.

"You look lovely," Oliver says, placing a hand at the small of my back and drawing me forward. "Doesn't she look lovely, Harrison?"

Harrison's jaw locks. "She's never *not* lovely, Oliver," he grunts, turning away to grab his keys. "Give it a rest."

Oliver winks at me once again, as if we are in on something together, but it's not entirely clear to me what we're in on. Is he flirting with me? Is he trying to set me up with Harrison? I have no idea.

Whatever is unsettled between them relaxes once we reach the restaurant. We enjoy a lovely meal at an outdoor table that sits right on the sand. The first bottle of red is empty by the time our entrees arrive and a second is ordered, while Oliver regales me with tales of Harrison's summer visits. I didn't realize how much time he'd spent traveling with his brothers, for years and years, or that his mother and stepfather own so much property—a vineyard in some little town called St. Antoine, a beach house in Biarritz, a cottage in Provence.

"You must bring her to Provence next summer," Oliver urges Harrison, turning to me. "Have you been?"

I'm sure Audrey has been to Provence a thousand times, so many times she can't be bothered to stop when she's passing through. "My family doesn't have *multiple vacation homes* kind of money. I've never even left the country."

He grins. "Even more reason to come, then. And if you have sisters for me and Matthew, bring them as well. You *must* bring someone for Matthew, or he'll steal you. He's definitely the best-looking and most charming of us all."

Harrison's eyes are growing dark.

"You're annoying Harrison," I tell Oliver. "He doesn't classify siblings according to hotness."

"That's because he'd be last," Oliver says, toasting him. "Clearly, it's Matthew, then me, then Harrison. So you'll bring your equally lovely sisters to France, and we'll stay in Provence for a week, with perhaps a visit to Île du Levant."

"Daisy has no sisters, and you sure as hell won't be taking her to Île du Levant."

I love listening to the way French names roll off Harrison's tongue. I love the way his mouth moves as he says them. It's just like Harrison to be fucking fluent in French and never even mention it.

"What's wrong with *Île du* whatever?" I ask.

"Nothing," Oliver answers. "Harrison is just quite American in his views on nudity. *I* think you'd love it."

I laugh, but Harrison does not. He *must* know his brother is simply baiting him, but I think it bothers him anyway.

I tap his foot. "I don't know about Provence next year. I might make Harrison take me to Costa Rica instead."

Harrison relaxes, as if the trip is really happening, as if I've just solved every problem he had. And my heart gives one hard, audible thump, because I make him happy and that makes *me* happy. I already know my heart will break when this summer ends and I'm alone again, but now I'm wondering how his will fare as well.

After dinner, we go to the nearest grocery store as Oliver has purchased nothing but wine since he arrived. We're standing in line when I run back to the freezer section for frozen acai.

"Hey, didn't I see you at Zuma Beach yesterday?" asks a guy nearby.

I shake my head. "I just arrived today, so it wasn't me."

He grins. "Sorry. You're blonde and tan...I guess there are a lot of women in California who meet that description. Where are you in from?"

I open my mouth to answer and am silenced by the arm that wraps around me, large and firm and possessive, the hand resting on my hip. "Do you have what you need?" asks Harrison, standing closer than he ever would normally, so close that his breath brushes against my hair when he asks the question. My nipples harden simply from his nearness, his touch, his breath, and I resent it. Since when does he wrap his arm around me *anywhere*?

I grab the acai and force a smile at the guy I was talking to. "Have a nice evening."

Harrison's arm falls away, but he remains close to my side as we walk back toward Oliver.

"What was that?" I demand.

"You can do better than a guy who's hitting on you in the freezer section based solely on your looks, Daisy," he grunts.

Oliver is laughing as we approach. "Did he save you from the bad man in the Stanford hoodie?" he asks. "I knew once I saw the fruit and paper towels in his cart that he was up to no good. Thank God Harrison stepped in."

I laugh while Harrison acts as if he hasn't heard us and starts unloading our cart.

It's pretty clear that Oliver thinks Harrison's jealous—and as crazy as it sounds, I'm starting to wonder too.

When we get home, they want to stay up with a bottle of wine, but I'm too tired to join them, and I figure they need some brotherly bonding time anyhow.

I throw my doors open to the balcony as I get ready for bed. The waves crash and their voices from the deck below reach my ear sporadically—laughing and bickering, mostly in French.

And then, clear as day, Oliver speaks. "Deny it all you want," he says in English. "The only one you're fooling is yourself."

I fall asleep dreaming of Harrison's arm around me in the grocery store, whispering French words that I somehow understand. "Do you see how it is with us?" he asks, and that hand grips my hip hard, a promise of things to come. "This was always meant to happen."

"I do," I tell him. "I was just waiting for you to see it too."

I wake up and stare at the dark ceiling. The words he spoke in my dream are ones he'd never utter in real life.

Whereas the words *I* spoke in that dream have been resting on the tip of my tongue for a decade, just waiting to be set free.

23

HARRISON

Over a bottle of wine, Oliver and I get reacquainted. We talk about the plans for the vineyard and Matthew's doomed relationship with a girl in Portugal.

And then we talk about my divorce, though I'd prefer not to. I'd probably have lied to my family about the situation just like I lied to everyone else, but Matthew was due in London a week after I'd arrived and I'd had to explain why I wasn't there. This topic inevitably leads where I knew it would: how wrong Audrey was for me, and how the *right* girl is currently one floor above us.

"You watch her constantly," Oliver says. "You realize this, yes?"

I swallow down a hit of irritation. "It's just a habit. We *did* have to watch her constantly when she was small, and that's hard to shake off. Plus, she's terrifying."

"*Terrifying*? In what way?"

"Have you not been paying attention, Oliver? We can't even walk into the fucking store without some creep following her down the aisle. She surfs until she's exhausted and tomorrow, I guarantee she'll be standing on one leg stretching next to the deep end of that pool. Anything could happen to her."

I don't miss the grin he bites down on, the flash of those dimples my mother is so enamored of. "Audrey flew to a foreign city and didn't see you for five months. You have no idea if there was an obsessed neighbor watching her during that time or if she was stretching next to the pool."

"Audrey didn't stretch," I grumble. "Nor did she have a pool."

"You are quite intentionally missing my point, which is that you're not worried about Daisy because she's *reckless*. You're worried because a world without her seems too painful to bear. But Harrison...fear of losing someone is part of the deal. It means she matters to you. Stop torturing yourself and give in."

I can't. Even if no one ever knew, where would it stop? Am I really going to sleep with Daisy for a week or a month and then go through the rest of my life pretending it didn't happen? "We're in completely different places, Oliver. I wanted to start a family years ago while she still doesn't know what she'll do when she graduates. Even if I was willing to risk two of my oldest friendships, even if I was willing to risk hurting *her*, there's no point in starting something doomed to end badly."

"You know why I didn't share my thoughts on Audrey when I met her?" he asks, pouring the last of the red wine into my glass. "Because I knew, no matter what I said, it was your little checklist for a successful life that would make the decision for you. You have always been too consumed with your plans, with staying on track, and where has it gotten you? For once in your life, I wish you'd just take what you want and let the consequences sort themselves out."

Except I'm not leading his charmed life, nor am I leading Matthew's.

And those consequences he's referred to so ambivalently?

They'd be terrible for me, but they might be even worse

for her.

～

I'M WOKEN by the sound of the blender.

I enter the kitchen to find Daisy making smoothie bowls while Oliver begs her not to make him try it. While I wish she wasn't making so much noise this early in the day, and I definitely wish she wasn't wandering around in a tiny brown bikini while doing it, it's impossible not to smile at the sight of her.

She's so...herself. She's got the doors wide open, the breeze blowing her blonde hair while her hips sway to the music coming out of her phone.

"Stop her," says Oliver. "She's insisting on making me healthier, and I don't care for it. Explain to her how anti-French this is. She's putting peanut butter in it, for God's sake."

I grin. "Has she claimed she's doing this for our health? She's really doing it because she wanted us both to get the fuck out of bed."

Daisy glances up, fighting a smile. "Well, since you *are* both up, I see no reason for us to lollygag inside."

My eyes meet hers. *She's perfect. She's exactly who I'd choose for myself if the timing was different.*

"Daisy, when I marry you and bring you back to France, you must promise to never tell anyone I ate this," Oliver says.

"You'd have to kill me first to make that happen," I tell him. "That would be the harder secret to keep."

"We can kill him. It'll be fine," she says to Oliver, shooting me a grin over her shoulder. "I'm good at keeping secrets."

I'm good at keeping secrets.

The words hit my stomach like a filthy promise, a delicious ache. If I truly believed something with us could stay a secret...I wouldn't be able to stop myself. I know it's impossible. Yet here I am, still trying to wish it into existence.

24

DAISY

I'm so exhausted that my legs are sludge as I carry my board out of the water. I barely have the strength to peel off my wetsuit.

"My God, how long were we out there?" Oliver asks as we collapse on our towels. "I don't have the energy to check my watch."

My eyes close sleepily as the sun warms my wet skin, but I feel Harrison's gaze and manage to turn my head toward him.

"Is something wrong?" I ask.

"Just making sure you're okay. We shouldn't have stayed out there so long."

"You worry too much," I tell him, and he doesn't reply.

It's as if the waves are slowly rising and falling beneath my towel. The imagined motion plus the warmth of the sand lulls me to sleep, and when I rouse again the sun is lower in the sky and Harrison is rolling a ball to this cute little kid in front of us.

I sit up, sleepily blinking at them both.

"Daisy," says Harrison, "this is Lincoln, who's just turned five and has been explaining to me why we don't need to worry about leprechauns stealing our gold."

"They can only travel by rainbow," Lincoln says.

"So, if there's a rainbow..." I begin.

Lincoln nods. "Then you need to worry. That's why I'm never going to Hawaii."

"The double rainbows there," Harrison explains to me with a grin. "Apparently, they're just a four-lane highway of theft."

I hide my laughter with a cough and lean back on my hands, as Harrison continues to roll the ball to Lincoln, and tease him. He's so good with this kid, so natural.

And that's exactly what he wanted, isn't it? He never had a true family of his own, with his dad always gone and his mother in France. He wanted the perfect wife, the kids, the stability. He'll find it with someone soon enough, and it breaks my heart that it won't be me. That even if I managed to fake Audrey's class and sophistication, the jig would be up in a month when I had to tell him I was returning to DC early and *why* I was returning early.

For everything Audrey did wrong, I guarantee she never got kicked out of school.

THAT NIGHT, the three of us make dinner together, though Oliver's primary contribution is refilling everyone's wine.

"Are you always this happy, Daisy?" Oliver asks, walking into the kitchen to top up my glass.

I hesitate before answering. I'd like to claim I am, but something went wrong with me last winter. I'm not sure I wanted to die, but I'm not sure I *didn't*, either. Was it the situation? Was it some genetic frailty inherited from my dad? The fact that I don't understand what happened means I can't swear it won't happen again. But I've been happy here. If I knew my life could consist of Harrison and surfing and sunlight and cooking, it would be pretty easy to tell Oliver that *yes, I'm always this happy*.

"We're on vacation. It would be hard not to be happy," I tell him instead.

Oliver's gaze lingers for a moment, as if he knows it wasn't exactly the truth, and then moves toward his brother. "Harrison manages to be quite unhappy on vacation," he says with a soft smile, "though I've noticed he's not at all unhappy on this one."

After dinner, they handle most of the clean-up and remain behind to drink more wine while I'm so tired I can barely stay upright. I retreat to my room, lulled to sleep by the sound of Harrison singing in French to make Oliver laugh.

If we never had to leave, I can almost guarantee I'd stay as happy as I am right now.

I WAKE in the morning but opt not to run the blender. Based on the number of empty wine bottles in the trash, they'll both be hungover, and I'd rather have them up and ready to surf by eleven than downstairs at eight but cranky all day. I've just finished exercising when Oliver strolls out, scratching his bare stomach with a cup of coffee in hand. "We might have had a bit too much to drink last night," he admits. "Entirely Harrison's fault."

I grin. "Yes, I've noticed how conservatively you drink when left to your own devices. *Harrison* is the problem."

"Speaking of my brother," he says, taking a seat, "how long have you been in love with him?"

My eyes widen. I'm horrified that I've been too obvious and hoping that he just used the wrong word, though he speaks better English than I do. "I've known him since I was a baby," I reply. "He's family. So always."

His grin is gentle, sympathetic. "This is not what I was

asking. I imagine you know how lovely you are. Have you not wondered why I don't hit on you?"

I brace myself. No woman is so secure that she welcomes a conversation about her flaws. "Harrison would argue that you've done nothing but hit on me all weekend."

"Harrison is ridiculous, and you and I both know it."

I shrug. "Then I'm not your cup of tea."

He rolls his eyes. "Daisy, you're *every* man's cup of tea, believe me. What stopped me is the way he watches you—as if you're all he wants in the entire world, and he knows that if he allows himself a single bite, he'd never stop." Oliver is likely wrong, yet my heart flutters and spreads its wings anyway.

I'd give up everything I want from life in order to make what he's said true. "He's just looking out for me."

Oliver stretches, then clasps his hands behind his head. "You know, our mother left him when he younger than that little boy on the beach yesterday?"

I wince. The thought of it pains me. It pained me even as a child. "I still don't see how she could have done it."

He sips his coffee. "But she'd have deprived the world of me and my younger brother Matthew if she hadn't gone. If you think *I'm* handsome, you should see Matthew."

I laugh. "I don't recall ever claiming you were handsome."

"It's too obvious to even bother debating," he replies with a grin, which slowly fades. "But my point is this: Harrison lost the person he loved most and *depended* upon most at a very young age, and he thought marrying someone like Audrey, someone he didn't care for too much, was an insurance policy. He wanted the *appearance* of a relationship without incurring the risks of one."

"None of that means he wants one with me. The only reason I'm here is because he still sees me as the toddler who's going to eat sand if he's not watching."

"He'd like you to believe that, yes," Oliver says, leaning

forward and dropping to a whisper as Harrison walks into the kitchen in nothing but swim trunks. "He'd like to believe it himself. But Daisy, he doesn't stop watching you. Not when you're surfing but also not when you couldn't be safer. When you lie in the hammock, he watches. When you walk to the bathroom, he watches. Even when you fell asleep on the beach yesterday, his eyes went to you. I doubt very much he was concerned about you eating sand."

My eyes move toward Harrison, fiddling with the coffee maker—his thick hair mussed from sleep, his eyes still drowsy. He's so lovely that it hurts to look at him right now, and that makes what Oliver's saying more terrifying than anything else. If someone as worthless as Christian could shatter me by ending things, how much worse would it be if the end came at Harrison's hands?

But how amazing would it be if it didn't end at all?

If I was the one he'd been waiting on all along?

25

HARRISON

I woke even more hungover than I was the morning before, though I barely drank, and it pisses me off. I wanted this final day with Daisy to be our best.

It pisses me off even more to find Oliver is already up and hanging out with her. She's in the blue yoga pants this morning. They cover far more skin than her bikinis do, but I'm seized by the desire to go wrap a blanket around her anyway.

I'm seized by several different desires, actually, and it's getting harder and harder to tell myself *no* to any of them.

He leans toward her, whispering something, and my irritation cranks up a notch. Last night he told me that if I didn't make a move, he would. I'd assumed he was joking.

Maybe he wasn't.

"You look a little rough," Daisy says, walking in with a smile, a *sweet* smile that banishes every concern because I've never seen her look quite the same way at anyone else.

"Nothing some aspirin and coffee can't take care of," I reply.

She brushes past me and refills her water, smelling of roses and coconut. "I should have stayed up last night to prevent you from having so much fun."

As if that would have helped. I'd have stayed awake the whole fucking night just to make sure she went back to her own bed and not Oliver's when it was done.

"It's a sad day when you're deemed the *responsible* member of the household," I reply.

"Yes," she agrees. "You and Oliver have set the bar unbelievably low."

We get out in the water early, trying to make the most of our remaining hours. When we break for lunch, I'm more tired than I was the day before. I'd prefer to just take a nap on the deck afterward, but Daisy is raring to go back out, and I don't want her out there with my brother alone for three hours. Do I trust him not to hit on her? Mostly. Do I trust him not to lay the groundwork for the future? I do not.

By the time the sun starts to lower, I'm fucking exhausted. I shouldn't have stayed up so late last night, but I think what's tired me most is this constant awareness of Daisy. Sure, I'm abundantly aware of her when she's in my home, too, but it's different here, when I'm seeing her through my own eyes and then through Oliver's. It's a double dose, and it's more than I can bear at present.

Oliver grins at her. "Harrison's about to turn responsible on us, isn't he?"

"Can we pretend we don't hear him?" she asks.

My smile is muted. "It's probably after four, we have a six-hour drive ahead of us, and we haven't even begun to pack."

Jesus, the idea of a six-hour drive is unbearable right now. I'd give anything just to go to bed and postpone for a day.

We each take a final ride into shore and reluctantly carry on to the house. I force myself to move into my room and throw my shit in a bag, then tie the surfboards on the car, but I've got nothing left when it's done. The trip back is definitely not going to be the rollicking good time the trip here was.

"Promise you'll come to Paris this year," Oliver says as we hug goodbye.

"We'll see," I reply. "You know how it goes."

Oliver walks to the other side of the car and hugs Daisy for far longer than is necessary. "You must come as well," he says. "Name the date, and I'll buy you a ticket."

My temper is a rope that has frayed until there's nothing left of it. Why the fuck is he offering to buy her a ticket? And then he whispers something, something I can't hear, and that last bit of rope snaps.

I climb into the car, fuming, and turn on the ignition before she's even inside. I say nothing to her as I back out and steer toward the main road simply because I can't. I know I'm overreacting. I know I'm exhausted from wanting what I can't have. Nothing that comes out of my mouth right now will be reasonable.

"You're sure you're okay?" she finally asks, her worried gaze darting my way.

My jaw grinds. *Let it go, Harrison. It doesn't matter what he said to her.*

"What did he whisper to you when we left?" I snap. I meant for it to at least sound civil, but it doesn't.

Her brows pull together in surprise, and then she flashes a grin. "He thanked me for the hand job."

I slam on the brakes and jerk the car to the side of the road. I'm ninety-nine percent sure it was a joke, but I don't have the capacity to deal with even one percent doubt. I'm too tired. I want too many things.

"For God's sake, Harrison!" she cries. "You know I was kidding. I'm not *that* bad."

I know this. I know. I don't understand why I'm suddenly so exhausted and so desperate for her at once. If there were a bed anywhere near us right now, I wouldn't have the willpower to stop myself. "Then what did he say?"

She rolls her eyes. "He basically said he wanted me to come to France so that *you'd* come to cockblock him, idiot."

"Ah." That does sound like something Oliver would do, and it would fucking work, too.

"Do you want me to drive? Because you seriously look like you could use a nap."

I swallow as some of my anger leaves and shake my head. I've seen the way she drives. No matter how exhausted I am, we're safer with me behind the wheel.

We reach the highway in silence. She fiddles with the music and convinces me to stop at a convenience store so we can get drinks. I'm too tired to even walk in with her. I'd thought I was hungover or strung out over Daisy before—now I'm wondering if it's more than that.

She brings me a water I can't seem to drink and then is quiet for the next hour. Joy is fizzing out of her with each mile that elapses.

"I'm sorry," I say with a heavy exhale. "I didn't mean to be so cranky when we left."

"It makes me feel like I've done something wrong," she says quietly, and there's a pang in my chest.

"What could you possibly have done wrong?"

She bites her lip. "That's kind of the problem, right? You never know what you've done. You only know that it's something."

"What do you mean?"

She stares out the window. "The last trip I took with my ex, Christian...everything seemed fine at first. Normal. And then it wasn't fine anymore. He spent the whole trip back to DC denying it, only to dump me a day later. And when that happens, you're stuck trying to figure out what's wrong with you, and it's like...it's *everything*. Everything is wrong with you." Her clasped hands tighten in her lap. "I realize that it's different with you. I mean, we're not dating or whatever. But it feels as if the bottom has fallen out, and I'm going to be the last one to learn it."

Fuck. I've been so caught up in my own thoughts about her that it never once occurred to me she might worry too. I reach out and squeeze her hand. "It hasn't, I promise." I let the pad of my thumb sweep back and forth over her palm. "I'm just really tired. I keep wondering if I'm going to be able to stay awake when we've still got four hours to go, and I have to figure it out fast because we're about to pass the last decent hotels until Carmel."

She squeezes my hand back. "Harrison, let me drive. I promise I'll be careful. You can sleep for the next four hours, and I'll have you safe at home in bed by eleven."

"I don't know that I have it in me to be in the car for another four hours." And as soon as the words are out, I know they're true. I can barely stand to be in the car for another five minutes. I unlock my phone and slide it to her. "Book us two rooms at a decent hotel in Pismo Beach."

She laughs. "It's ridiculous to waste money on two rooms. I'll just get us two double beds."

Oh God. I might be tired, but I'm not so tired that I wouldn't make a disastrous mistake if we were sharing a fucking room. I bet I'd get a second wind in two seconds if the opportunity presented itself. Especially after an entire weekend of built-up lust from watching Daisy in a bikini and having no opportunity to, uh, discharge it.

"Two rooms, Daisy," I growl. "Please."

She directs me to a very pretty hotel in Pismo Beach. I get us checked in, but I'm barely clinging to life as we reach our doors.

"I guess you're going straight to sleep?" she asks.

I'd like to. But there's also a selfish piece of me that doesn't want to say goodnight to her yet, plus I'm worried she'll freak out about the cost of room service and skip dinner if she's left to her own devices.

"Now that we're out of the car, I'm feeling better. Why don't you drop your stuff off and come to my room? We can order dinner and watch a movie."

I regret that offer the moment I make it. I've got one bed and Daisy will think nothing of climbing in beside me, stripping down to the little she's got on under her sweatshirt, and making some comment about blowing me in exchange for dessert—one I won't be certain is a joke.

Tonight, I lack the will to resist any offer she makes, joking or not.

26

DAISY

I'm *relieved* that Harrison is sick, as terrible as that is, because the things I was thinking before he admitted it were so much worse.

It all felt a bit too much like the end with Christian. Things were fine during that trip in November, and then suddenly something flipped, and I was never sure what it was. Did he dislike that I'd asked him what he was doing for Thanksgiving? It's not as if I'd hoped he'd invite me to meet his parents. Was it that I was a little stressed about finals? I'd spent so much time letting him treat me like a sex toy that I'd been ignoring my schoolwork, so my final exams mattered a lot more than they should have. I hadn't blamed him for it, but maybe he thought I had. I'll never know. But given that I saw him with his girlfriend a few weeks later, the one he swore he was done with, it stands to reason that I wasn't enough, and she was.

And as devastated as I was when he dumped me, having Harrison ask me to move out would be a thousand times worse.

He's already lounging on the king-size bed when I walk through the door he left ajar, huddled beneath the blankets with the menu in hand.

I strip off my sweatshirt and climb in beside him, though he hardly seems to know I'm here. We put on *The King's Man*, which has violence for him and Aaron Taylor-Johnson for me, and I deal with room service when it arrives and bring Harrison his food, begging him to eat a little bit.

He falls asleep sitting up, his food untouched, before I've even finished half my risotto. I move his food to the floor and watch the movie alone, but it has far less Aaron Taylor-Johnson than the trailer implied.

I curl up beside him. "I'll just close my eyes for a second," I promise. I sort of mean this, and I sort of, just once in my life, want the experience of sleeping curled up beside Harrison, smelling his shampoo, memorizing his even inhales and exhales. I'm asleep before I've memorized nearly enough of them.

I'm not sure when I wake but the TV is off and he's whispering my name in the darkness. I assume, at first, that he's telling me to leave. But no...he's whispering my name as if he's asking a question.

As if he's asking *permission*.

He rolls me beneath him before I can reply, his body heavy and solid atop mine. The only thing he's got on is a pair of boxer briefs, and I was pretty sure I knew what question he was asking, but those fitted boxer briefs leave no doubt whatsoever about what it was. He's hard as nails and every bit as deliciously oversized as I suspected he was.

His lips move to the point where my neck meets my shoulder, and the heat of his breath has me arching before his mouth has even begun to graze my skin. He uses a knee to spread my thighs, and while it seems like the kind of thing we should discuss and the kind of thing he in particular would discuss to death—ground rules like "your uncle can never know" and "this won't happen again"—it's been a long time, and I want this, and if he's not going to insist on ground rules, why should I?

He lifts my tank and his lips move up and up over my rib cage while he wrenches my shorts down.

It's hot, how assertive he's being, but I'm still thrown by how unexpected it is. When does Harrison *ever* just take what he wants? He's tugging off his boxers, and he hasn't even asked if this is okay, hasn't even asked if I'm on birth control. And when did he strip down to his boxers in the first place?

He palms my breasts and I arch, reflexively, seeking more. His cock grazes my clit and his teeth latch onto a nipple—a pulse of pleasure-pain that stabs me while his groan drives every intelligent thought from my head.

Yes, whatever. Who cares that he doesn't want to discuss it? Yes.

"Those fucking blue yoga pants," he mumbles, sliding a forearm under each thigh to spread me open wide.

I'm meeting his thrusts—now separated only by my panties —even as the first flicker of true concern pinches me.

"Yoga pants?" I ask. I peer up at him in the darkness. His eyes are closed. *Wait. Fuck.*

Does this make sense? No. *Nothing* about this makes sense. Harrison would never, ever, just try to fuck me without a *conversation* first.

"Harrison?"

He doesn't seem to hear me. He's in his own little world, apparently. One in which I'm wearing the blue yoga pants, and he's just removed them. I reach a hand to his forehead—his skin is burning to the touch.

"God, those pants make me crazy," he mumbles. "I've wanted this for so fucking long."

He's positioned between my legs, his erection a deliciously heavy press, and I'm already soaked for it. But he doesn't even know it's *happening*.

I want to go back to five minutes ago, when I was an innocent party in all this. His fingers slip beneath my panties—a light, teasing touch that I'd kill to have him continue.

But I can't. Goddammit. He'd hate this so much if he was aware of it.

"Harrison, stop," I say, forcefully. I push him hard, and after a moment he rolls to the side, collapsing on the pillow beside mine. My body is on fire—and it's *not* with fever—and my clit is so swollen that even lying here is a form of torture. His hand lands on my stomach and starts to creep toward my panties. I've got to get the hell away before I allow him to do something he'd never forgive me for.

I firmly place his hand on the mattress between us and force myself out of the bed, going to the bathroom for a wet washcloth. I grab ibuprofen from his travel kit and return, holding the pills to his mouth.

"Daisy," he mumbles, "what's going on?"

"I think you're sick, baby. Take these."

He follows my directions obediently and even drinks a little of the water I offer him before he collapses back to the pillow.

I place the washcloth on his forehead. He grabs my hand. "Will you stay?"

I lie down beside him, placing my hand on his chest. "I'm not going anywhere, I promise." His shoulders settle with my words, as if half his illness was simply worry about me, and he falls into a deep sleep while I lie awake with my heart beating hard.

If he remembers this in the morning, he'll feel guilty about it—perhaps so guilty he'll finally insist that I leave. And he'll also be aware that I was going to let him do it.

God, was I ever going to let him.

I can feel his weight on top of me, that long, thick cock heavy against my abdomen, and the way he stripped my shorts off like he'd die if he wasn't inside me. I can feel the warning press of him between my legs, the fullness of it.

It's embarrassing that I thought it was genuine on his part. It's embarrassing that I could have believed Harrison would ever just fuck me without a word of conversation about it first.

And yet...he very clearly knew it was *me* beneath him. The words coming out of his mouth sounded like ones he'd said a hundred times before.

So, how do I get him to say them again?

27

HARRISON

The sun is pouring into an unfamiliar room, and Daisy is curled up beside me with her hand on my chest. Based on the bare legs twined with mine, she appears to be wearing very little aside from a camisole. And I have no fucking idea where we are, why she's in my room, or what godawful thing I might have done last night to allow this to happen.

I remember saying goodbye to Oliver and how pissed I was that he was whispering to her. I remember her not at all funny joke about giving him a hand job, and the way I wondered if it was possible to make yourself *sick* with desire for someone. I think I told her we needed to stop for the night. There's really not much beyond that.

I pull a washcloth off my forehead, and she starts to rouse.

"Hey," she says sleepily. "Let me get that for you. You need a new one."

She sits up, pushing messy curls out of her face, looking decadently flushed and pouty and disheveled, the way I imagine she'd look if she'd spent the whole night letting me have my way with her.

I was already hard, and that thought doesn't help. I reach down to adjust myself and discover I don't have a stitch of clothing on.

"Daisy," I rasp, "why am I naked?"

"The roofies I put in your dinner worked better than I could have hoped." She climbs from the bed, taking the washcloth with her, wearing nothing but a camisole and the tiniest shorts as she walks toward the bathroom. *Jesus.* "You gave me the night of my life."

I grip myself tight beneath the covers and will away my body's reaction.

She emerges a moment later with a wet washcloth and places it on my head. "You were burning up. I think you probably shed your clothes in the middle of the night. I stayed to keep an eye on you because you were a thousand degrees."

She leans over me to glance at the clock on the nightstand. Her breast is brushing against my chest. One tight nipple grazes my skin, and I have to hold myself rigid not to react. "It's nearly eight," she says. "What do you want to do? My shift isn't until one. I can get someone to cover me pretty easily if you're not ready to go home."

"Daisy," I hiss between my teeth, "can you stop leaning against my chest?"

"Sorry," she says hurriedly, leaning away, and I feel like an asshole. She took care of me all night, and now she's apologizing because of *my* raging libido.

"We should get back," I reply. "If you could just give me a few minutes to shower, I'll be ready to go."

"Oh, sure." She blushes. "Sorry. I'll go to my room. Just text when you're ready."

She climbs out of bed, grabs her sweatshirt off the floor, and walks out. I go to the bathroom and turn on the shower, gripping myself as I picture her on the deck of my house, bent over in the blue yoga pants. I imagine the wet feel of her as I spread her legs wide, that moment just before I push in. The water in the shower isn't even hot before I'm coming to the thought of it.

WE MANAGE to get back to Santa Cruz in time for her shift, though she only leaves after I swear that I'm fine.

I'm really feeling much better, but I called in sick anyway because I'm not in the mood for Baker's bullshit—he'll be annoyed that I'm coming in at midday, so he might as well just be annoyed that I didn't come in at all.

I rinse the surfboards, clean out the car, and then go to Daisy's beloved *rich people store* and get stuff for dinner. It's a weak *thank you* for the fact that she dropped everything to come along with me this weekend when she didn't have to and then spent the night in my room, putting wet washcloths on my head and politely ignoring me while I apparently took off all my clothes.

It's a weak *thank you* for the fact that I've allowed her to take care of me for weeks when she didn't have to. She'd argue that she's staying here for free, but she went above and beyond— she got me back to being the person I was not just before I discovered Audrey was cheating but the person I was before Audrey was ever in the picture at all.

I'm still putting together why I gave up everything I enjoyed for a marriage that didn't make me happy, but the important part is that I'm ready to fix what went wrong, and I'm not sure I would have been if it weren't for Daisy making me see it.

I'm reading the paper with a beer in hand when she gets home that afternoon. "If you're taking off work to sit home and drink, I may have gone too far in my quest to make you relax a little," she says, walking onto the deck.

I turn toward her, my gaze immediately falling to her rack, though I'm hardly at fault for that. The goddamn shirt they make her wear at work pretty much *demands* you look at her rack.

"I fucking hate that job," I tell her. "They need to give you more clothes."

She takes the seat beside me. "That would be counterproductive. The lack of clothes is the only reason I'm earning so much there."

I hate that too. I hate that some creep is drawing pornographic pictures of her, that a thousand other creeps are imagining God knows what. "Just quit. I can help you out next semester."

"You're already letting me live here rent-free. I'm not taking your money."

Take it as a favor to me. I really don't want you at that damn job, in that fucking shirt.

She climbs to her feet, side-eyeing my beer. "In spite of the exquisite care you're taking of your immune system, you probably ought to get a solid meal tonight. Let me shower and then I'll run to the—"

I wrap my hand around her wrist to stop her. "I already went to the store. I'm making us steak, and it's marinating right now. Stop trying to take care of me all the time. It's my turn to take care of you instead."

Her gaze meets mine. I didn't mean for it to sound sexual, but it sort of did, and she's not about to let it go. "How exactly are you going to *take care* of me?" she purrs, licking her lips.

I laugh. "I knew you'd go there. By feeding you, Daisy."

"What are you going to *feed* me, Harrison?"

I groan, discreetly placing the paper over my lap. "You truly can make anything sound filthy, can't you? It's a skill."

"Too bad it's not a skill I can be paid for."

"You could be paid an awful lot for that skill," I reply as she walks away. "Don't get any ideas."

"Too late!" she calls back. "I'm applying right now."

She goes to shower, and when she returns—barefoot, wet hair knotted atop her head, sun-kissed from the weekend outdoors—it hits me all over again how right this feels with her, how easy it is to have her around. It's a dangerous line of thought—one I'm allowing myself to have far too often when it absolutely can't happen.

We make dinner together. I want to inhale the smell of her shampoo every time she passes. How the hell did that idiot in DC ever let her go?

"The guy you told me about in the car yesterday," I venture as we sit down at the table. "Is he why you swore off men?"

She looks away. I fucking hate that she's hiding something from me when she's too goddamn open about almost everything else. I hate that she's hiding this in particular. *Is she not over him?*

"He's part of it, yeah."

"What's the other part?" It comes out sounding regrettably jealous.

She stares at her hands. "It wasn't the first time it happened. Men...they convince themselves I'm something more than I am."

My brow furrows. "More?"

"They have this ideal. Like Griff, the guy who keeps drawing me at work in those costumes. He obviously wants some sexy warrior princess with huge knockers, and he sees it in me." She pushes the steak around on her plate. "Another guy will want something entirely different, and he'll think he sees *that* in me, but over time, it all falls apart. They want some combination of porn star and mystery girl when I'm really just a shitty student who isn't especially good at anything—and they don't want that."

I want to tell her that she's simply had a little bad luck, but in some respects, Daisy's looks are a *form* of bad luck. In any movie, she'd be cast as the siren, the sexpot luring every guy to his doom. I've seen the way men look at her, and they're not seeing a sunny girl who just wants to be out in the water and make a nice smoothie bowl when it's done.

I rub a hand over my eyes. "Daisy, your ex sounds like a jerk. If he didn't appreciate you for who you are, he didn't deserve you."

"It's more than that. I'm..." her words die off. "When some guy comes in acting like I'm *everything*, I start to hope maybe there's more to me than there appears, and then he takes it all back, and I wind up a lot lower than I started. I just want off the treadmill."

I hate this conversation. I hate that the way to fix this problem is by forcing her to give some *other* guy a shot. "There's a lot more to you than any of these exes of yours seem to realize, and a million men who would feel like they'd won the lottery if they got you exactly the way you are right now—whether or not you go to law school or become the head of the UN or whatever bullshit your mother hopes for. You need to date someone you *know*, not some guy who sees you and decides who you are based on your looks alone."

Her gaze meets mine, and for a moment it's there between us, that tension, that pull. Because yes, *I* know her. *I* like her barefoot and dancing while she makes a sandwich.

"Not now, obviously," I say, looking away. "I'm guessing this breakup was really recent, and maybe you need a few months off from dating, but when you get back to school..." I trail off awkwardly.

I was trying to say *it can't be me, but I also don't want to watch it happen.* I'm not sure I really conveyed it, however.

"It wasn't that recent," she replies, not meeting my eye. "We broke up last November."

I stare at her. "You're telling me you haven't dated anyone in...eight *months?*"

She laughs. "You're pretty judgmental for a guy who hasn't dated in six."

"Except there's a world of difference between the dissolution of your marriage and a college breakup. At twenty-one you kind of bounce back, normally."

Her smile falters. "Why would I bother, though? How many great relationships have you seen? Your parents divorced; Scott makes my mom miserable. Caleb and Kate were a shitshow, and so were you and Audrey."

"My mother and stepfather are absolutely besotted with each other, and it's nearly been three decades," I counter. "And even if you never want to get married, there are other benefits to a relationship."

"Sex?" She rolls her eyes. "I'm going to say something, and you're probably going to argue or think I'm crazy, but sex is *really* overrated."

The desire to say *let me prove you wrong* is already so strong it's nearly choking me. I knew I shouldn't have introduced the topic. I swallow. "How so? You sure bring it up a lot for someone who doesn't like it."

I both do and do not want her to describe once again how good she is at getting herself off.

"I like it on my *own*." The quiet, embarrassed words hit just the way I knew they would. I subtly adjust myself beneath the table.

"But guys have a foreplay card," she continues. "And there's variation, but it's all roughly the same."

"A foreplay card?" I ask. "I'm certain I'd have heard about this by now if it were really a thing."

She hitches a shoulder. "It's just like this list, like you all are pushing buttons or checking boxes. You grab a few things and then rub something too hard or just poorly. Half the time it's uncomfortable or doing nothing, and even if it's okay, you're so impatient after a minute or so that it moves along to sex...and then it's over."

I shouldn't have a hard-on, listening to her describe what were clearly abysmal sexual experiences. I have one anyway, of course.

I channel some calmer, more adult version of myself to give her the answer I should give her instead of the one I'd like to. "Daisy, I think maybe you've just had a run of really bad luck."

She shrugs. "Maybe, but am I supposed to keep putting up with it while some guy slowly tears me down and makes me doubt myself? I'm tired of jumping through hoops to win someone's approval and failing, all for a bunch of supposed benefits that never arrive."

I inhale through my nose, preparing to say something I *already* regret. "When you get back to school, find a guy who already knows you and won't put you on a pedestal. Someone who doesn't expect you to make his wildest fantasies come true. Maybe...just have fun. Just enjoy yourself, and don't get swept up into some big, serious relationship."

She laughs. "Wow, I can't believe Mr. Overprotective is suggesting I just fuck around. If Liam heard this conversation, you'd be in so much trouble."

Liam couldn't possibly hate it as much as I do. "You need to be with someone who cares about you enough to make it worth your while but who isn't expecting the performance of a lifetime. Someone who will take his fucking time building up to —" I stop myself. A description of how this mystery guy should take his time would get way too graphic, and would basically just be a list of all the things I've pictured doing to her. "Someone who realizes foreplay is ninety percent of it. And if you can't tell a guy that what he's doing isn't working, you shouldn't be with him in the first place."

She glances at me. Maybe she's asking why I can't be that guy.

I guess there's a part of me asking why I can't be that guy too. All the answers I once had are mattering a little less by the minute.

28

DAISY

I'm lying in bed, but I don't see myself falling asleep anytime soon.

All the things he started last night still beg for completion. My nipples ache for the sting of his teeth. I picture his weight above me, his cock grazing my clit, and I buck upward against the air. That's how real the memory is.

You just need the experience of being with someone who cares about you enough to make it worth your while but who isn't expecting the performance of a lifetime. Someone who will take his fucking time building up to—

Building up to what? There was a clench in his jaw as he said it, a flicker of what seemed an awful lot like...frustration. As if, perhaps, he was thinking of *himself* and the way *he'd* take his fucking time building up to whatever it was.

Maybe he doesn't care about me the way he's supposed to, but he *does* care. And I bet he knows *exactly* what he's doing in bed—those fingers of his moved with expert precision last night before my moral compass came in to cockblock us both. So why shouldn't it be with him? Why shouldn't *he* be the one who proves this supposed truth to me? He made it abundantly clear last night that he wants to.

I flip on a light, climb out of bed, and come to a halt at the sight of my reflection. My pajamas are as unsexy as they could possibly be—tank top, flannel bottoms. If I actually had sexy lingerie here, I'd consider putting it on, but it's better this way. How humiliating would it be to prance in there wearing lingerie and still get rejected?

I take a deep breath, as if I'm about to jump into ice-cold water, and then I pad down the hall to his room.

"Harrison?" I tap lightly. "Are you up?"

"Yeah." His voice is already wary. I should take that for the warning it is and turn my ass around, but instead, I open the door.

He turns on the lamp beside him as he sits, all the visible parts of him deliciously bare. I glance at the bunched-up covers, hoping for a glimpse of his lower half, while he fumbles on the nightstand for his glasses.

When he turns to me, that knot in my stomach tightens. Jesus Christ. Harrison, shirtless in those glasses, should be his own category of porn. There's nothing he could ask of me right now that I wouldn't agree to.

I cross the room and take a seat on the end of the bed. "I didn't know you wore contacts."

He raises a brow. "Is that what you came in here to discuss in the middle of the night?"

"No. I'm sorry. Did I wake you?"

He shakes his head, something miserable in the gesture. "No. I couldn't fall asleep. So, what's up?"

I take a deep breath, tugging nervously at the hem of my tank top. "You know how you said I just need to meet someone who knew what he was doing but also knew *me*?"

He freezes. I haven't even stated my request, and it's already clear this is going to end badly.

"Well," I continue with a forced shrug, "what if it was you? I mean, I know you don't like me that way, and you're still getting over Audrey, but you seem like you could perform if you *chose* to, and you aren't dating anyone, so..."

He places a palm over his face and keeps it there for far too long. "Oh my God, Daisy. Did you seriously just come in my room to ask me to fuck you?"

My eyes narrow, and I cross my arms over my chest. "Well, not *just* that. You're the one who talked such a good game about foreplay."

"Daisy," he groans, "if Liam and your mom knew we'd even had this conversation, they'd never speak to me again, and if we acted on it, they wouldn't be *able* to speak to me again because I'd be dead seconds after Liam learned about it."

I brace my hands on my knees and stare at the ground. I knew I wasn't going to be great at seducing Harrison, but I'm not sure we could possibly be having a less sexy conversation than this one.

"I wasn't asking you to have sex with me a *million* times. Just the once. Maybe twice, if there's really as much to sex as you've implied. Okay, three to four times to cover most of the basic positions, but it's not like I'm planning to give Liam the play-by-play in the morning."

"These things have a way of getting out eventually." He pinches the bridge of his nose, as if I'm a child who's frustrating him. "I think you better go back to your room."

Great, and now he's *dismissing me* like a child, but the situation is a thousand times more shameful because I basically threw myself at him first.

He's full of shit, too. If he was actually scared about it getting out, he wouldn't have let me stay here in the first place. No one is ever going to believe we *didn't* sleep together if they hear about this summer.

"Don't blame it on Liam." I swallow down a horrifying

desire to cry. "You just aren't interested. That's all you needed to say."

I walk out the door and close it behind me. He doesn't try to stop me, though I guess a part of me was hoping he would. I get back to my room, sink onto the edge of the bed, and press my face to my hands.

It was so fucking stupid to think that I could just waltz in there, ask him what I did, and have it miraculously *not* be awkward tomorrow. What did I think was going to happen? It's almost too dumb to admit it to myself:

I didn't want him to sleep with me once. I was hoping he'd sleep with me, and it would be so magical and life-altering that the age difference and his friendships would no longer matter. It was absolutely crazy. If I had an ounce of sanity left, I'd start packing my shit right now.

Footsteps creak in the hallway, interrupting my train of thought. Is he *leaving? He has work tomorrow, and now I've—*

There's a knock on my door.

"Daisy? Can I come in?"

"Please go away," I beg, but my voice cracks. It's bad enough that he's rejected me. I won't survive pity from him afterward.

"Daisy," he croons from the other side of the door. "Shit. I'm coming in." He steps inside and his face falls. "Honey, why are you crying?"

I brush at the tears on my face. "I just made a fool of myself in front of you and got shot down in the worst way. Why the hell do you think I'm crying?"

He sits beside me on the bed. "It's not like I didn't *want* to say yes, Daisy. But your mom and Liam would never, *ever* forgive me."

"Please just stop." My voice is a bare rasp. "If you wanted to, you would have. Liam and my mom wouldn't find out, so you're just making excuses."

He sighs. "Daisy, I assure you—I want to. If you had any

idea how many times I've jerked off thinking about you bent over doing your stretches you'd feel a lot less rejected. But it would be wrong. It's one thing to let you stay here, but—"

"You jerked off thinking about me?" My tears are forgotten.

He laughs. "I think you focused on the wrong part of what I said. But, yes, I have. I'm probably going to jerk off later just to the thought of you asking me about jerking off."

I glance at his crotch, and he elbows me. "Eyes up, Daisy. But for the record, hearing you say anything vaguely dirty makes me hard, and this conversation is no exception."

"How hard?" I ask, my voice laughably breathless and eager. My gaze drifts to that bulge in his boxers again.

"Please do not ask me *that* question in *that* voice when I'm trying to do the right thing," he says between his teeth. "You have the voice of a webcam girl even when you're not trying."

Harrison fucking Reid has jerked off thinking about me. I'll never recover from the shock of it. "I'm a little less familiar than you are with webcam girls apparently."

His laughter sounds slightly pained. "I've never paid one. But if I had, I imagine she'd sound just like you."

"If you were going to pay one, what would you have her say to you?"

He groans. "I'd probably just ask her to repeat this conversation verbatim." His thighs tense as if he's about to stand. "Well, I should—"

"So when you think about me bent over stretching," I say, cutting him off as I scoot backward, leaning against my pillows at the head of the bed, "what is it you picture?"

His gaze flickers to me, his eyes narrow. "That hardly seems like the kind of thing we should be discussing when you're in that tank and I'm in nothing but boxers. I've admitted enough for one night."

He braces to rise again but I slide my foot out to nudge his hip.

"I put myself out there, and you rejected me. The least you could do is put yourself out there a little too. So, tell me what you picture."

He releases a heavy sigh, his hand fisting his hair. "I have several different fantasies about you. Some involve walking up behind you when you're in that one pose..." he trails off with a strangled noise. "The one where you're down on the ground with your ass in the air. I assume you can figure out the rest. And that night you mentioned how easily you can find your own clit has occupied many of my thoughts in the shower as well."

I bite down on a smile. "So you like the thought of me getting myself off?"

He laughs, more to himself than me. "I'm a guy. Of course I like that thought."

I settle back against the pillows and let my legs open a little bit more. Never in my life have I masturbated in front of someone, and I can't imagine why I'm considering it now when not two minutes ago I was crying about the way he rejected me, but...he's already admitted he wants to see it. He's already admitted jerking off to the thought of it.

I slide my hand into the waistband of my pants and down between my legs. "So you just picture watching me like this?"

His eyes are dangerous now, hazy and feral. "Daisy, what the fuck are you doing?"

I shrug. "I'm pretty sure you know exactly what I'm doing. I'm sliding my finger along my clit, then—"

I slide one finger inside myself and my head falls backward. I started this just to torture him, but find myself strangely turned on by the whole experience too.

He swallows. "I should go."

"I want you to watch," I reply. I'm growing bolder by the minute.

He winces, nostrils flaring as his head turns, as his gaze

drifts to that hand between my legs. "Do you have a finger inside yourself right now?" His voice is pure gravel.

When I nod, he groans, his jaw grinding. "Oh, God."

"Do you want me to do it again?" I ask. "Should I add a second one? Because I want to. I'm pretending it's your fingers sliding inside me."

He gives his cock a hard squeeze, as if he can't stand not to be inside me while I do this. When I run one hand over my tank top and pinch a nipple, he leans closer, his exhale reverberating over my skin.

"Do it again," he whispers, wrapping a hand around my ankle. "I want to watch you make yourself come."

I could argue that if he's going to watch me, he might as well participate, but I'm too far gone. I do it again, my fingers slipping in and out easily now, and suddenly he's kneeling between my spread legs, grasping himself tight, his eyes on me as if I'm something that could vanish at any moment.

"Take off the pants," he growls. His hesitation has vanished entirely. He's every bit as demanding, as *certain*, as I thought he might be.

I tuck my thumbs into the waistband of my pants and lower them. Air hisses between his teeth when he realizes I'm not wearing panties and he yanks them the rest of the way down my legs.

"Touch yourself," he says, his voice low and guttural.

I battle a wave of stage fright—somehow it was different when he couldn't see precisely what I was doing, but I go ahead and slide my hand over my stomach again and between my legs, where I am so soaked that I'm a little embarrassed by the sound as I circle my clit again and push my middle finger inside myself.

The expression on his face—eager, desperate—emboldens me. I let my knees fall open and his sharp inhale in response leaves my body tightening, clenching on air.

While I normally come pretty easily on my own, it doesn't happen this fast, but I'm already close. His hand starts to slide up my calf.

"How is it, Daisy?" he asks. "Tell me how it feels inside that tight little cunt of yours."

"Oh, God," I moan. "Say that again."

His grip on my calf tightens even farther. His other hand is fisted around his cock. "You like that, do you? You like that it gets me off, imagining what it'd be like inside your tight cunt? I've been thinking about it every day since you fucking arrived. Thinking about how hard I would fuck you, how hard I would make you come."

"Harrison. *Fuck*." I go right over the edge at the words, my eyes squeezed shut. He utters a curse under his breath, and that hand on my ankle is the only thing keeping me tethered to the bed. He didn't even *touch* me and it's still the best orgasm of my life.

I have to fight to return to reality. Under heavy lids, I take in several things at once—those avid eyes of his, his cock pushing hard against the elastic of his boxers, which he grips as if he's in pain. He's so goddamn desperate for it.

"Your turn," I purr. "You owe me one now."

I fully expect him to offer some tedious explanation about why that can't happen, but instead he tugs the boxers down and thrusts into his fist, inhaling through his nose.

"Jesus," he whispers. "I'm already close."

I stretch, wishing he'd push inside me or crawl up and demand I take him in my mouth.

"Tell me what you were thinking about just now," he says as his hand moves faster. He slides my tank top up with the other. "Tell me what you were thinking about when you came."

"I was thinking about you above me, about to push inside me." *Like you were last night, though you don't remember it. Hard as steel, aggressive, certain you wanted it.* "I was thinking about how tight it would be, how you'd barely fit—"

"Fuck," he hisses and then he leans over me and lets his orgasm spray out across my stomach in three long bursts, his hand still flying over his cock.

My thighs clench. I just came, and I'm so turned on again that it's as if I haven't finished in a year.

He's still breathing fast when his eyes open. He takes in the design he's just painted all over my stomach as if he's never seen anything hotter.

"Well, it's a good thing we didn't have sex," he says with a quiet laugh.

"We could have," I reply. *I know you want to.* "We still could."

His gaze meets mine. There's so much indecision there, and though I desperately want him to crawl over me and end the torture, I'm not at all surprised when he rises from the bed instead.

"I can't," he says. "You have no idea how much I want to, Daisy, but I can't."

He walks out of the room, and nothing feels finished. I'm every bit as worked up as I was before I went to him, but I suspect he's pretty worked up too.

And I haven't even put on the blue yoga pants yet.

I BLINK AWAKE.

For a second, I wonder if I dreamed last night, but no... there's still a trace of him on my stomach, and it was way too good for even *my* very active imagination to have fabricated.

It's still early. I consider heading out to surf, which seems easier than sitting through the inevitable lecture from Harrison about how sorry he is and how it shouldn't have happened, especially as I plan to derail his good intentions as fast as humanly possible.

Except...if he doesn't get the tedious lecture out of the way, will he spend the entire day going into a tailspin over it? Will he feel guiltier and guiltier? That won't help my cause either.

I brush my teeth, throw on a sweatshirt, and leave my room...only to discover that his door is open, though it's not even seven, and he's never up this early unless we're surfing. Downstairs, there's a coffee cup in the sink and his keys are gone.

My stomach knots. The only reason he'd be gone this early is if he was trying to avoid me. And if he can't even face the conversation we need to have, it sure doesn't bode well for what that conversation will entail when it happens.

I didn't want to listen to him apologize—but it never occurred to me until now that he might ask me to leave.

I surf just to clear my head before I go into work, but it doesn't help as much as it should. I keep expecting a text from him. Some version of "*Hey, sorry, I know we need to talk, but I had a meeting*"...anything to explain why he wasn't there, but it doesn't come.

The more I wait, the more disturbed I am by his silence. My waitressing skills—never laudable—are worse than ever. I can't focus on anything but the question of what he's thinking and why he's gone dark. People angrily ask for drink refills and that side of mayo they requested ten minutes ago, and I don't care. If Harrison's this quiet, he's either apartment hunting for me or he's fled the fucking country.

Griff, the artist, is the only one who doesn't mind my substandard serving abilities. Today, he's drawn me in a micro-mini with black stars covering my nipples—I've noticed that I'm wearing fewer and fewer clothes in these drawings of his—and the breasts he's given me exceed anything a human female could carry while remaining upright.

"If you ever wanted to come pose for me, I could do a much more detailed one," he says as he pays the check.

I force a smile. "I'd have to ask my boyfriend."

The excitement in his face dims a little, as I'd hoped it would. "It wouldn't have to be a big deal," he offers. "Not necessarily nude or anything if you weren't comfortable with it."

I know exactly how Harrison would react if his girlfriend or wife was asked to model in a strange guy's home, not *necessarily* nude. I guarantee the words "that's not fucking happening" or "over my dead body" would be uttered. I can't think of anything I'd love more than to be the person he wanted to keep for himself, something he was determined to protect, and a tiny part of me last night dreamed it was possible. Sure, I knew he'd feel guilty and might backtrack a little, but I figured he'd give in again. And then he'd give in more. And eventually, after weeks or months of giving in, maybe he'd see that the age gap isn't that big a deal.

But there's not been a peep from him by the time my shift ends, so that's definitely not happening. Is he going to ask me to leave? Or is he going to fabricate something that calls him out of town until the summer's end?

I fish my phone from my pocket as I close out my tables, no longer able to stand the suspense.

> Are you coming home to surf?

He doesn't answer right away, which could mean nothing but bothers me anyhow. And the answer—which doesn't arrive until I've already biked home and changed into my bikini— bothers me more.

> HARRISON
>
> Baker is on the warpath. Not sure when I'll be back but it'll be late.

I stare at the phone. So, not only is he avoiding me...he isn't even going to reference what happened. I'd bet a hundred bucks when he finally gets in tonight, he's going to tell me this just isn't going to work out. My heart is already splintering at the thought.

I think of a thousand follow-up texts, but I don't send any of them, hoping that if I just wait long enough, he'll clarify. He doesn't. I don't want to feel this way. I don't want to be this weird, desperate girl who thinks a guy is her boyfriend just because he jerked off on her stomach—jerked off under *duress*. But I'm apparently that girl anyway. I wanted more, it's not coming, and I've got no idea how to salvage the situation.

Or if he's even going to give me the chance.

WHEN I WAKE the next day, I can't tell if he came home.

I limp through my shift. Working at Wharf Seafood has never been a heavier burden than it is today and when I return to the still-empty house afterward, I've never felt more alone.

Yes, I wanted more from him. I wanted so much more. But what we had here when we were simply friends or unwilling housemates was good too. And I don't know how I'm going to get that back.

> Hey, your silence is freaking me out. Can you just tell me what you're thinking?

The text seems so mature and grounded until I've hit *send*, and then it seems clingy and adolescent. I might as well have sent him a note asking, "*Do you like me? Check yes or no.*"

And he doesn't reply at all to that one. Which means that what he's thinking is bad or needs to be said in person. *Fuck.*

I go out to the break. Surfing won't necessarily improve the situation, but it sure won't make it worse. Jon, the guy who invited me out with him and his friends a while ago, is there. He's friendly, funny, chill—exactly the kind of guy Harrison was describing when he suggested I see someone casually. Jon isn't glorifying me into someone I'm not, and I wouldn't need to play a role with him. I could tell him what wasn't working for me.

And if I were seeing someone, maybe Harrison wouldn't feel like he had to kick me out. Maybe I can still salvage this. In spite of my stupidly needy text, if he gets home from work to discover that I'm perfectly fine and possibly going on a date, perhaps it'll dial back the panic I've definitely set in motion.

He won't have to make up a reason to leave. He won't give me the "it's not you, it's me" talk that will be equal parts humiliating and heart-breaking.

I float closer to Jon. Our conversation is entirely surf-related. I tell him I just went down to Malibu and he says *oh, you should have surfed at Rincon on the way* and I think *yes, I know*.

"We're heading to a bar down in Capitola tonight," he says. "If your *uncle* is willing to let you out of his sight."

I laugh as I give him the finger. And then I agree. If dating someone else can fix things with Harrison, it's a sacrifice I'm willing to make.

29

HARRISON

OLIVER

Just landed in Paris. How is my future wife?

I have no idea because neither of us have met her.

If you let the luscious Miss Doherty leave for DC without making a move, I assure you I will fly there directly and refuse to leave until she's mine.

That's referred to in this country as "stalking." It's frowned upon. And she is NOT available.

You finally grew a pair? Maman will be so pleased.

You did not tell Mom.

> You brought a young Brigitte Bardot with you on our weekend trip and couldn't take your eyes off her. Of course I told her. I also sent pictures of her to both Maman and Matthew. Matthew has called dibs, which is patently ridiculous as he can't even afford a ticket to DC.

> P.S.: Do not lend him money for a ticket. I've already said no.

F uck. The last thing I needed was my family aware of my current situation, but what's done is done. So, like the infatuated sap I am, I make the situation worse.

> What photo?

He forwards a picture he took of Daisy on the beach, grinning at the camera as she walks alongside me, the wind whipping her hair. She's so lovely that she's hard to look away from.

I had the best of intentions when I went to her room, but Jesus—when she slid her hand into her waistband, I was a dead man. Just remembering it has me hard as nails, so I don't know how the hell things can ever be normal between us now. They can't be. And if I were a better man, I'd tell her I was going out of town for work and get the fuck away before I made things worse...except I'm not a better man.

I don't want to lose the rest of the summer with her. I don't want to be in that house if she's not going to be out on the deck, torturing me in blue leggings. I don't want to be there without her off-key humming as she slices apples, the way she dances in the kitchen when she cooks, the sound of her quietly cursing as she walks into things while getting dressed to surf in the dark.

I can't let her go. But how the hell am I going to survive having her walk past me in nothing but a towel now? How am I going to watch her dance around my kitchen in a bikini and keep my hands to myself after what happened? I can't do that either.

I was thinking about how tight it would be, how you'd barely fit.

Goddammit. I can't go home to her, and I can't *not* go home to her, so what the fuck do I do?

I pick up my phone to reply to Daisy, but I've got no idea what to say. I wish there was an emoji that said *I'll never lay a finger on you again, even if I'm dying to. Also, please don't leave.*

Perhaps it's for the best that no such emoji exists, because I'd be selfish enough to send it if it did. I barely recognize myself around her anymore, but I'm certainly not the man I thought I was. Every high-minded principle goes right out the window when I think of her the way she was in her room, coming with my name on her lips. Looking up at me from under her lashes while my cum dripped down her stomach.

A tap on the door grabs my attention as Baker walks in for the second day in a row. He's furious that I didn't come in Monday and probably furious that I went away for the weekend, but since he can't *technically* begrudge me a sick day or a fucking weekend, he's simply going to unload on me in a more general fashion, just like he did yesterday.

"I need you to go to this client happy hour in San Jose," he announces. I'm too in my own head about Daisy to even form a response as to why I can't.

I know I need to get home and talk to her. I know I need to apologize and see if we can fix things. I just can't come up with a good way to do it when all I really want to do is peel her clothes off and pick up right where we left off Monday night.

My phone vibrates and I glance down at it...Daisy is texting.

Baker raises a brow, annoyed that my gaze flickered even briefly toward the phone while he's delivering this vital lecture. "Do you need to get that?" he asks, his voice sour with sarcasm.

Yeah, take a seat. I'll just be a minute. I barely hold the words in, but I've spent my entire life being the responsible son, the responsible friend, the responsible spouse, and reining myself in is second nature.

Aside from when Daisy's involved, anyway.

"It can wait," I reply, flatly. "I assume you were nearly done."

This pisses him off, of course, and he proceeds to reiterate the same goddamn points he's already made: that he went to bat to get me this position, that he never had to worry about me in the past, that he knows divorce is hard—he's done it twice—but we didn't even have kids so I really need to pull my shit together if I plan to remain at the firm. I always thought Baker and I got along great, but the second I started actually enjoying my life, he decided it was a problem. I'm billing as much as anyone here, but he wants the return of Harrison the Robot, who set a standard no one else came close to. And why would I do that? Why *especially* would I do that for him when he's been such a fucking prick the past month?

Fuck it. I'm not going to fucking San Jose. I'm going to surf with Daisy and talk this out and—

"You're on thin ice, Reid," he says, leaving. "Pull it together or find a new job."

I sink back in my chair. There's a reason he's used *that* as his parting salvo—because there's not another reasonably sized firm in Elliott Springs, and I wouldn't have clients to bring with me even if there were. I'd be starting from scratch, and every case I took would be the worst of what I deal with now. Disputes between neighbors or defending a guy on his fourth DUI.

I spend the afternoon and evening driving to fucking San Jose and charming Baker's clients. It's after nine by the time I head home, working on my apology to Daisy the entire way. *I shouldn't have come into your room. I shouldn't have asked you to take off your pants.*

No, not that. I can't reference specifics. Because if I do and she gives me that look, as if she's remembering...I'm probably going to fuck up again.

"*I shouldn't have come into your room,*" I'll say. "*It was a mistake and I really hope we can just go back to the way things were. I like having you here, but if it's uncomfortable, I can help you find somewhere else.*"

Better, but still insufficient somehow. Mostly because I don't want to find her somewhere else to stay. I want her with me for as long as I can keep her.

Her car is on the street when I arrive at home, but the lights are off inside. The house is entirely silent as I climb the stairs and my gut is in knots. I don't want to discover that she's sick. I also don't want to enter her room and fuck up everything I've resolved to do if she's *not* sick.

Her door is open, the room is dark, and the bed is still made.

A chill runs down my spine. She went surfing. She went surfing alone because I was too goddamn busy jumping through Baker's hoops. I take the stairs two at a time to the garage, my heart hammering, and sink to the stairs in relief when I see her surfboard is leaning against the wall.

Except...she's still missing. As much as I didn't want to have the conversation we still need to have, this is worse. And I'm annoyed, even if I shouldn't be.

> Where the fuck are you?

DAISY

> The way you ask a question leaves much to be desired. The way you answer one does too.

My teeth grind as I type my next text.

> I apologize. Where the fuck are you?

DAISY

> Oddly, that's not much of an improvement. I'm nearly home. Chill.

I go upstairs and pace the family room, watching the road until a car stops in front of the house and Daisy climbs out of the back. A moment later she is clambering up the stairs in the same oversized sweatshirt she always wears.

But there's also a hint of makeup, which she almost never wears.

I swallow. "You went out?"

She sets her keys on the counter and lifts a piece of paper. "I left you a note," she replies.

I was too agitated to even look for a note. "Where'd you go?" I snap.

Her arms fold across her chest. "How very paternal you're acting, under the circumstances. And how demanding, given that you couldn't even bother to answer my text. I went to a bar with a few of the guys who surf across the street and took an Uber home."

I'm the one who told her she should have a social life. I'm the one who suggested she should probably fuck around for a little while. But it turns out I was full of shit because I can't stand the idea of her dating, and I sure as hell can't stand the idea of her *fucking around*.

I fill a glass with ice, pour the bourbon to the top, and take a healthy swallow. "Was it a date?"

She shrugs. "I don't know that tonight was a date, but one of the guys asked me out to dinner tomorrow."

Pressure builds at the back of my head, dimming the sides of my vision. I set the bourbon down too hard on the counter. Liquor seeps from the bottom of the glass, and I don't give a shit.

"I mean, that's okay, right?" she asks, pouring herself a

glass of water from the fridge. "You were the one who suggested it, and it seemed like the best way to keep your virtue safe."

I'm supposed to say *yes*. I'm supposed to ask what kind of guy he is and insist that she drive herself just in case. But I can't fucking stand the idea of anyone seeing her the way she was last night. I can't stand to have her saying, "*I was thinking about how tight it would be*" to anyone but me.

The thought sends every ounce of responsibility I've ever possessed flying out the window.

"No," I say, stepping toward her. I take the water from her hand and set it on the counter before I press her to the refrigerator. "No, Daisy. It's not fucking okay."

And then I kiss her. I kiss her hard, the way I wanted to last night. The way I've wanted to every goddamn day since she arrived. Her mouth is even softer than I pictured it would be, and when it opens beneath mine, the desire for more hits me like a hammer. It's as if every version of myself who's been denied over these past few weeks has formed an army and is storming the castle. I will never get enough of her tongue, her inhales, her curves beneath me.

My hand slides inside her sweatshirt to cup one breast through her bra, decadently heavy in my grasp. God, the number of times I've dreamed of doing this...hundreds? Thousands? She gasps as my palm glides over one nipple, then the other.

Jesus fucking Christ. I never imagined myself to have a particular type, but I do, and that type is Daisy. It's the exact weight of her breasts in my hands, the tiny waist, how tight and wet she'll be when I'm finally inside her. Her proportions defy logic, and being with her is going to ruin me for other women, but so be it.

"We need to close the curtains," I grunt, grinding against her helplessly as her hand reaches for my belt. We should go to my room, but I can't. I can't wait the length of time it would take to get her up the stairs.

"Just hit the lights," she says, as impatient as I am.

I find her mouth again, pushing her shorts to the floor. "No. Lights on. I want to watch you stretch to take every fucking inch of me."

"Alrighty then," she says, pulling my belt free at last. I groan as her hand slides into my pants and grips me. "Forget about the curtains. Let everyone watch."

I want to agree to this because I'm already so hard it hurts, but the sight of her naked is something I want to keep to myself, always.

"Couch," I growl against her mouth. "Now."

I march to the far wall to hit the curtains, and she saunters to the couch, removing her sweatshirt as she walks. I move fast toward her, pulling her against me, finding her mouth again.

Her fingers tug at my tie then start to work on the buttons of my shirt. I need her skin against mine faster than she can get it there. Buttons skitter across the floor as I wrench the shirt off myself.

She reaches inside my boxers and I have to stop her, jaw grinding as I try to regain control. "Give me a minute, Daisy, or this just won't last." I pull the tank over her head. She reclines on the couch in nothing but her panties.

Fuck. Yes. She is definitely going to ruin me for anyone after her.

"Take everything off," she purrs. "I want to see you."

I push the pants and boxers to the floor, fling the T-shirt somewhere behind me, and drop to the far end of the couch on my knees. "Spread those legs, Daisy," I demand, and she complies with a quiet gasp.

I run my index finger over her, from her clit to her entrance and back. "You're dripping for me," I say, sucking a finger into my mouth.

"I've been like this for weeks," she says with a shaky laugh, and Jesus Christ, those words alone could probably make me blow.

I push her thighs farther apart and bury my face between her legs the way I desperately wanted to the other night.

"You don't have to," she breathes.

"Why not? Am I missing your clit like everyone else?"

Her laugh turns into a gasp as my tongue resumes. "No. No, I'm pretty sure you've found it. Jesus."

My tongue flickers as I circle her entrance and she moans, so I do it again, applying more pressure. I slide one finger inside her and then a second. It's such a tight fit that I hiss between my teeth at the idea of getting inside her.

"Let me make it good for you," I tell her. "Too hard? Too soft? I want you to tell me exactly what you need."

She sucks in a breath. "I just—oh God, Harrison. That's good. Like that. You don't have to keep going, but—"

I push two fingers in again, against her inside wall, and let my tongue resume.

"Faster," she pleads. "With your fingers. Oh, fuck. Yes. That's perfect."

She's arching to get closer to me, her hand palming my scalp, tugging my hair. Her breath comes faster and faster. My tongue picks up speed, in time with my fingers.

"I'm already close," she whispers. "Oh, God."

She clamps down on my fingers as she goes over the edge, her head falling backward. There are certain things you can't fake, and the way she's convulsing against my fingers is among them.

My pride in this is almost indecent. It's every best moment I've ever had combined—my biggest wave, my first aerial, graduating. It's all of them together and twice as good, and I'm so fucking hard as she curses and tugs at my hair that I can't even exult in it too much.

Her eyes open slowly, and she gives me a crooked grin.

"Okay, that was worth it." Her hand slides down to stroke me. "I wanted to be the one doing this Monday night," she says. Her thumb runs over the head of my cock, spreading the moisture there. She strokes me again, and I wrap my hand around her wrist.

"You've got to stop," I groan.

She frowns, already wounded, and I laugh. "I'm not saying I *want* you to stop. I'm just saying I'm going to come if you keep going, and I'd rather be inside you."

Her mouth curves and her legs open. "Then by all means, get inside me."

Fuck. I can see why the men she's been with have been such a disappointment. Who could possibly last when she's smiling the way she is, when she's demanding I get inside her in that raspy voice?

I climb above her. "Do I need anything?"

"No," she says, suddenly breathless. "Just please—" She raises her hips, urging me to hurry, and I slam inside her in a single hard thrust that knocks the breath from us both.

My mouth finds hers as I thrust again, my hand sliding up to palm a breast, to pinch her nipple. "Fuck, Daisy, this is not going to last."

"I don't care," she says, and it frees me to stop caring too. We become tongues and teeth and grasping hands, and when my teeth clamp down on her nipple and she cries out, I nearly lose it right then.

I want to watch, but I know it'll put me over the edge. I want to make it last, but it's too wet, too good, too urgent. I come hard inside her with a low groan against her neck. I can't say I've ever had sex I'd consider bad, but this is something else entirely. When I collapse on top of her—still hard and certain that I'll need more from her in a minute or two—it's as if I've come home.

30

DAISY

I was wrong.

Sex is not overrated.

Sex is so magnificent that I'm not sure how people who are already aware of this fact even function on an average day.

Four times last night, and once again at dawn, and I'm still not done. He's moving through his morning—pod in the coffee maker, protein shake tucked into a pocket of his briefcase—while I'm wondering how I can convince him to do it again, to do it a hundred times more and never return to his office.

"Stop looking at me like that, Daisy," he warns, "or I'm not going to get out of here."

I climb on the counter. I picture pulling him to me by his tie and wrapping my legs around his waist. Would he like that, or would it make me seem too young, too clingy?

A part of me is scared he's already thinking it, that we might *already* be over and I'm the only one who doesn't know it.

He sets the travel mug into the coffee maker and then turns, raising a brow. "What's with the sudden darkness, Goth Barbie?"

I smile. That much-hated nickname is a little more palatable now that it's not reminding me of the age difference. "No darkness," I reply. "Just planning my day. I assume you'll be late again."

"Baker can go fuck himself," he growls. "I'm coming home."

I shrug. "Well, I mean, there's no rush, really. I've still got my date."

I don't. I already texted Jon to explain, but Harrison doesn't need to know this just yet.

He turns toward me, his jaw unhinged. "*What?*"

"My date. I told you about it last night."

His nostrils flare as if he's scented prey. "Daisy," he says quietly, "that had better be a fucking joke."

I bite down on a grin. If he's going to pull a disappearing act, at least it won't be today. "Yes, it was a joke."

He crosses the kitchen and pushes my knees apart so he can stand between them. "It wasn't a funny one," he says against my mouth.

I let my hand press to his fresh-shaved jaw. "It made *me* laugh. It's still making me laugh."

"I can think of a few ways to make you stop laughing."

I gasp as his teeth sink into my lower lip, and he yanks me to the counter's edge. Between us, my favorite bulge in the whole world is growing.

"That sounds like an empty threat," I reply.

He undoes his belt and pulls my hand down to grasp him. "How empty does it sound now?"

I inhale. I love how feral he is when he lets go of all that restraint. I love that we've barely started this conversation and he's already thick and hard beneath my palm.

I slide my hand under the waistband of his boxers to grasp him, to stroke, and his eyes fall closed, his forehead leaning against mine as if the pleasure is so intense he can't quite keep his head upright, and then I squeal in surprise as he lifts me and heads for the stairs. "We don't have to," I argue. "You're going to be late."

"I don't *have* to?" His mouth moves to my ear, and his voice drops as he starts taking the stairs two at a time, with me still wrapped around his waist. "Daisy, I've never cared less than I do right now about being late for work."

HE GETS HOME EARLY, but for obvious reasons, it takes us a while to get out to the break, and we don't last long there either. I pull him into the outdoor shower with me afterward. When we're done there, he carries me straight to his bed and tosses me onto the mattress.

"So tell me," I say, collapsing on my back, "that erection you got the first day I was on your deck...was that actually about me or was it just some random A.M. occurrence?"

He laughs, running a hand over his face. "Suffice it to say that any of the erections you've witnessed since you moved in— and I'm pretty sure there have been several—were entirely because you have an incredible ass, among other attributes, and tend to wear very few clothes."

"I'm amazed by your restraint."

"In retrospect, I'm amazed too. But, you know..." His smile slowly fades. "This is something your mother and Liam would never forgive me for. They still see you as a kid, and I think they always will. They would trust me *not* to do exactly what I've done."

I sigh. "My mother kills herself trying to keep me safe and shape my life but is seemingly untroubled by the fact that the guy she married is so awful I had to move out."

He rolls toward me, running a hand over my hip. "Are you ever going to tell me what he did? Because it was more than him being a dick. I know you that well at this point."

It's a truth I've never told anyone since I first suggested it to my mom, mostly because I couldn't stand to have one more person fail to believe me.

"Scott cheats. A lot. I knew it even before they got married because he hit up my friend's older sister on a dating site right before the wedding."

Harrison doesn't appear to be surprised. "I kind of figured. He seems like the type. Did you tell her?"

I shrug. "I was going to, but she was having this big brunch for the bridesmaids and was all excited about it, and there was just never a good time. She was so happy, and after the brunch she had her bachelorette, and the rehearsal dinner, and I didn't know what to do."

He squeezes my hip. "So instead, you dyed your hair and let everyone call you a brat. Including me. God, I'm so sorry."

"Don't apologize. I *was* being a brat. I just didn't know how else to handle it." I swallow. "But then I caught him a month later. He was supposed to be out of town, but I saw him with some chick at Long Point. So I *did* tell my mom, and it all went really badly. He'd driven all the way back to the airport, had her pick him up, and they'd gone to dinner after—I assume he saw me, too, and was covering his bases."

"So she didn't believe you."

I flip on my back. "No, it was worse than that. She started crying and begged me to go to counseling. Scott..." I hate this. I hate saying it out loud. "Scott had been pointing out ways I was like my dad, so me coming to her with some wild story about seeing him at the beach was one more sign. And if I suggested he'd seen me, that he'd driven back to the airport...I'd have sounded even crazier, so I was just screwed."

I glance at him, waiting to see doubt in his face. Waiting to see that question there: *Is she like her dad? Are there signs I've missed?* Anyone can be made to look insane if you selectively choose their worst moments—you list out the depressed times, the angry times, the irrational thoughts spoken aloud, even in jest. Except in my case, it's also possible. And I won't know until it happens. Maybe I won't even know then.

His lips press to my head. "Jesus, Daisy, I'm so sorry."

I blink back tears, not at the retelling of the story, but at being believed. Yes, he's only the second person I've told, but he's the first one who's taken what I said at face value.

"After that, he was watching for me to slip up. If I cut school, he somehow knew immediately and told my mom. Then my stuff started going missing or was messed with. My surfboard wasn't where I left it, my toothbrush disappeared and reappeared, my laptop would be unplugged and dead when I got home though I never unplugged it. When I accused him, he and my mom just shared this look, like *'oh here's another sign.'* Eventually I just moved in with Liam."

"Daisy," he groans, "I wish you'd told her. Or me. I'd have believed you."

I shake my head. "Scott was too good at it. He'd already made me look jealous and crazy, and me telling her that he was hiding my stuff and trying to make me look worse...it would just have been a bigger argument that he was right."

"You could explain now, though."

"What's the point? He's listed every single thing I've done wrong for seven years. She has a mountain of evidence that I might be ill somehow. And even if she believed me, I'd just be ruining all those memories for her. If her marriage to Scott is the only romance her life will ever hold, I'm not going to destroy that."

He pulls me against his chest, a place I probably wouldn't be if Scott hadn't been such a dick.

Right now, it's impossible to wish any of it had gone another way.

31

HARRISON

Things turned bad with Audrey a year into our marriage, when her brother died, but even before that they were never especially good. She wasn't hungry for things the way Daisy is—she wanted jewelry on our anniversary, a photo of us that would make a good Christmas card, the mortgage refinanced when rates dropped—things that would satisfy her for five minutes and then mean nothing again.

And she was bothered by the most trivial shit while pretending the big issues weren't there. "She's wearing white a *month* after Labor Day," Audrey said of a woman we saw at dinner. We'd had nothing to say to each other through the meal, we hadn't had sex in a month...but the fact that someone was breaking a stupid fucking fashion rule was an issue worthy of notice. She remained irritated by *that* for hours.

If she hadn't cheated, I'd have stayed with her forever because it would have been the right thing to do, and I'd have been miserable, while what's occurring with Daisy is unequivocally the *wrong* thing to do and it makes me happier than I've ever been before.

We surf most nights. We have sex on every surface of my home. Even the garage floor isn't left unscathed, which is what happens when Daisy insists on "helping" me out of my wetsuit.

I now arrive at the office each morning exhausted from the lack of sleep and riding a wave of dopamine that leaves me feeling as if I could lift a car over my head.

If her previous relationships were anything like ours, I understand why men put her on a pedestal—it's almost impossible not to. Being with Daisy is like sinking into a warm bath when you didn't know you were cold—I'm stunned by how good it is. I'm stunned by how such a simple thing can also be this blissful, this indulgent. I want to stay inside her and never leave.

It has to end—she and I are still in completely different places in life, and we will remain so for the next decade at least —but there's a part of me that would give up everything to keep her with me forever.

SHE HAS to work a double shift on Friday, the only reason I stay at work myself. I tell her I'll pick her up because I don't want her biking home in the dark, and I arrive early because I'm too goddamned eager to see her. Inside, the hostess is gone and most of the tables are empty. There's no sign of Daisy.

The guy behind the bar is drying glasses. "Can I get you something?"

Is this the kid she'd be dating if she wasn't living with me? He's got the same early-twenties overconfidence I had at his age, the kind you acquire after realizing almost no girl is out of reach if you play your cards right.

"I'm, uh, picking Daisy up."

His double take is subtle, over in a flash, but I see him trying to put together who I am. She looks young for her age while I'm clearly in my thirties. The whole thing appears sketchy as hell.

He nods. "She's with the manager. I'll call to the back—who should I say is here?"

"Her uncle," I reply, though I don't know why the hell I've said it.

He picks up the phone while I go to a bench near the hostess stand, one that probably held tired parents and squirming children earlier in the day when the wharf was busy. I thought I'd be one of those parents by now. The fact that I'm waiting on a twenty-one-year-old to get off work makes that dream feel further away than ever.

Daisy walks out of the kitchen, says something to the bartender, and turns toward me...and all those thoughts fade away.

Her smile—*fuck*. The way she smiles at me, and only me, is something I want to keep forever. And I want to keep it entirely to myself.

She goes behind the bar and leans down for her bag. The bartender continues drying glasses, but his gaze is on her ass the entire time, and it's still on her ass as she crosses the room to me.

"You told him you were my *uncle*?" she asks.

I usher her out the door. "I felt like I needed to explain myself."

"Well, now we both have some explaining to do because *I* told him you were the guy who came on my face this morning."

My head jerks toward her and she laughs.

"Oh my God, you really thought I'd say that to someone?"

"You say shit like that to *me* all the time."

She shrugs. "You're different. At first, because it was fun to mess with you, and now because you really do come on my face fairly often, so it'd be weird if I never addressed it."

I laugh unwillingly. I'm not sure how she manages to get me

hard while making me laugh while annoying the shit out of me all at the same time.

I hold her door. "Does it bother you? That I said I was your uncle?"

She tilts her head, seeming to think about it. "Nah," she says finally. "It's for the best that they all think I'm single anyway. I'm a terrible waitress. Being theoretically available means I get forgiven a lot more than I would otherwise."

I shut the door behind her and go to the other side of the car, my jaw grinding. "Is that why your manager called you to the back?" I ask, my voice calm by force. "Because you're *theoretically* single?"

"No," she says, pulling her hair out of its ponytail and running her fingers through it. "He surfs. He was just showing me pictures of this place in Panama he might buy."

"You know, I don't call my employees in at the night's end to show them pictures of the homes I might buy."

"Of course you don't. You didn't even tell your wife." When I don't laugh, she elbows me. "It's not a big deal. I think he's got a little crush. I'll live. It's an occupational hazard. I'm used to it."

She's used to it because she looks…like Daisy. Because she looks like every man's fantasy, and she's spent way too many years of her short life fending men off. I don't want her to have to fucking do that. And I'm hung up on the fact that she's got to do it even now, when she's living with—and *fucking*—me. Her manager is still calling her to his office to look at his photos, and the age-appropriate bartender is staring at her ass every time she bends over.

I possess something that every man wants, and even if Daisy and I were coming clean about what was going on between us, it wouldn't stop any of them. They'd know she was too young for me. They'd know they just needed to wait for it to run its course. I can't fault them. Having Daisy for even a brief window of time is like winning the lottery—you know the odds are bad, but you still want to play.

ON SATURDAY, we surf early, and she makes us smoothie bowls afterward. "Don't tell Oliver I put peanut butter in it again."

I cross to where she stands and pull her against me. "God, I was in agony that entire weekend."

"Oh?" Her voice is a soft purr against my skin while her hand slides into my shorts. "I wish I'd known. I'd have taken care of it for you."

I pull her to the couch, helping her out of the clothes she just put on, going down on her until she's seconds from coming before I slide inside her.

My eyes fall closed as I bottom out. "I want to stay inside you the whole goddamn day," I growl.

She arches, her legs wrapping around me. "Then do. I don't want you anywhere else."

When we wake hours later, the midday sun is blazing through the windows, dirty dishes are all over the counter, and the couch now possesses a new white stain I doubt is going to come out.

I love the mess, I love the ruined furniture, I love the way her hair has dried in tangles. I wouldn't change a thing.

"My couch now possesses a mysterious stain."

"Something to remember me by," she says. "I have no idea why you bought a velvet couch. At the beach, no less. If it's not already full of sand, it will be. And, uh, it appears it's not good for having sex on, either."

"Audrey chose it." Audrey, who'd *never* have had sex on a couch and would have been disgusted at the mere suggestion.

"Now that you're entering your sex-crazed bachelor days,"

she says, walking naked toward the kitchen and grabbing a paper towel, "I'd suggest you consider leather instead."

I flinch. I want to ask how she knows this. I want to ask how many times she's been fucked on a couch, and I know I'd be angry at the answer.

This is supposed to be a fling. I don't know why I'm incapable of treating it like one.

32

DAISY

The problem with swim trunks is that they're so easy-access. Even on the days when we have agreed in advance that we are heading straight out to surf as soon as he gets home...those roomy swim trunks demand a very different outcome.

And thus we are racing to get to the break tonight before we've missed high tide entirely.

"If I haven't mentioned it yet," he says, grinning over his shoulder at me as we paddle out to the lineup, "I'm grateful you so ruthlessly blackmailed me when you came back to California."

I laugh. "Do you mean that, or is it the hand job talking?"

"The hand job certainly didn't *hurt* your case."

"I actually have a great deal of experience blackmailing older men," I reply, straddling my board.

His eyes darken. "This conversation is taking an unpleasant turn."

I lean back on my hands. "Liam was the first...non-sexy blackmail of course. He was sleeping with one of my teachers and *also* sleeping with my soccer coach. It's not like he was lying to anyone, but they wouldn't have been pleased."

He grins. "Is that how you weaseled your way into his home?"

I wave a hand. "I'm delightful. I don't have to weasel my way into anyone's home. Okay, I did have to weasel my way into yours, but you were drinking too much to realize how delightful I am."

"I fully realized how delightful you are—I was just trying hard to forget." His gaze drifts over me in a way that leaves me clenching my thighs. "So what did you get out of Liam?"

I shrug. "He had to sign something saying I had counseling every Friday and could leave at eleven for the day."

He raises a brow. "And *did* you have counseling?"

I nod at the board beneath me. "If this counts as counseling, then yes."

A wave is approaching. We both lie down and turn to face the shore. "And how long did that go on for?"

"All four years of high school. Liam dated a *lot* of women. One day you'll have to compare blackmail stories."

I regret the words the moment I utter them. Did I really just forget that he and I have to stay a secret? That next month, when I leave, all these weeks with him will be a moment in our shared past, one neither of us can even allude to?

I did. But based on the way his smile wavers, he hasn't forgotten for a minute.

THAT NIGHT, he orders in dinner and brings it to his room where I'm lounging, naked and wanting more.

When soy sauce drips down my stomach, he leans over to lick it off. "I've never eaten naked before, but I'm starting to see the advantages."

I raise a brow. "You've never eaten naked?"

He raises a brow right back. "You *have?*" His eyes are dark. I suspect he won't be happy with my answer.

I lean over the sushi to kiss him. "Not with anyone who made me come three times first."

"Well, I guess there's that," he grumbles. "It had better not have been with the guy you dated at age fourteen."

I laugh. "It was not. And please don't tell me you're jealous of a high school senior I dated seven years ago."

His grin is sheepish. "It's a guy thing. We always want to believe we're the first to land somewhere."

"It's a *people* thing, not a guy thing. But it would be pretty hard for me to believe I was your first when I know the last person you were with. Or...was she?" I wince at the line of questioning I've introduced—I'm not sure I want the answer—but persist with it anyway. "Did you not even have, like, a one-night stand?"

He blows out a breath. "I thought about it. I thought about it a *lot*. But I knew I was going to be a little fucked up over the divorce for a while, so I didn't want to give someone the wrong idea."

"The wrong idea?"

He shrugs. "The impression that it meant something."

I swallow and pretend I'm focused on swirling wasabi into my soy sauce so he doesn't notice how much that hurt. It's not *supposed* to hurt. We both know this will end in August, and I guess that's the perfect situation for him: time-limited, without expectations.

But I'd thought he was going to be the one guy I didn't have to play a role for, and it isn't true.

I'm playing the role of someone who doesn't mind that this is going to end, and I do.

I already do.

33

HARRISON

The following weekend, the waves are mush, and Daisy talks me into going for a run instead of surfing. She gets an ice cream cone once we reach the wharf, and we walk along the beach. It pisses me off, the way men look at her when she walks past. I want to announce to every last one of them that she's taken, which is a problem because she's not.

She needs those post-college years to make the same dumb mistakes I did, to figure out what she actually wants from life. The person you are at twenty-one is entirely different from the person you'll be a decade later. She can't possibly know what she'll want by then.

"You know what you need in your dumb mansion?" she asks, licking her ice cream cone.

"The dumb mansion where you live for free?"

She gives me a lopsided grin. "Yes, that's the dumb mansion I was referring to. A sauna."

"Why the fuck would I get a sauna?" I ask, my hand linking with hers. "I hate saunas."

"They're good for your quality of sleep, which is highly correlated with longevity."

"I'm too young to worry about how long I'm going to live," I reply. "I'd say the last few years felt a little *too* long."

She elbows me. "Don't say that."

I swoop her up in my arms. "You're a very violent little thing, did you know that?"

She looks up at me from beneath her lashes and takes another lick. "I'm pretty sure you like it when I'm violent. I'm pretty sure what made you come so hard last night was my nails on your back."

"I think we should put that to the test," I begin, but before I can say another word, there are two children running at us, one of them shouting my name.

I set Daisy down so quickly that she stumbles and drops her cone into the sand.

"Shit," I hiss. "Sorry."

Caleb's soon-to-be stepkids, Sophie and Henry, run up to us. And Sophie, who never keeps a thought to herself, is staring at Daisy. *Shit.*

"Is she your girlfriend?" Sophie demands, pointing at Daisy.

Fuck. I knew it was possible that I would run into an acquaintance down here and have to come clean, but Caleb's a bad one to come clean with. Especially when I was just carrying Daisy like a bride.

Caleb and Lucie approach with strained smiles—it's pretty fucking clear they saw everything.

Caleb gives Daisy a hug, introduces her to Lucie...and then he turns to me. "What's going on, man?" Caleb asks, eyes narrowed. "I thought you were spending every weekend in LA."

I sigh. "It's a long story."

Lucie nudges Caleb. "Did you tell him we're renting his dad's old place?"

Caleb swallows, struggling to make small talk. "Yeah, your

dad's beach house is a rental now. We're having a big office party there in a few weeks." He looks between me and Daisy. "So...what's going on?"

The tension in his voice tells me he already knows exactly what's going on and there's nothing I can say that will make it okay. He's looking at Daisy the way I *tried to* when she first arrived: like the little girl in pigtails we taught to surf. The toddler who couldn't pronounce the letter "t" and who called her favorite restaurant *Kenfucky* Fried Chicken.

Lucie's smile is nervous. Her hands flutter to her sides. "What if you guys chat for a minute? I'm going to take the twins back up to the wharf and get them some water."

"I'll come with you," says Daisy too quickly.

They're not twenty yards away when Caleb releases a groan. "Dude, tell me this isn't exactly the way it fucking looks, which is that you've been lying to us about some girlfriend in LA while hooking up with Bridget's *kid*."

"It's not like that," I reply, because even if it is precisely like that now, I can't admit to it when it would definitely get back to Liam. It might anyway. The truth about London, however, seems pretty mild compared to the much greater lies I'm telling him now. "Audrey and I didn't break up the way I implied. I sort of fabricated a girlfriend. I know I should have told you the truth. I just...I needed to lick my wounds for a while."

His nostrils flare. Caleb's never hit me before, but I can tell he wants to. "That doesn't explain why you're licking them with *Daisy*."

"We're just friends. She got in a fight with Bridget and needed a place to stay."

"You and I have been friends for twenty-five years, but you've never swept me up in your arms while we took a romantic stroll down the beach."

I tug at my hair. "For fuck's sake. It wasn't a *romantic* stroll. She made me go running, and we were playing around. Can you please just let this go? She'll be back in DC next month. It's not a big deal."

He raises a brow. "Not a big deal for *you* or for her? Because you're a decade older than she is, and she's had a crush on you since she was old enough to walk."

Did Daisy have a crush on me when she was little? I'm not sure if that would make this better or worse. "That's not true."

Caleb shoves his hands in his pockets. "You're an adult, and she's *sort of* an adult. Just be careful. We've all had a romantic relationship that has really put us through the wringer at some point. Me with Kate. Beck with Kate. You with Audrey. Don't be that for Daisy, okay?"

"I wouldn't. I won't."

I'm far less certain about it than I sound, however. How many villains start off by proclaiming that what they're doing isn't all that bad?

I'm pretty sure it's most of them.

34

DAISY

HARRISON

Tide's in at 5. I'll be there.

I just got cut. That's a very long time to wait. How should I pass the time?

I can think of several ways.

It's not really the same without you jerking off on my stomach afterward.

Filthy girl. Now I'm hard as a rock. It's going to be very awkward if my boss walks in.

I could take care of that for you. You could hide me under your desk.

Now I'm gonna need you to take care of it for me as soon as I get home. Be waiting. Panties off.

I'm giddy. Even if it's all pretend, this pretense makes me happier than any *real* thing I had before him.

I'm at home, showered and waiting just before he's due. When my mom calls, I consider not answering but we never talk for long, and I've got a few minutes 'til Harrison gets here. Besides, if I talk to her quickly today, I won't have to talk to her tomorrow, and the less we speak, the fewer lies I'll be forced to tell.

"I have to go soon, Mom," I warn. "I've got an, um, date."

"Anyone special?" she asks.

"No." The lie is necessary. It's what she wants to hear, and I sure as hell don't want the questions that would come if I answered in the affirmative.

"Good," she says, as I knew she would. "The next six months are too important to be getting distracted. Did you see that article I sent about tricks for taking the LSAT?"

"Yeah, thanks." I wish I could tell her the truth—that it's hard to get geared up to take an exam for law school when you're not even sure you're going to be graduating from college.

"So the reason I was actually calling is that I wanted to make sure you're coming to the opening of the theater next week," she says.

"Huh? Didn't it open weeks ago?"

"That was the soft opening. They're doing a big thing to celebrate."

"I don't—"

"Honey, you have to go. Liam did the restoration. This is his night."

Downstairs, the garage door is opening.

"We'll see, Mom," I say, desperate to end the call. "Oh, there's someone at the door. Can I—"

"Liam and Emmy would appreciate it. I seriously think he's

going to wind up marrying her. I've never seen him like this over someone."

Harrison climbs the stairs and takes me in like something he's starved for. He comes to the end of the couch, raising a brow at the shorts I'm still wearing, wrapping his hands around my ankles and spreading my legs.

"Mom, let me call you back," I squeak, hanging up the phone before she can continue.

He tugs at my shorts. "I thought I told you to have the panties off." He leans down, pulling my thong to the side. The heat of his exhale ghosts between my legs before he presses a gentle kiss to my clit.

"I was working on it," I reply breathlessly. "But it felt a little weird to keep going once I got on the call with my mom."

He tugs the panties off and runs his tongue over my center, letting it circle, then dip inside me.

"You still deserve a little punishment," he says, sitting up. "Come here."

I pout. "I kind of liked where we were."

His grin is positively feral. "You'll like this too. Probably." He pats his lap. "Ass up."

I suspect I know what's next, and I'm already soaked from the idea of it.

I climb over his lap. His palm rests on my back. "So tell me what was so pressing about this call that you couldn't take off the panties?"

He smacks my ass hard and I gasp at the sting, but before I can complain, he's letting a finger slide back along my center.

"Ohhh," I murmur. I'm losing track of the conversation, and he's barely begun. "She wanted—"

He slips a finger inside me and I gasp again. He adds a second one and begins to slowly fuck me with his hand.

"She wanted what?" he asks calmly.

"She wanted—" Oh, God, it's so hard to think when I've been craving this all day long. "Go to the theater opening."

"I thought the theater already opened." His other hand slides between us and reaches my clit while his fingers continue to move.

"Harrison," I groan. "More."

His laugh is low and menacing and makes me want him even more than I already did. He smacks my ass again, but that finger on my clit never stops circling. "Greedy girl. You're still explaining why you didn't follow orders. I'm the one who decides when you get more."

"It was a soft open."

I brace for the sting of his hand, craving it in a weird way. He delivers, and I groan.

"Oh God, I'm going to feel so weird about coming while you spank me. That would be weird, right?"

The bulge in his pants throbs beneath me. "That sounds like a challenge, Daisy." His hand lands on my ass again. "Should I attend this premiere too? Should I finger you during the movie but never let you come?"

I can see it. His hand lands again, harder this time, and I barely notice because I'm too consumed with the idea of him fingering me in a theater, refusing to let me get off.

I sit up on my knees. "I'll do it back to you."

He opens his belt, unzips his pants, and pulls his cock from his boxers, long and swollen and ready.

"Show me what you'd do in that theater, then," he says, and he gasps as I lean over and pull him into my mouth.

"I'll go straight from work," he hisses. "You won't have been fucked for at least twenty-four hours, and you'll be so wet that it's dripping down your thighs."

Smack!

Fuck, it feels so real right now. His cock is hitting the back of my throat, already close. It's as if we're in that theater, and the idea of it is so fucking filthy that when he jams two fingers inside me, I come apart.

"Fuck, Daisy," he hisses, holding my head, unmoored by the fact that he's made me come this way. "*Swallow*."

He floods my mouth with a groan. It takes him a moment to come back down, to realize he's got my hair in a death grip. "Jesus, sorry," he says with a breathless laugh, releasing me. "That was a lot. I need a new couch now, don't I?

I laugh, collapsing on my side and holding my arms out for him to join me. "Probably. You needed one anyway. Audrey decorated this place like the combination of a really boring museum and Lady Havisham's moldy old tomb in *Great Expectations*."

He pulls me against him, pressing his smiling lips to my neck. "A boring museum?"

I shrug. "You know—the ones with really plain sculptures and where all the rooms are mostly empty, and everyone murmurs quietly about how brilliant the shit is when it's, like, a rectangle made of marble? I don't know how hard it is to work with marble, but I guarantee that I could make a rectangle out of one if I'd taken a class or two."

"So how would I turn this place into a house that isn't half boring museum and half Lady Havisham's moldy old tomb?"

I reach for my phone and begin scrolling. This is something I've actually given a fair amount of thought to, perhaps because I want to rid his life of any remaining signs of Audrey. "First of all, ditch the velvet couch, because that just doesn't work at the beach. I'm shocked it's not already full of sand. Something like this." I show him an oversized couch with plump cushions. "And ditch the coffee table too. I don't even understand why you bought it if you guys wanted kids. That thing's an accident waiting to happen."

He frowns. "I brought up the table corners with Audrey. She

said if we had kids visiting, their parents should be watching them."

Hope flares inside me: *maybe he's realizing how wrong she was, how right I am.* I banish the thought as soon as I note it. No matter how true those things are, I'm not the girl he winds up with. I know that.

I continue showing him all the other things I'd change. The soft area rugs I'd buy, new light fixtures, a suede platform bed, a big oak table so he could have friends over.

He reaches to the floor for his pants, grabs his wallet, and hands me a credit card. "Order it."

My brow furrows. "*What?* The nightstand? It wouldn't really work unless you—"

"All of it," he says.

I stare at him. "Dude, all this stuff will cost a hundred grand. If you want to spend that kind of money, you should probably call a designer and—"

"Please just order it," he says. "I don't care about the money. I just want it done as soon as possible. This is all shit Audrey picked out anyway. I don't need the reminder."

The euphoria of a moment before drains away. He doesn't need the reminder of Audrey, which means her absence still bothers him. And I'm only here as a bridge between Audrey and whoever comes after me, a woman who'll be older and smarter and more sophisticated. I am simply the rebound fuck, a pleasant memory he'll one day shake his head at...somewhat appalled by his decision-making once he's come through the other side.

If I'd gone out with Jon, it would have been smooth, like riding a wave into shore. I might have vaguely enjoyed it, but I'd have had no regret when it was time to jump off and call it a day. With Harrison, though, I'm at the top of a wave that's beyond my skill level. I know the crash is coming and that it will be ugly. But I'm already inside it and there's no turning back.

"She's gone dark again," he says softly. "What are you thinking about?"

I'm thinking this is a fling for you, but it isn't for me.

I'm thinking this is going to ruin me when it ends.

"Reverse cowgirl," I reply. "I've never done it, but it looks fun."

He studies me for a long moment—I worry he's not going to let me distract him—and I'm relieved when he finally pulls me close. "I guess the furniture can wait."

Yes, it can.

Everything can wait. I'm already inside the wave, and it's too fucking late. I might as well enjoy the ride.

THE NEXT MORNING, I follow him downstairs, dressed to surf but unwilling to leave before he does. Something's been bothering him since last night and the uncertainty makes me want to cling, a deeply unattractive quality. I'm trying hard not to let it show.

"When do you go back to school?" he asks as he makes his coffee for the ride to work.

Why is he asking? If he wanted to get rid of me, he couldn't now. Maybe he's just waiting for me to leave.

"I'm not sure," I reply. He stiffens, as if he senses the lie. "I've got to figure it out. I don't think my car is going to survive the trip back. Why?"

He's silent just a second too long before he meets my eye. "You barely talk about school. I'm wondering if there's more to the Lazy Daisy nickname than I realized. Or if there's just shit you're not telling me."

It's in his expression and tone more than it is his words: a slight irritation with me that he's trying—and failing—to repress, which is exactly how Christian was at the end. He started picking fights and it was only in hindsight that I realized the problem wasn't that I'd done something wrong or that I'd begun to fail, but simply that he was tired of me.

Is that what's happening now?

Or maybe it's that I'm lying to Harrison. I'm lying to everyone.

"Why would I talk about school?" I reply. I sweep my foot out and let my toes curve around his belt to pull him my way. "We have so many better things to do."

His hand wraps around my ankle, gentle but firm, and he removes my foot.

"It would be nice," he says as he grabs the travel mug and his keys, "if you'd stop trying to distract me with sex when you don't want to answer a question."

He walks out, and my stomach drops. Is this how it begins —with some vague displeasure and fault-finding on his end... and then suddenly I'm dumped?

He thinks he wants the truth, but if I told him, he'd run as fast as he fucking could.

I still haven't decided what to do when he texts to say he's not coming home tonight. *A client thing,* he says, without explaining why a client thing would require him to be gone until morning.

Maybe it's nothing, or maybe the end is already here.

At least I'm not pregnant this time around.

35

HARRISON

This morning didn't go the way I'd wanted it to. I reacted badly to Daisy's response—or lack thereof. I need to apologize, yet...those pieces of Daisy she hides away are an itch that only gets worse when scratched.

There was something going on with her when we discussed the furniture. There was something going on when we spoke about school, too. The ex-boyfriend? Someone else? I have no right to ask for those pieces of herself that she's hiding, but I want them anyway. I want them a little more every day.

I nod along to the guy talking on the other side of my laptop and have just picked up my phone to text her when the receptionist hands me a note.

Someone's here about your friend Liam. She says it's an emergency.

I hang up the call and brace myself for the worst, but the woman who enters my office—Liam's new girlfriend, who I've only seen once—is texting as she walks in, and appears more irritated than upset.

"Hi. I'm Emerson Hughes," she says, shaking my hand. "I'm a, uh, a friend of Liam's."

"What happened?" I demand. "Is Liam okay?"

She waves me down as she takes a seat. "Nothing happened to him. He's fine."

I stare at her. *She must be fucking kidding me.* "Did you seriously tell my secretary that Liam had an emergency just so you could get an unscheduled appointment? I was in the middle of a conference call."

"Liam does have an emergency," she says without apology. "He just isn't aware of it."

I sigh. Every minute she sits in my office for this unscheduled meeting is a minute I won't be spending with Daisy this afternoon.

"Liam's going to lose Lucas Hall," she says. "You know how long he's worked on it, but they're putting it to a vote tomorrow, and my company has made it impossible for him to win."

Liam has talked for years about turning the property into a hotel. I'm disappointed on his behalf, but what good can I possibly do twenty-four hours before the hearing? "I'm not sure what magic you think I can wield to fix this," I tell her. "I'm not on the town council, and I don't have any sway with them."

"I need you to get an injunction," she says. "The building has historic significance and the only way it can be torn down is if structural defects make it unstable. We paid off a shady inspector—I can get you proof that the report was incorrect, enough to get the state to put the vote on hold."

She's making it sound far easier and less time-consuming than it will be. I'd have to go to San Jose and argue with fifteen clerks before I got to the right person, all while the work I was *supposed* to get done today sits on the back burner —which means no surfing with Daisy tonight, or watching her peel her wetsuit off, or following her into the shower afterward.

I scrub a hand over my face. "To clarify, you're asking me to cancel everything and do unpaid work on your behalf *all day* to solve a problem *you* created for my friend."

"All day and all night," she says, and at last, there's a *hint* of apology in her voice. "I think I've got a guy who will invest in this and give Liam the money he needs, but I'll need you to come to LA with me and write up the agreement tonight once you've gotten the injunction."

For fuck's sake. "I'm not going to LA. You can figure that out on your own."

"Don't you have some girlfriend there you never want to be away from?" she asks. "I'm offering you a *private plane* to go see her. I'll even stay until morning if you want the night there."

"My plans are here."

She was in *persuade* mode before, but suddenly her expression...wobbles. She swallows as she looks away, as if she's trying not to cry. "Please. It's important."

I want to say *no*. But this is for Liam, who's been one of my closest friends for most of my life and to whom I now owe a debt—one I hope he never gets wind of.

But God do I regret the way I left things with Daisy. Those minutes in the kitchen I'd spent upset were minutes I could have spent being grateful I had the pieces of her I did.

I gave them up. And now I'm about to give up even more.

FOR TWENTY-FOUR HOURS, I'm so busy I barely have time to think. There are multiple meetings in San Jose, and I wind up at a judge's home at sunset to get the injunction signed. Every time I pick up the phone to call Daisy, I get sidetracked by conversations with Emerson and the investor in LA.

When I finally walk out of the hearing about Lucas Hall the next day, I've had no sleep and almost no food, but all I want is Daisy...I want all of the hours I missed yesterday and the hours I've already missed today, and I don't know why the hell I left things with her on such a bad note but I'm going to do my best to make up for it.

I stop into the office after the hearing to grab my stuff. Baker says we need to talk, and I don't even reply. I just walk out into the sunlight and head to the only place I want to be in the whole fucking world.

36

DAISY

I used to have a nightmare in which I'd walk into a final exam only to realize I'd forgotten to attend class all semester.

When Christian dumped me right after Thanksgiving, I lived it.

All semester long, I'd let him have everything his way. I was at his apartment each night instead of the library. He didn't like DC, so every weekend we went away—his parents' place in Stone Harbor, a friend's apartment in New York City, an Airbnb in St. Michael's—and since he only had Tuesday/Thursday classes, they were always *long* weekends. I knew I should be studying, and I knew I shouldn't be skipping class, but it felt *uncool* to say it aloud.

When it ended, the bottom fell out from under me in a number of ways. I was single. I was also no longer this special object of Christian's obsession—no longer magical or gifted. I was nothing but an unwanted twenty-year-old who was barely passing most of her classes. It was the moment when I needed to pull my shit together, but I woke every day exhausted and sick to my stomach with circles under my eyes that makeup couldn't hide, that no amount of sleep got rid of.

Finals began two weeks later on the day I discovered I wasn't simply depressed and overwhelmed—I was pregnant.

The only person I wanted to discuss it with was my mom, but how? She'd spent my entire life talking about raising children as if it was an unfortunate choice, one she hoped I'd avoid. She thought I was destined for bigger things, but none of those bigger things had ever appealed to me. The idea of becoming a mom, though? It was like this tiny sparkling hope in my chest. It felt right in a way nothing else had. And I knew she'd never understand.

Christian didn't answer when I texted him, so I waited until Creative Writing and followed him out of class.

"I should have fucking known," he seethed. "You planned this all along, didn't you? You and your low-rent mom are exactly the same."

"Low rent?" I repeated hoarsely. I hadn't expected him to be happy. But I also hadn't expected him to turn vicious.

"Gold diggers. You both get knocked up and make some guy take care of you because you're not capable of taking care of yourselves."

My father hadn't contributed a *dime* to my upbringing, but what really hurt was that my background was something he'd *comforted* me about when he was still infatuated...while apparently thinking far less of me than I'd even thought of myself.

But what really did it was when I told my mom how poorly finals were going and that I was probably going to be on academic probation—and she burst into tears. It was so minimal compared to the pregnancy, yet she was destroyed. After everything she'd given up for me, I just couldn't imagine disappointing her even more than I already had.

So I spent the holidays alone in DC, recovering from a

breakup and an abortion and trying to come to terms with all the ways I'd failed in my short life.

I kept waiting to rebound, to feel better, but that moment didn't come, and when I went back to the student health center about it, they prescribed me the same freaking antidepressants my father had been on when it all went bad.

It took me most of the spring to recover, but eventually, I forced myself out of bed and added a new exercise each day. I got a part-time job, and asked the school if I could come back. I still wasn't on firm footing when I returned to California, but things have been so good here that until yesterday, I'd begun to think it was just this...blip. This strange anomaly.

Except that darkness is swirling inside me again now, which means it wasn't a blip. It wasn't an anomaly. If things end with Harrison—no, *when* they end with Harrison—I'm going to be right back where I once was.

His car is in the garage when I return from work. I shower before I go up, mostly to put off what happens next. Who am I going to be after we talk—my father? Something in between?

I arrive on the landing to discover him on the couch, asleep in nothing but boxers.

He blinks at me as he sits up, frowning. "Hey. Is everything okay?"

I swallow. The world is caving in on me again. "I don't know. Is it?"

He holds out his arms. "It'll be a lot better when you're not all the way across the room."

Those words lift me up as if he's cast a magic spell. The wave is still going to crash.

I'm just so relieved it isn't crashing today.

37

HARRISON

D aisy and I get up early to surf since it'll be our only chance today. I resent the premiere tonight already —it's a solid three hours I'm going to have to sit multiple seats away from her, and if I know Daisy, she'll spend each of those hours tormenting me in any way she can.

She gives me a smile when we get back to the house that tells me exactly where her head is at.

"You sure you don't want me to shower with you?" she asks. "You know, to take the edge off before the movie?"

Just the suggestion of it has me hard. Or maybe it's the sight of her unzipping her wetsuit. The two things run together, honestly. "This is a terrible idea. You know that, right?"

"Getting you off before work?"

I adjust myself. "That's generally an amazing idea except when I'm going to be late," I reply, throwing my wetsuit over my board and heading for the outdoor shower. "No. I meant tonight. We're tempting fate."

I try to shut the shower door, and she groans. "Seriously, Harrison? You're going to make me stand outside? I'm freezing."

I grin as I step out of my trunks. She's impossible in the best sort of way. "You can come in, but leave the bikini on and keep your hands to yourself. I've got a client meeting in forty minutes."

Her eyes gleam. She's wrestling with the desire to torture me, and I'm both relieved and chagrined when she opts not to.

"How are we tempting fate?" she asks as I roughly shampoo my hair.

"You're going to be standing there looking luscious while everyone asks what we've been up to all summer, Daisy. So I'm going to be struggling to answer, and you can't lie for shit."

"I'm an *amazing* liar."

I open one eye to raise a brow at her.

"I'm going to practice lying all day," she amends. "I'll be incredibly good at it by tonight."

I laugh as I rinse my hair and spin her so she's fully in the hot water as I head to the door. "Okay, Daisy, lie to me. Let the practice begin."

"I don't want to suck your dick right now," she says from beneath her lashes.

I wince as I reach for a towel. "That sure seemed like a lie."

"Of course it was a lie," she says with a grin. "I always want to suck your dick."

I'm TENSE ALL DAY. Yes, I'm worried we're going to be obvious. I'm worried some guy is going to hit on her and I'll wind up throwing a punch in the theater, or that she'll whisper something in my ear about sucking my dick in front of her mom and uncle. Mostly, though, I just want her to myself. I don't want her smiles given to anyone but me. I want to slide my palm against hers and brush my lips over her neck, and all those things are off-limits for too much of our goddamn night.

I gather my shit at six-thirty to leave for the theater. I'm on my way out and passing Baker's office when he does that finger thing, the one that means "wait," as if I'm his fucking intern.

I stand, fuming while he chats to someone on the phone. Why the hell am I still at this job? I denied it before, but Daisy was right. I don't *have* to work. I could never work another day in my life, and as long as I didn't start blowing all my money on drugs or exotic travel, I'd be just fine.

I'm here because I didn't want to be my parents, and I also didn't want to be some trust-fund asshole burning money while he jumped from one thing to the next. But is it making me happy? Did choosing the responsible career and marrying the "right" girl bequeath any of the benefits I was certain they would?

I'm the happiest I've ever been in my life because of the most irresponsible, unethical thing I've ever done. So fuck Baker, and fuck doing the right thing. Fuck anything that keeps me from Daisy.

Baker watches, bug-eyed, as I walk out the door.

I drive fast downtown. It's nearly showtime when I get to the theater and I'm not even inside yet but Daisy already exerts a pull, as if we are magnetized.

I walk in, scanning the packed lobby for her and only her. She stands at the far end of the concession stand a few feet from her mom, talking to friends and wearing a tiny, flirty little dress so sheer I could shred it without even trying, so short that it offers blissfully easy access to the panties I *hope* she's wearing. I won't be laying a finger on her when her mom and uncle are here, but if she's not wearing panties, I guarantee she'll let me know and the next few hours will be agony.

"Look who finally showed up!" Liam shouts, walking over and giving me a one-armed hug with Emerson's hand clasped in his. Across the room, Daisy's gaze meets mine, and she smiles.

"Yeah, place looks great," I say, my heart sinking as Caleb and Lucie approach.

"Long time, no see," Caleb says, raising a brow. I guess he could have said something worse, but the attitude still leaves something to be desired.

"When was the last time the three of us were even in the same room?" Liam asks.

I sigh. "It's been a very long time." Entirely my fault.

My phone chimes and Daisy grins at me. I shouldn't try to read the message which is undoubtedly from her and undoubtedly *trouble* with Liam two feet from me.

I do it anyway.

DAISY

I'm not wearing panties.

My eyes fall closed. I knew she'd do this. I both love and hate that she has. More love than hate.

I'm going to punish you for this when we get home.

DAISY

I'm already wet at the thought.

"Ellis was really impressed with your work," Emerson says. "If you're ever looking to switch jobs, let me know. I'm almost positive you could do most of your work from home."

I picture it—working from home with Daisy there, constantly undressing and dancing around the kitchen and asking me if I want to surf. It would be my ultimate fantasy and, simultaneously, absolute disaster—I wouldn't get an ounce of work done. But why the hell is my first thought of Daisy when the topic isn't related to her in any way? When she'll be gone at the end of the next month? Why is it that my whole fucking world didn't include her at all in May and now revolves around her? And right on the heels of Baker's bullshit, I should be jumping at this. It's the old, ever-responsible voice in my head that keeps me silent, a voice that says *you can't quit again. What if the new job doesn't work out? Are you going to crawl back to Baker a second time?*

"Thanks," I tell her. "I'm not sure I'm—"

Daisy's gaze hardens suddenly, and I lose my train of thought.

It's a look I've never seen on her face before—suspicious, full of hatred, and I follow it to find Scott at the other end of the room, looking at her.

Scott has never especially bothered me—he was simply Bridget's worthless husband, a bad choice she made that we were all forced to put up with. Now, though, he's someone who's hurt Daisy, someone who's been worse to her and Bridget than they ever let on.

Daisy's lip curls as she turns her back, continuing to talk to the girls on the other side of her.

"Scott showed up?" I ask, jaw clenched.

Liam rolls his eyes. "You think that cheap fucking asshole was ever going to turn down a free ticket? Showed up and invited two friends."

I'm telling myself to ignore Scott until he starts heading in Daisy's direction. He's not starting shit with her on my fucking watch.

"Excuse me," I say, pushing past everyone and jumping over the red velvet rope to follow him.

"Sir, you can't cut the line," says some officious kid in a red vest.

"Try to stop me," I reply, moving faster.

I reach Daisy and Bridget just after Scott does. He extends a hand, and I accept reluctantly. "Harrison!" he says heartily. "How long's it been?"

"It's been a while," I reply between my teeth.

"I was just telling Daisy that we've missed seeing her this summer. We have no idea if she's sleeping on the street." He turns her way—she is already bristling. "And I bet you haven't been to mass once since school ended, have you? Or gone to confession? You know your mom lights a candle for you every Sunday."

It's a role he's played for years—upstanding guy doing his best versus wild, thoughtless stepdaughter. I fucking hate that I ever thought it was genuine.

"Some people are good humans all on their own, Scott," I grit out. "I've never seen Daisy do anything that warrants confessing. Maybe you're just a little guiltier than she is."

There's a flash of anger on his face before he laughs and hits my shoulder as if I was joking. "If you believe that, you haven't been keeping up."

How am I only seeing now that this is what he's always done? He implies that there's more going on, and we're all too polite to call him on it and thoughtless enough to sort of believe him.

Now I know better. And I'm done letting him get away with it.

"Tell me what I haven't kept up with, Scott," I say.

He shoots what is no doubt supposed to be a *fond* smile at Daisy, still playing the role of kind-but-concerned stepfather. "We don't need to get into all that here."

I catch Daisy's eye, willing her to stand up for herself, to call him out. To say, "*No, Scott, let's go ahead and get into it.*"

Instead, she looks away. "I'm going to save us seats," she tells Bridget.

"I'll go with you," Bridget replies, squeezing Daisy's arm.

The last thing I want is to be left with Scott, but here we are. "Look, I didn't want to embarrass Daisy," Scott says once they've walked away, though that's exactly what he just tried to do, "but you know...she took off this summer and won't even tell us where she's staying. Bridget's worried sick."

I straighten. Scott thinks I'm the reasonable member of Liam's friend group. He could use a reminder that I've still got five inches on him...and I'm not always reasonable. "Maybe Bridget shouldn't have convinced her to come home under false pretenses, then. My understanding is she came out here because you guys had separated."

"Look, dude, I'm not sure why you're choosing to believe Daisy over me, but for all we know she's spent the summer living out of a car like her dad used to. Let's just say...the apple appears to have not fallen too far from the crazy tree, if you know what I mean."

I've got him by the collar so fast that I'm not sure which of us is more surprised by it. "I know exactly what you mean, asshole, so let me explain something to you: I'm not your friend, I think you're a lying piece of shit, and if I ever hear you imply that again I'll make you really fucking sorry."

Caleb's got a hand clapped on my shoulder before Scott can even reply. "Everything okay here, bro?"

I hold Scott's gaze for one long moment before I let him go with a shove. "Yeah, I think we're good."

"Asshole," Scott says, fixing his collar with a scowl as he enters the theater.

"What the fuck was that?" Liam demands, approaching with wide eyes. "I thought *I* was the only one who hated Scott."

I turn toward him, my jaw grinding. "He was implying, heavily, that Daisy is like her dad."

Liam shrugs. "I think he's just worried because they don't know where she's staying, and she's also not graduating on time."

My laughter is an angry bark. This is why Daisy says nothing—because all the people in her orbit can easily make a case of her failings, the same way I did when she first arrived.

Daisy, you ate sand. Daisy, you crashed a golf cart and cut off all your hair. Daisy, you're graduating late. Stupid, meaningless bullshit that keeps getting thrown in her face. "What the *fuck*, Liam? *You* didn't graduate at all."

His eyes narrow. "Yeah, I'm aware. I dropped out to help raise *my* niece, who had both me and her mother on her side, so it's unclear why you're suddenly involving yourself."

I know I need to dial it back. I'm too invested for a guy who theoretically hasn't seen Daisy in years. I just can't do it. "If you were actually on her side," I reply, "you wouldn't allow anyone to imply she's mentally ill just because she's fucking graduating late, and you sure as fuck wouldn't be the one doing it."

Liam releases a quiet laugh. "Dude, I don't know what the hell's going on with you, but I haven't seen you this close to throwing a punch since we were in fifth grade. That girl in LA has changed you into...me."

By force, I release my clenched fists. I really wanted to hit Scott...and I really want to hit Liam too. I never understood why my friends would get so emotional when they were dating someone—why Luke would throw a punch in the lineup over Juliet, why Caleb beat the living hell out of Lucie's ex-husband, consequences be damned.

Now I get it. I don't simply want to destroy anyone who gets in her way...I want to destroy anyone who isn't in her corner.

And that's not how I should feel about a fling.

It isn't even how I felt about my wife.

38

DAISY

When I wake the next morning, I've got two missed calls from my mother, and the phone is ringing with a third.

"Sorry," I tell her when I pick up. "I was surfing." It's easier than saying *I was sleeping in because your childhood friend Harrison was insatiable all night.* "Is everything okay?"

"Scott's gone," she says firmly. "For good this time."

She sounds pretty certain, but we've played this game before, and I'll be damned if I'm going to give up what I have right now just so she can slip back into her old ways a week or two hence.

"Mom, I'm sure it'll work out—"

"It's different this time, Daisy," she says, and she doesn't sound upset—she sounds *resolved*. "I spoke with Liam last night, after the movie, about Scott. Honey, I had no idea he was..."

"He was what?" I demand. Because she sure as hell knows he's been cheating by now.

"He made a comment last night to Harrison about you being...like your father."

My stomach sinks. "Based on what?"

"Nonsense," she replies. "I was pretty upset about the stuff Scott said to Harrison when we were both there. But I never knew he was saying things like that behind your back and mine. For him to imply you've got a problem over these entirely normal incidents..."

I dig my hands into my hair. "Mom, he's been doing that for nearly a decade and it's only bothering you now? Who cares if he's saying it behind my back? It's that he's been saying it to you and that you fucking agreed with him that's been the issue!"

"You're right." Her voice is strained as if she's about to cry. "And I'm sorry. But I never knew, when you were little, how things were going to turn out. You *are* a bit like your dad with the surfing and wanting to be outside all the time and the way you haven't always cared about consequences. Which doesn't mean you'll turn out like him, but Scott spun things in a way that...I *wanted* him to be wrong, Daisy, but I'd have felt like a bad mother if I assumed he was wrong and didn't get you the help you needed."

I'd probably have done the same thing in her position, but I'm still not quite ready to let her off the hook. "So you didn't believe me when I said it, but you believed *Liam*?"

"No," she says. "No. It's just that...I've seen enough proof of my own that you were right about him cheating, and last night he proved he doesn't have your best interests at heart. It's one thing for him to express some concerns to me. I'm your mother. To twist the truth to a bunch of people he barely knows...that's sick. So it's done. That man is never returning to my home. Ever."

I've wanted this moment for years. Except I don't want her to get rid of Scott for me. I want her to get rid of him for herself —because he can't stop cheating and because he's unreliable and narcissistic. Selfishly, I don't want her to get rid of him at *all* right now because I know what she's going to ask next.

"I'm going to Harrison's office this afternoon to have him draw up the separation agreement," she says. "Will you come back home?"

Yes, that's what I knew she would ask. And under the circumstances, I don't see how I can tell her *no*.

These past weeks here have been the happiest of my life—weeks that made up for all the dark months that preceded them. I love this house; I love surfing. Mostly I love Harrison, and the experience of being with someone who likes me exactly the way I am. I won the lottery here, and now I'm being asked to hand the prize back. Will he even want to keep seeing me if I'm not conveniently waiting in his home? My mother lives a half hour away...it's not as if I'd just happen to be around, and there'd be no point in continuing to work at Wharf Seafood when I'd barely earn enough to pay for gas and parking.

"Sure, Mom," I reply quietly, and it feels like a sort of death.

After today, there will be no more mornings on the deck, no more early morning and late afternoon sessions at the Horseshoe.

And there will possibly be no more Harrison.

It's that last one I'm struggling to face.

BY THE TIME Harrison gets in that night, my mom has set Scott's stuff in her front yard, and the separation agreement has been filed. It's really happening, and there's probably no going back.

Harrison's gaze brushes over me as if checking for injury.

"Did you talk to your mom?" he asks, undoing his top button.

I want to yank him to me by his tie and tell him to shut up. I want to say, "*Don't ruin this.*"

"Yeah." I cross the room to him. "She said she was meeting with you?"

He nods, and for the first time I notice the circles under his eyes. "I assume she wants you to come home?"

I swallow. "Yeah. I told her I'd be there tomorrow."

And then I wait. I want him to ask me to stay. The arguments he could make would be selfish ones. I've been making them all afternoon myself: *I've given up enough on behalf of these breakups with Scott; she's a grown woman, and she'll be just fine.*

I think, even if he said all of this, I'd wind up leaving—my mom has given up too much on my behalf to not be there when she needs me—but I wish he'd try anyway.

Instead, he lifts me onto the counter, spreading my knees and stepping between them, and then he kisses me as if I'm something he's about to say goodbye to forever.

HE'S efficient and no-nonsense in the morning as he gets ready for work. The coffee is made. The protein shake deposited in the side of his bag. But when it's finally time for him to leave, he tosses the keys from one hand to the other, stalling.

"I'll see you soon, yeah?" he asks. There's a flicker of worry in his dark eyes. "Your mom probably wants you around this weekend, but if you can get free, let me know."

I blink back tears. We never addressed it last night, and I'm not sure we're really addressing it now either. But at least he wants to see me again—I wasn't entirely sure if he would.

"Don't drink all the bourbon before I get back down here."

He steps close. "I'll be fine. Just take care of your mom. And yourself."

I force my mouth not to tremble. I want him to be happy in my absence, but he mourned for Audrey for months—it would be nice to think he's going to mourn for me, even if it was only for a few days.

His lips brush mine and then hold there. "Be good, Daisy," he says, swallowing as he walks away.

There's something about it that feels very final.

After he's gone, I pack everything but my wetsuit—I'm leaving it here in the hopes that I'll get another chance to use it —and then I go to the deck, where I say a silent goodbye to the house, to the water, to all these amazing sun-soaked moments I've spent here with him. It went too fast. And I'll be back here again, but it won't be the same. It won't feel as if it's mine, and maybe Harrison won't feel as if he's mine either. Which is probably for the best since he never actually was.

My mom's still at work when I get to her house, which is okay because I need a moment to process my disappointment as I walk in the door. I need a moment where it's okay to admit that I miss the sight of the ocean, the sound of waves crashing, and, most of all, how much I already miss Harrison. That I'm more than a little heartbroken at the fact that I won't see him tonight, that I'll be sleeping in my childhood bed alone.

I place my stuff in my room and scrounge around in the fridge for dinner. I find frozen chicken and cream and pasta and whip up a casserole. As miserable as I am, cooking soothes me somehow. I play my music and though I'm too sad to dance and sing...I feel slightly better by the time the dish goes in the oven.

Mom sniffs the air when she walks in a half hour later. "You cooked?"

I shrug. "I made a chicken casserole—it should be done in a few minutes."

"You didn't need to do that," she says with a frown.

I swallow down my irritation, but I wish to God she'd just... give it a rest. Why is it the end of the world if I take some time to make a meal? "I like cooking, Mom."

She waves her hand dismissively. "One day, you'll be like Doctor Thomas. You know she doesn't even do her own laundry? She has someone in her house full-time to take care of everything. All the cleaning, the cooking, the shopping—that's going to be you eventually."

She says this with a wistful smile, the way someone might talk about winning the lottery. Except...I like to cook. I like to go shopping. Is there a single thing I actually enjoy that my mother would approve of?

After dinner, we watch *The Notebook*. Ryan Gosling repeats that same move—the full-on kiss, Rachel McAdams' face gripped in his hands. I picture Harrison calling it assault. Saying he's never kissed anyone like that. I would like to be the first, the one he feels that much for.

Is he eating? Is he working late? Is he setting up a dating profile, ready to re-enter *that* world? Maybe I got him over the hump. If I were a better person, I'd be happy about it.

I pick up my phone to text him and put it down. Telling him I miss him is clingy and puts him in the awkward position of needing to say it back. He'd probably worry I was getting too serious, was forgetting the impending end date.

Or I could say something so filthy that he'd beg me to come see him. So filthy that he'd be desperate for it.

I glance sideways at my mom to make sure she's thoroughly engrossed in Ryan Gosling. She is.

What's the dirtiest thing I could possibly say? What's something we haven't done yet? There are a few things, not many, but I'm fully prepared to offer one up. I lift my phone...just as a text arrives from him.

Harrison: When can I see you?

My chest floods with sunlight. It's better than anything he could have said. It means he misses me and wants this and that I'm marked safe, for today, from being the needy, childish nymphette he wishes he hadn't met.

> Are you asking for a naked pic or my actual presence?

HARRISON

> I'll take one of each if both options are on the table.

> Sunday morning? My mom will be at mass. I'll tell her I'm surfing.

> And the picture?

> Coming soon. (Imagine me saying that in my dirtiest voice.)

> You say everything in your dirtiest voice.

> And you love it. I'm surprised you didn't ask for a video.

> I'm new to this. If I'd realized video was a possibility, I would have.

I smile to myself. It's not the same as being with him. But it's not as bad as having nothing of him at all.

39

HARRISON

Baker is thrilled that I'm working on a Saturday.

The condescending little *"good to have you back"* he sends my way grates like nails on a chalkboard. I'd like to ditch work for a week just to make him understand I'm simply here to avoid an empty house and not because of his threats.

I thought I'd recovered my love of surfing, my appetite, my anticipation of weekends and evenings and hours off, but they've again lost their appeal in Daisy's absence. I need them back. I need her back.

She arrives on Sunday morning smelling of coconut and rose and sunlight. She's got a bikini on under her sweatshirt, and I'd assumed we'd surf but I want too much from her in the limited time we have.

No sooner has she reached the main floor than my mouth is on hers and I'm tugging that sweatshirt overhead.

"I'm sorry," I groan as I lift her onto the counter. "If you're dying to surf—"

She laughs, reaching into my shorts. "I came here for something else entirely, I promise."

I untie the bikini and groan as I palm her breasts, leaning down to pull one tight nipple and then the other between my teeth.

I slide her shorts and bikini bottoms off and sink to my knees, pushing her thighs wide. She leans back on her forearms. "Fuck," she hisses, sliding her palm along my scalp. "So much better than surfing."

It passes too quickly. I'm flicking my tongue over her swollen little clit one moment, moving her to the couch, taking her to bed—and she's gone the next. And in her absence...what is the point of anything? Why am I working? Why am I living alone in Santa Cruz? What did I even want from life before she entered the picture?

And how am I going to continue like this?

On Tuesday morning, I tell the office I've got a meeting, and she arrives after her mother has left for work.

I've already got my wetsuit on, a concerted effort on my part to make this not all about sex.

She drops her keys on the counter and grins. "Are you serious right now?"

"You said you wanted to surf," I counter.

She crosses to where I stand and pulls at my zipper. "Going forward, just assume it's a euphemism."

Later, when she's collapsed above me, her sweaty chest clinging to mine, I run a hand down her spine.

"Cabo," I tell her. "That's where we'd go if it was possible."

"Mmmm," she says dreamily. "Is this before or after the trip to Costa Rica?"

I laugh. "After. And then we'll go to Portugal and surf there."

She presses upward, smiling. "And will we stop at Île du whatever-it-is that Oliver suggested?"

"No," I whisper, cupping a breast, pinching a nipple. "I want this view to be mine alone."

She sighs, glancing at her phone. "I should go. You've got to actually be at work, and my mother's never going to believe I was surfing for four hours if she comes home for lunch."

"When will I see you again?" I ask, pulling her back to me.

"Sunday, I guess." I hear the disappointment in her voice and it matches my own. Sunday is too fucking far away and I'll get too little of her when it arrives.

I throw on clothes and see her to the door, watching from the deck as her car sputters down the road. When I turn to head back in, the emptiness of the house hits me hard, along with the pointlessness of it all. Why am I here? Why am I at a job I hate? How did I end up in this fucking place, where the only thing I want from life is the one I can't have? I distract myself by ordering the couch Daisy picked out before I get ready to head to the office.

I suspect I'm mostly doing it to feel like there will be a little of her still here after she returns to school, and I already know it won't be enough.

The following morning, Caleb calls. I've been expecting a lecture about Daisy ever since that day I lost my shit at the theater.

"Hey." My voice is cautious. "What's up?"

"Had a few things I wanted to run by you," he says, "but I thought I'd better check in anyway. I just heard Daisy moved back to Bridget's. You good?"

"You're worried now? You didn't seem too happy a few weeks ago."

He sighs. "I wasn't. It's still weird. But as Lucie pointed out, she and Daisy are only a few years apart. I think it's just that she was always so much younger than us. That's how I knew her."

"Yeah, I get it," I tell him. "And I'm doing fine. What did you need to run by me?"

"I was wondering if you might want to come out to your dad's place on Saturday. Our office party is Friday, but we had to rent it for the whole weekend. Lucie thought it might be fun to have everyone over since the twins will be with their grandparents. We'll surf, maybe go to a beach bar? Just like old times."

I silence a groan. It'll be two couples and me, and they'll spend the whole goddamned weekend grilling me about Audrey, trying to set me up and acting besotted with each other. I'm just not in the—

"Daisy's coming," Caleb says. "Daisy and Bridget."

Oh. "That's a weird thing to add, given the way this conversation started."

His laugh is rueful. "Lucie's behind that too. I'll survive."

How am I going to spend a day by her side without making my obsession apparent? It's the worst fucking idea ever.

"Sounds great," I reply. "I'll be there."

It's the worst fucking idea ever and wildly irresponsible. I'm smiling for the first time since she left.

When I get to the beach on Saturday, Liam and Caleb are already in the water while Lucie and Emerson sit on the sand. There's no sign of Daisy or Bridget, but I don't feel like I can ask where they are.

"Daisy and Bridget are on the way," Lucie says with a knowing smile, lowering her glasses.

I act as if I don't see it. But Jesus, I hope she and Emerson don't start comparing notes.

I carry my board out to the water where Liam proceeds to grill me about his sister's divorce, asking for details I can't share.

"I just want to know why, man, and she's not admitting anything," he says. "I'm not asking you as her lawyer. I'm asking you as her friend. Because he must have done something wrong."

"And as both her friend *and* her lawyer, I'm telling you to discuss it with her. I have nothing to say."

"If Scott cheated on her, he and I are going to have words." He frowns. "Daisy's coming. We'll talk more later."

Her name alone is enough. My gut clenches as if it's being squeezed in a fist, and I turn to watch her wading into the water. Her gaze meets mine and holds a half-second too long as she climbs on her board and starts to paddle out. Everything she feels is written all over her face. I'm sure it's written all over mine as well.

We're never going to pull this off.

"Little Lazy Daisy finally got out of bed," says Liam as she reaches us. "Took you long enough."

"Little Lazy Daisy wasn't the issue," she grouses. "It was *Busy Bridget*, who needed to bake a fucking pie before we drove out here."

I laugh, remembering all the summers when Daisy would arrive here fuming because Bridget had moved too slowly for her liking. Some things never change.

"You sure you even remember how to surf, Miss East Coast College Girl?" Liam asks.

Her gaze meets mine on the way to his. "Unlike *you*," she says, turning her board as a wave approaches, "I have youth on my side."

She grabs the wave easily and even catches some air going over its back. I can't help it—I'm grinning.

"Damn," says Liam, disappointed. "I assumed she'd be a lot worse. Watch. She's going to give me the finger in three, two—"

Daisy gives him the finger, and we both laugh. And then I sigh. How the fuck am I going to stay away from her all weekend? She's the only part of it that matters to me.

~

IN THE EVENING, we go to a dive bar down the street—a shack with a roof but no wall facing the beach, where we take over a long picnic table in the sand, away from the noise of the dance floor inside.

Daisy is across from me, pink-cheeked and glowing. She's impossible to look away from, though I do my best. I picture her cheek against my palm, her breath against my neck. The way she gasps when I go down on her. I can't even look at her now without wanting to act on it.

"So, what's up with the girl in LA?" Liam asks me.

Every head turns my way.

I shrug. "It ran its course."

He raises a brow. "Ran its course? You sure acted like it was a bigger deal than that a few months ago. Anyhow, you need to get back on the horse. Try some dating apps."

Daisy was smiling before, but she isn't now. Her gaze drops to her plate. She doesn't want to think of me getting *back out there*. I know this because the thought of *her* getting back out there makes me sick to my stomach.

"I just got out of a five-year marriage, Liam. There's nothing wrong with taking some time to figure things out."

"Of course not," he says. "But that's what I mean. You figure things out by doing a little experimenting. You were always in a relationship with someone. Have a couple one-night stands, followed by a couple of threesomes—" He looks over at his niece, who's gone pale beneath her tan. "Cover your ears, Daisy."

Her laughter is forced and unhappy. "A, you're supposed to tell me to cover my ears *before* you say the offensive thing, and B, I'm twenty-one, Liam. I've actually heard of both threesomes and one-night stands. I might've even had some."

Liam groans the way I'd *like* to. If I can barely stand the thought of her with one guy who isn't me, I sure as hell can't stand the thought of her with two. At once. *Fuck.*

"Do not even joke about that," Liam warns her before he looks back at me. "My point, Harrison, is that you've always tended to be a little too monogamous. You met Audrey and that was it. So don't make the same mistake again. Don't fall in love with some chick and marry her just because the sex is good. Live a little first."

"Look who's suddenly an expert on relationships," jokes Emerson. "You're thirty-two, and I'm your first serious girlfriend."

He wraps an arm around her. "That's because I waited for the *right* girlfriend."

"Who should I set him up with?" Bridget asks Liam. "What about Holly?"

I'm about to stop her, but Daisy's already rising from the table. "There are some guys from high school inside. I'm gonna go say hi."

Bridget and Liam continue discussing Holly while I sit frozen. I can't follow Daisy without attracting attention, and what would I say if I did? Even if I've got no desire to *live a little*, as Liam suggested, I still want marriage, stability, children—and that's all a long way off for Daisy.

"I'm not interested in being set up," I say firmly, and the topic moves on at last, but I'm no longer listening...because Daisy's now at a table full of guys, chatting with some douchebag in a backward baseball cap, and I fucking hate it.

She's a foot smaller than him—anything could happen to her. He could follow her into the bathroom or lure her away with the promise of a party down the road. The fact that it's going to happen a million times in the coming years without me around at the night's end kills me. Every night for the rest of her damn life, I won't be there to stop it.

And my desire to stop it is exactly why I shouldn't have begun this in the first place. This is what she's *supposed* to do— spend a few months dating some dumbass from high school in a backward baseball cap, then dump him to date some other dumbass, and continue the cycle until she's certain of what she wants.

The guy she's talking to rises and pulls her toward the dance floor. My gaze is laser-focused on his hand, which slides from her rib cage to her hip. Other people join them, and his distance from her shrinks until they're maybe two inches apart at most. My hands wrap around the bench to keep myself in place.

"Do we trust this kid?" Liam asks Bridget, finally fucking aware of a situation I haven't been able to *cease* being aware of.

She bites her lip. "He's not the one who was accused of raping that girl on the soccer team, right?"

She and Liam are getting out their phones to check, but I'm not willing to wait that long.

"I'll handle it," I say, rising from the table before anyone can stop me. They'll assume I'm just being Harrison, the upstanding citizen and all-round good guy, when it's the fucking opposite. I no longer care.

I march inside, pushing through the crowd on the dance floor to tap the guy Daisy's with on the shoulder—though *tap* might be underselling the amount of force exerted. "Can I borrow her for a moment?"

He looks like he wants to argue, but something in my expression must make him decide against it. Daisy's eyes narrow, but she doesn't argue either as I guide her across the room to the back side of the bar, where we're blocked from view.

"Shouldn't you be out sowing your wild oats?" she asks, arms folded protectively over her chest. "Enjoying a variety of threesomes and one-night stands?"

I roll my eyes. "Liam's an idiot. You know I'm not interested in that."

Her tongue prods the inside of her cheek. "I didn't see you shutting it down."

I reach out to squeeze her hip. This situation is impossible, and what I'd really like to do is throw her over my shoulder and walk out the back door when I shouldn't even be touching her. "Daisy, obviously that's not what I want. But Lucie and Caleb already know about us, and I think Emerson suspects something too...I'm doing my best not to make it any more obvious than it already is."

Her shoulders begin to relax. "Then why are you in here, pulling me off the dance floor?"

"I think it's pretty obvious why I cut in," I reply. "It's because Liam and your mom think that guy is a rapist."

She grins. "And *you* weren't concerned at all. What a good guy you are, selflessly coming over here to cockblock me."

I look over my shoulder before I lean toward her. "I've got something to fill your mouth with if you keep smirking at me like that."

She looks up at me from beneath her lashes. "You say that as if I don't *want* my mouth filled, Harrison."

Jesus. "Don't do that to me with your mom and your uncle twenty feet away."

She bites down on a smile. "Don't talk about how I want you to fill my mouth? All the way to the back of my throat?"

It's too much, and she knows it's too much. There's a part of me wondering where we can be alone—not later, not next week, but right this fucking minute. My hand tightens on her hip. "Tomorrow, after we leave, come to Santa Cruz."

"I can't. My mom's doing some big Sunday dinner."

"Then Monday."

Her eyes dance. "You're going to make me wait a full forty-eight hours?"

She's right. With the way she's looking at me now, waiting even five minutes feels nearly impossible. Maybe there's a bathroom in the back of this place where we could...*no, fuck*, I've already been gone too long, and one of them will be in here any second now to see what's up.

"I'm gonna try. And come back to the table with me. I don't want you talking to those guys."

She leans into me, her breasts brushing my chest, and goes on her toes. "Kiss me and I'll consider it."

God. "Daisy, *anyone* could see us. Your baseball friends are watching. Please come back to the table."

"Admit you were jealous."

"I'm pretty sure you don't need me to admit it. Anyone watching us over the last five minutes is well aware."

She waits with her brow raised.

I squeeze her hip one last time. "I was jealous. I've never been so fucking jealous. Now, for the love of God, go back to the table. And stop looking at me like that."

She goes back to the table with an extra sway in her hips, and I tug at my hair in frustration.

There's no way I'll make it until Monday.

40

DAISY

Every minor irritation for the rest of the night is burned away by Harrison's feral, hungry gaze.

Liam referring to me as Lazy Daisy is inconsequential. My mother telling anyone who will listen that I'm not studying enough for the LSAT is almost amusing. And I'm not sure where it's going to happen, but there's not a chance that Harrison's waiting forty-eight hours to touch me. I can tell just by that grinding jaw and the way his gaze keeps flickering to me as we return to the house that he's trying to solve the impossible. That even as we walk in the front door, he's picturing pinning me to the foyer floor.

Inside, Emerson excuses herself to make a work call while Liam cracks open beers for the guys. "Let's stay up all night drinking and surf at dawn the way we used to," he suggests.

Caleb laughs. "We did that *once*, dude."

Lucie yawns and then presses her lips to Caleb's cheek. "That sounds awful. I'm going to bed."

Caleb watches her walk away longingly. A hundred bucks says he now regrets inviting us all here.

"It's after eleven, Daisy," my mom says. "You should get to bed too."

I guess the minor irritations aren't so inconsequential after all. "I'm twenty-one, Mom. I actually choose my bedtime pretty successfully on my own and was already heading there."

"Goodnight, hon," she says, blowing me a kiss. "Don't forget to brush your teeth."

Oh. My. God.

I go to my room, brush my teeth—which I'd actually have done *without* my mother's reminder—and then lie in bed, desperate for his weight above me.

Eventually, the noise downstairs quiets—I'm guessing Liam didn't get anyone to stay up—and I'm still wide awake and full of bad ideas.

What if I texted Harrison and we met on the beach? What if I went to his room?

I'd seriously consider either option if it wasn't for the fact that *he'd* be the only one who'd lose things if we got caught. Liam and my mom will still view me as naïve and easily led when I'm fifty—I'm apparently not even to be trusted with my own dental hygiene yet. It's Harrison they'll blame for all of it.

I lie awake for another fifteen minutes and then...the door opens with a barely audible creak. I smile as his shadow stretches across the room, as he locks the door and climbs into the bed behind me, wrapping his arms around my waist. "I'm sorry," he whispers. "I couldn't stay away. I'm only here for a second."

I reach behind me, letting my fingers slide through his hair, urging him closer. His lips press to my neck, and air hisses through his teeth as my ass brushes quite intentionally against his erection.

He groans quietly. "We can't. Someone will—"

I grab his hand and slide it inside my shirt until it's covering my breast. My nipple hardens, and I grind against him. "We could be really, really quiet," I say, reaching back to palm him through his shorts.

"Fuck." His breath is hot against my ear. "This is such a bad idea."

He tugs my panties down and his hand slips between my legs. I'm so wet I don't even need foreplay. I lift my leg and when I can't get his shorts down one-handed, he takes care of it, rough in his haste.

I cry out as he thrusts inside me.

"Quiet, Daisy," he warns.

I bury my face in the pillow as he does it again.

"This is how we should have spent the whole fucking summer," he grunts. "Just like this. Right from the start."

My hips push back toward him, wanting more, and his hand slides from my breast to my stomach and between my legs. It's like an electric shock, that addition of his fingers. I gasp again.

"Tell me how to do this, Daisy." His voice winds tight as he gets close. "Tell me how to be in the same room without wanting you, without needing to be buried inside you."

I push back harder and gasp again as my orgasm bears down on me. "Cover my mouth." He does it with not a second to spare.

His teeth sink into my shoulder as he explodes, holding himself still inside me, his groan muffled by my skin.

"I'm not done," he says, as his breathing begins to slow. "I need more. I feel like I'm never going to be done."

Me neither. But I guess we mean that in entirely different ways.

HE LEAVES my room just before dawn and when I wake a few hours later, I'm deliciously sore...and euphoric.

It felt different, last night—in his reluctance to leave, in the way he curled against me in his sleep. As if perhaps he's finally realized that I matter to him. As if, as crazy as it is, he saw a future for us. Or maybe it's just that *I'm* starting to see a future for us, which is the last thing I should allow myself to do.

We get a few hours of surfing in before we have to clear out. "Meet me at the wharf tomorrow night," he says as we leave the water. "I have a call at six, but I can get there by seven-thirty, and we'll go out to dinner after."

My mouth opens and he cuts me off. "I know you're about to say something dirty and I'm begging you not to. This wetsuit shows everything."

My mouth closes. I was, actually, about to say something dirty.

We throw our boards in the sand near Liam, who's lying on top of his, resting.

Liam squints into the sun as we remove our wetsuits, his smile fading as he stares at me. And at the mark Harrison left last night. "Dude. What the hell happened to your shoulder?"

Harrison and I exchange a glance. *Shit.*

"That's old," I lie. "I got bit by a dog on the beach."

His jaw falls. "You got bit by a *dog*? What the hell? Was it on a leash?"

"No, it was some stray dog running around. Super old. He was just being playful."

Liam sits up. "Daisy, are you serious? A wild dog bit you, and you didn't even check it out? It could have had rabies, for fuck's sake."

"It wasn't rabid," I say.

Harrison raises a brow. "Just super old."

"Barely had any life left in him."

Harrison's mouth twitches. "It appears he had a *little* life left in him."

Liam glances between us. "Rabies isn't a fucking joke.

Remember that girl Shelley who was a year ahead of us at Prep? She got bit by a rabid bat and died."

"This wasn't a bat," I reply.

Harrison grins. "Just a dog."

I nod. "A really old one."

Liam groans. "I hope one of you dies of rabies just to prove my point."

41

HARRISON

> Where are you? I just parked.

It's Monday night, and I'm impatient. The minutes have dragged since I left her side yesterday at the beach. I climb from the car, frustrated that the call coming in is from Audrey rather than Daisy. She called over the weekend too. I was too preoccupied and too uninterested in what she had to say to answer. And why the fuck is she calling anyway? She knows I prefer to communicate in writing.

"Sorry," I tell her briskly. "I saw your call and forgot to call back. But this is a bad time. Can I call you later in the week?"

"Sure," she says. "But you're good? Things are going well?"

They say that the opposite of love isn't hate, it's indifference, and I get that now. Because questions like this from her once annoyed the shit out of me, had me thinking *you lost the right to ask me about my life when you started fucking your boss.* But now I'm not mad at her. I just couldn't care less what she wants or how she's doing.

"Things are amazing," I reply. "We'll talk next week."

I hang up before she can reply, just in time to receive Daisy's text.

DAISY

Look up.

I do as she's said and there she is, ahead of me. There's a grin on her face as she licks the ice cream cone in her hand—intentionally voracious and filthy. Every man in the vicinity turns to watch.

If I could choose any superpower right now, it would be the ability to make her invisible to everyone but me.

"Want a lick?" she asks with a sly smile, holding the ice cream out. I grab it and throw it in the trash in a single motion, and then my mouth lands on hers.

It's not that hands-cradling-face kiss she thinks is so magical, but it sure isn't tentative either. It's a kiss that says *I'm going to fuck the hell out of you the second we're alone,* and I'm sure we're drawing attention, especially when I'm in a suit and clearly a decade too old for her.

I don't fucking care. All that matters is her mouth against mine, the way she sways into me as if she can't help but move closer.

"Wow," she teases. "It's almost as if you missed me."

"You fucking know I missed you," I growl. "I haven't been able to think about anything else."

Her palms spread over my shirt. She reaches up and tugs on my tie. "We should have met at your house, then."

I push her hair back behind her ear. "It's not about sex." She raises a brow, and I laugh quietly. "It's not *not* about sex, either. I'm going to spread you open as soon as we get home. What I'm saying is...it's more than that. I'm not sure what it is, but it's a lot more than that."

It's the kind of admission I should have kept to myself when it can't go anywhere, but I don't regret it until she glances away, blinking back tears.

"What's wrong?"

She shakes her head and forces a smile. "Nothing. It was just a sweet thing to say."

I hold her gaze for a long moment. I know when she's not telling me the truth.

And right now, she definitely is not telling the truth.

AN HOUR LATER, she's in my bed, naked and radiant, having convinced me we should go home and order pizza rather than wasting "precious time" in a restaurant.

I press a kiss to her shoulder. There's a bruise left from where I bit her. I have to fight the temptation to bite her again, to make the mark permanent in some way. "I need a whole weekend of just this. Somewhere far away."

"Where would we go?" She sets her paper plate on the nightstand and rolls to face me. "Cabo?"

"Dominical." I reach for my phone and pull up the photos —deep blue water, white sand, palm trees. "Really consistent surf, and the water never gets colder than eighty degrees."

Her eyes fall closed. "God, wouldn't that be amazing?"

I push her hair back behind her ear. "We'd get a little cottage with some privacy, right on the beach. We'd be naked the entire time."

She laughs. "We can't be naked *all* the time. At least not while we're surfing."

"It's my fantasy. We can be as naked as much as we want."

"Is board rash not a thing in this fantasy world of yours?" she asks, trailing a finger down my sternum.

"As a matter of fact, it's not. And after Dominical, we'll go to

Cabo, or the North Shore, or Bali, and we'll surf naked there too."

As mythical as it sounds, what I've described is entirely real, and possible—aside from the naked surfing—and I crave it in a way I've never craved anything in my life. And what the fuck is stopping me? I've got the money. I've got the leave, too, even if Baker doesn't want me to take it. We could spend a week in Costa Rica if nothing else. I'm not sure what she'd tell Bridget, but we'd come up with something.

"When do you have to go back to school?" I ask.

She stiffens. The hand that was sliding over my chest stops moving entirely. "I have to be back right after Caleb's wedding."

That's mid-August—only three weeks from now. There's no way the semester is starting *that* early, and I can tell she's keeping something from me simply by her stillness, her reserve. A thousand questions come to mind, questions I have no right to ask: Is it actually over with the ex-boyfriend? Is there someone else?

Her palm is moving over my rib cage. She's trying to distract me with sex, and I don't want to be fucking distracted.

My hand bands around her wrist to stop her. "Why are you going back early?"

She shrugs. "I just have some stuff."

Fuck. I shouldn't ask, I shouldn't push, but it bothers me, these tiny pieces of her she won't let me have. It's bothered me all fucking summer, the way she suddenly turns dark and gloomy, the way she looks away or lies when I ask her what's wrong.

"Daisy," I hiss, hating myself. "I need to know."

"Know what?"

I roll to face her. "Whatever it is you're not telling me. Whatever it is you're hiding. I can tell every fucking time you don't want to say something. You could try to distract me with sex, and there's a possibility you'd succeed, but I really...I just need the truth, okay? This time I need the truth."

She bites her lip. For a moment I'm certain she's going to make a joke, attempt to laugh it off.

"I'm going back early because I have to," she finally whispers. "I lied to you about some things. I've been lying to everyone."

42

DAISY

I wanted to avoid all this.

I will never be his perfect wife Audrey with her immaculate nails and her flat-ironed hair and the way she knew things I never would—the best airline to take to Dubai or the difference between champagne and prosecco—but I'd thought I could hide the uglier parts of myself, and now he's going to see those too. He had eighty percent of me this summer, and he liked it well enough. But I've never been able to see how he could cope with the twenty percent that remains when I still can't.

"The guy I told you about? Christian?" I can no longer meet his eye. "Well, he ended things right before Thanksgiving, and I found out I was pregnant a few weeks later."

He grows entirely still. I can't let myself think about what that might mean right now. My throat is tight as I continue, the words hoarse. "I wanted to keep it." It's all I can get out before the tears start to roll down my face. "I wanted to and—"

I only exist because my mother *didn't* make the decision I did. I want to explain what happened before Harrison distances himself and I'm crying too hard to do it.

He pulls me to his chest, crooning my name as if I'm young and injured, and he can barely stand that for me. "I'm so sorry. Daisy. I wish I'd known."

My chest is still raw but the gentleness in his voice is a balm. He doesn't even know *why* I did it and he's already not holding it against me. It's the kind of forgiveness I haven't even been able to offer myself.

"Christian accused me of doing it on purpose. He called me a gold digger. And when I told my mom I'd bombed my finals, she just completely fell apart. I just couldn't stand to disappoint her."

"How could you have been so careless? Don't you know how lucky you are?" she'd cried and I just couldn't imagine telling her that I was pregnant on top of it. That I was about to be a single mom, just like her. That I probably wouldn't graduate at all.

"I'm so sorry you went through it all alone," he says pressing a kiss to the top of my head.

I'm crying again and it's half grief over what happened, but it's also relief. He truly doesn't hate me for it the way I've been hating myself.

"Afterward it was like I was in this hole I couldn't climb out of, and that I'd given something up that I actually wanted, but I *still* wasn't going to be able to make my mom happy. I got really depressed and I just couldn't shake it off."

His hand runs over my back. "Did you talk to anyone?"

"The school tried to give me the same antidepressants that caused a reaction in my dad." I laugh miserably. "I have no clue if I'd be wandering the streets now like he is if I'd taken them. Or if it's something that's just going to happen down the line, whether I take them or not. I couldn't get out of bed, and eventually, I dropped all my classes. I—" My tongue prods my cheek. Should I keep talking or leave the rest held inside me?

His hand curves around my hip. "You...?"

"I'd go to sleep hoping I didn't wake because I knew all my lies were going to catch up with me. I still don't know if they're letting me back into school, and how the hell do I tell my mother I might not be graduating because I couldn't get out of bed? I can't even explain it to myself."

"She might understand better than you think. People go through this stuff. I mean...when you arrived, I was blackout drunk and had lied to everyone rather than admitting that my wife left me."

I laugh through my tears. "Yeah, yours is worse." After a moment, though, I sober again. "You fixed things, Harrison. You're back at work. I kept loan money for a semester of school I didn't attend, and I postponed the hearing about getting back into school when my mom asked me to come home, so I've got no idea if I'm returning." It was so fucking stupid.

"And it's been weighing on you this entire time," he concludes.

God, I've made such a fucking mess of everything, and it sounds even worse spoken aloud than it did in my head. "I think I was just scared of what they'd say. There's a significant possibility that they won't let me come back, and I'm already getting mail about the loans."

He tips my chin up to face him. "I happen to know a lawyer who could accompany you to this hearing."

I raise my eyes to him. "Really? I mean...do you think it would help?"

"Daisy, you were a frightened student to whom the school did not provide appropriate guidance. They put a struggling, emotionally damaged kid—"

"I don't love being described as *emotionally damaged*."

He presses his lips to the top of my head. "I don't care if you were the most psychologically stable human in the last forty years. For the purposes of my argument, you were a struggling, emotionally damaged student who was placed in a really unfortunate position and was offered no fucking help when she asked for it. They will *definitely* be letting you back into the goddamn school, especially once they know you've got a lawyer involved."

I'm relieved. And I'm also horrified.

Because I told him most of the story. Just not all of it. Not the part he'll hate.

$\sim$

I PROVIDE Harrison copies of all the relevant documents: my grades, the report from the health center, the receipt from Planned Parenthood, and the letters regarding my student loans. He gets the hearing scheduled for Friday. As much as I'd like to put it off, I can't come up with a good reason to do so. It's not as if I can tell him that my biggest fear is no longer that the school will kick me out but that the school will press for answers, answers I'll have to provide in front of *him*.

I tell my mom I'm surfing with friends for a long weekend —we'll only be in DC for one full day, but there's no reason to look a gift horse in the mouth. If I'm going to lie about a trip away, I might as well make the lie big enough to encompass a night or two at Harrison's while I'm at it.

Harrison sleeps soundly on the red-eye to DC while I remain awake, a nervous wreck.

Dear God, just let us get this over with. Let it all turn out okay.

My entire future is riding on what takes place over the course of the coming day. Twenty-four hours from now, I could still be the woman Harrison respects. A college senior nearly done with her degree, ready to make her mother proud.

Or I could be none of those things.

When we land in DC, he instructs the driver to take us to the Mandarin Oriental. I glance up at him. "Why are we going to a hotel?"

"The hearing isn't until one," he says. "I need to shower and get a suit on. And you need to do whatever's necessary to look innocent, lost, and scared."

I give a sad laugh. Most of those things are already true. Though I guess *innocent* is a stretch, under the circumstances.

We check into our room and take turns showering. By the time I emerge, wrapped in a towel, he's already buttoning up his shirt. I glance at the bed and raise a brow.

He laughs. "Absolutely not. We've got the whole weekend for that once this is behind us, and I need to focus, while you need to look as if you weren't fucked within an inch of your life by your attorney."

I remove the towel. "You wouldn't have said it *that* graphicly if you weren't already thinking about it."

His nostrils flare, and he adjusts himself. "Daisy, I'm always thinking about it, but this matters too much to take a risk. Get some clothes on, and then we'll go over everything one last time."

Reluctantly, I do as I'm told. My most innocent dress is probably not innocent enough, so I cover it with a cardigan. It's brutally hot and stiflingly humid outside, the way it always is in DC during the summer, which means I'm going to be sweating my ass off the whole way there.

"Take a seat," Harrison says when I come back out, fully clothed. "I just want to get my facts straight."

I go to the desk chair, my stomach in knots, as he paces with a notepad in front of him. "You dated Christian all semester?" he asks.

"Most of it," I reply. I haven't lied, but it already feels as if I have.

"And he broke up with you by text," Harrison confirms. "What exactly did he say?"

I swallow. "Just that he felt things had run their course, and since the semester was ending, it was a good breaking point."

"And you had no idea prior to this that he was going to end things?"

I hitch a shoulder. "We'd just gone away together before Thanksgiving. It seemed like everything was fine until we were on the way home. I thought maybe he was annoyed that I'd referenced winter break, but until then, I didn't have a clue."

I'd looked back on it, of course, and seen the small signs. The way he'd snapped at me over dinner the week before. His brief irritation with me in class over something minor. But that's the problem when someone is losing interest: you can convince yourself of anything. You can convince yourself his irritation is just a sign that he's comfortable with you, or that he's finally realizing something you've known all along—that you're not that great and don't deserve the care and consideration he showered you with at the start.

"You were ill for how long prior to the onset of finals?" he asks.

"I'd been under the weather for a few weeks. I started throwing up about three days before finals began."

"I'm going to ask you, when we're in there, to tell us verbatim what they said at the health center and what happened at the clinic when you went. I'm also going to ask you to describe your father's history of mental illness and what you went through during the spring. I need you not to minimize it, okay?"

I nod, clutching my clasped hands to my stomach.

"Great," he says, glancing at his notepad again. "You discovered Christian had been lying to you about the girlfriend and went into a tailspin while he walked away scot-free. I presume he's now graduated?"

I stare at him, frozen.

The truth could ruin things, but lying about it and getting caught *definitely* would ruin things. And what if the hearing committee demands names and numbers and addresses and texts? I have to tell him the truth. As much as I don't want to, there's really no choice.

"I never said he was a student," I whisper.

Harrison freezes. "What?"

I bury my face in my hands. "He wasn't a student. He was my professor."

43

HARRISON

Christian Cooper writes the kind of books in which a lot of words are used to describe very little, where nothing much happens, and that's the point because nothing much happens in life either. Critics use words like *incandescent* to describe his writing, but they're still books no one actually wants to read, which is probably why he took a teaching job, though I'm sure the abundance of vulnerable young females didn't hurt either.

He's good-looking, cocky, and not old, but certainly nowhere near Daisy's age. I'm sure he had plenty of students throwing themselves at him, but she's the one he wanted.

She explains, haltingly, that he invited her to some writing group. She'd gone because he'd told her she was talented and because the ex-boyfriend who'd dumped her the summer before was so impressed that she'd been asked. And on the way out, Cooper told her she was his muse. That his writer's block had ended the day she walked into his classroom. He'd dated celebrities and there he was, wanting *her*. He'd been shortlisted for prestigious prizes, had had a novel optioned by HBO, and yet he was insisting *hers* was the fresh, unsullied voice.

I get how it happened. I just can't *stand* that it happened. And I'm here as her lawyer, but it's hard to do that job when I am fucking spiraling right now.

That one little detail changes everything. I see a pattern where I didn't before. Older men have been preying on her for the better part of the past decade. The eighteen-year-old boyfriend, the manager at work, Cooper...

And me.

I pinch my nose. *Focus, Harrison.* I need to pull my shit together because we've got thirty fucking minutes before we enter this hearing, and no matter what else happens today, she's leaving here with her future restored.

I sink onto the edge of the bed, pressing my hands to my face before I force myself to look back at her. "Daisy, this changes everything. Why didn't you say anything before now?"

"Because I didn't want you looking at me the way you are at this precise moment. I had no idea he was still dating that doctoral student."

I shake my head. "*She* isn't the issue. It's that he was your professor. Between that fact and the school's gross mishandling of your pregnancy and your depression afterward, you could sue. You *should* sue. This isn't a discussion we should be having thirty minutes before the fucking hearing. I'm going to cancel the meeting and—"

"No," she says, twisting her hair. "No. Look, I don't want to sue. I don't want everyone to know I was sleeping with a professor and got pregnant. These are things that—" Her voice is choked. "These are things I want to take to my grave. I sue, and they become part of my public history."

"Not necessarily. Your identity could be protected." I grab her hands to make sure she understands how important this is. "Daisy, it could be worth a *lot* of money. I'm talking millions, if we found you an attorney who specializes in these kinds of cases. And it's such a slam dunk the school would settle before it even went that far."

She laughs, brushing at the first tear that rolls down her face. "Harrison, how would I explain that I suddenly have millions of dollars to anyone? How would I finish my degree if I was sitting in a courtroom half the time? I don't want that money. I knew what I was doing. It's not like he pretended to be a student or blackmailed me into sleeping with him. I made a bad decision, entirely on my own, and yeah...the school should have better resources for students in my position, but I don't want to *profit* off the fact that they don't."

There was an imbalance of power. That's what she's not acknowledging. That's perhaps what I wasn't acknowledging all summer either. She depended on me for a place to live, for God's sake. She knew me as her uncle's most responsible friend.

And I manipulated all that to my benefit. "Daisy—"

"I would pay two million dollars right now if I had it just to make this whole problem go away," she says, her voice breaking, her eyes bright with unshed tears. "I'd pay two million dollars just to not have failed those classes, to not owe them money, to be able to get my degree and never have my mom or anyone else know about the way I fell apart."

"Fuck," I groan, pacing, dragging my hands through my hair.

She's making the wrong decision, and I'm certain that if she was willing to discuss it with Bridget and Liam, they'd tell her the same thing. But she's not willing, and ultimately, it's her call.

"You don't waive any rights," I tell her. "We go in there, tell them what happened, but at no point do you agree to an NDA or waive a single right to come after them later on. Are we agreed?"

"But what if that's the only way they'll let me finish?"

"It won't be. They wouldn't fucking dare, under the circumstances. No matter what they say, my response will be 'I'll discuss it with my client' and you don't agree to *anything*, okay?"

"Okay," she says, swallowing. "Okay."

We take a cab to the school and walk to the administration building, side by side, not touching. We wouldn't touch anyway, given that I'm here as her attorney but I also need the distance from her. I need more distance even than I've got. We're led to a large room you'd find in almost every old university: tall windows, ancient hardwood floors, wood chairs for the hearing panel, and shitty folding chairs for the two of us.

I continue to plan out what I'll say but it's nearly impossible when that one little piece of information is rewriting every moment we spent together. Because which part of it can I claim I did for her? None of it. I brought her to Malibu because I didn't want to be away from her. I slept with her that first night because I was jealous. Again and again, I went out of my way to ensure she couldn't be with anyone else.

It was all so fucking selfish, so much worse than I'd realized at the time.

Jesus. I *spanked* her.

I can barely stand to remember it now.

The committee members look bored as they file in. They're thinking about what they'll do once they get out of here, whether there's time to run to the store on the way home or if they should just get takeout.

They're about to lose that boredom.

They're about to get real fucking nervous.

The head of the disciplinary committee begins reading from a sheet of paper in front of him. "Miss Doherty was on scholastic probation during the fall semester and then proceeded to drop all her classes in the spring after failing to ever attend most of them. This appears to be pretty cut and dry unless there's information we're lacking."

"There is," I say, rising, shoving the shitty chair backward because I'm furious with them and with the situation and with myself. "You don't seem to have it anywhere in those notes that Miss Doherty was repeatedly victimized by this institution, and by one of your cherished professors most of all."

Suddenly, no one's thinking about whether they can go to the fucking store.

I begin to detail the treatment Daisy received at the student health center and the way no one ever inquired about a family history of mental illness before quickly tossing her a prescription. When I name Christian Cooper, there are glances shared. I'd guarantee it's not the first time they've heard a story like this. They've let him get away with it because he's someone the university could brag about in the admissions brochure, and that makes them even more culpable than they already were.

When I get to the things Cooper said to her when told she was pregnant, the university's counsel cuts me off.

"This is obviously a very serious allegation," he says. "One that exceeds the purview of this committee. I need to discuss this with outside counsel before it proceeds further."

Daisy stiffens. I place a hand on her shoulder, silently telling her not to worry.

"Before it *proceeds*?" I snap. "I really hope you're not about to tell me that a student who was repeatedly abused by this institution and flew across the country for this hearing is going to leave here without an answer when the semester begins in three weeks."

The man's eye twitches. He glances at the woman heading the committee.

"Obviously, Miss Doherty is invited to return," she says promptly. "I see no issue with her returning to school. We'll see that last semester is wiped from her transcript and any tuition she paid is reimbursed."

It's the least they could do, and they know it. Christian Cooper used a position of power to leverage a sexual relationship with a significantly younger female without giving a damn who he hurt when he did it.

And I did the same goddamn thing.

44

DAISY

When someone loses interest in you, it's like a light switch has been turned off by someone insisting the lights are still on. You wonder if the problem is you. Perhaps you are deeply insecure. Perhaps you need more validation than other girls, or you're a narcissist who makes someone else's bad mood all about you.

And so you don't push back when he tells you the lights are still on because asking about the lights too many times will make you sound *crazy*. It will drive him away. But it always, always turns out that the lights were off, and it was done, and he just didn't want to say it to your face.

On that final drive back to DC with Christian, I fought myself to stay silent. He'd given me an excuse that sounded like bullshit, but what was I supposed to do?

I couldn't keep asking without sounding needy. I wanted to bring up winter break again. I wanted to apologize for bringing up winter break at all. I wanted to tell him I hadn't meant to pressure him—I'd just needed to book my flight—and I also wanted to say something, anything, that would tell me he wasn't ending this.

And now I'm reliving it. As Harrison and I walk out of the hearing—a hearing I just *won*, a hearing I should leave feeling ecstatic—he can barely meet my eye. He acts as if he's just busy calling us a car, checking on our flights, but he does it as if I'm not even standing beside him. Or as if he wishes I wasn't.

"What's wrong?" I ask. *Why are the lights off?*

"Nothing," he says. *The lights are on. You're crazy.*

I squeeze his hand, urging him to look at me. "Harrison, I know what you're thinking. I don't have an older man fetish." I simply like guys who are confident, and that tends to be found in men, rather than boys. Nico, the guy I dated before Christian, was my age, but being a senator's kid and having a lot of money gave him a head start. "I think I was attracted to Christian because he reminded me of you in some ways."

He winces.

"Not the bad stuff," I continue hurriedly as the car pulls up to the curb. "Just the responsible, pulled together, confident part. But he wasn't you. He was never even close. It was entirely different with him, and I never felt the way I do now."

Students passing turn toward us, perhaps hearing the desperation in my voice...the pleading of a girl who already knows she's lost.

"Let's talk about it at home," he says, holding the door for me.

My gaze meets his as I step inside. I can't read the look in his eyes. Is it sorrow? Is it guilt? Is it anger?

The only thing that's clear is this: the lights are off, and I can't turn them back on.

~

WE'RE on the flight home and he's on his laptop. He enlarges a photo someone sent, one I can't help but see. The bluest water, amazing surf.

"Where's that?" I ask.

"Peniche. In Portugal." His voice is quiet. He barely looks at me as he responds. "Oliver was just surfing there."

I wait for him to suggest that we could stay there, after Costa Rica and Cabo and the North Shore. I wait for him to tell me we'd rent a house on the beach, that we'd be sandy and naked and utterly alone the entire time.

But he doesn't say a fucking word. He closes the laptop and looks out the window instead.

He drives me to the parking lot where I left my car and stares at his steering wheel once we arrive. "I really fucked up, Daisy," he says. His voice is rough. "I've fucked up so badly that I don't even know what to say right now. The minute you showed up at my house, I should have just come clean to everyone."

"Why?" I demand. I knew the end was coming, but it's different, hearing it confirmed. I hold my hands over my stomach as if he's just punched me. "I was happy all summer, Harrison. It's been the happiest summer of my life. And you were happy, too, so why are you acting like it was all a mistake?"

He swallows. "Because it was. I was fooling myself into believing there was nothing predatory about it, but of course there fucking was. Your history is littered with predatory men, and now I'm one of them. You depended on me for a place to live—"

"I blackmailed you into that, and you did your best to make me leave!" I cry. "And I'd been there for a month before you ever laid a finger on me, and I had other places I could have gone. It wasn't *predatory*."

I'm not entirely sure why I'm even arguing. The only relevant facts are these: he wanted me before he knew the truth, and now he doesn't. That's what's driving this conversation, whether he admits it or not.

He exhales. "We could argue about this all day, but you're

never going to convince me I didn't do the wrong thing. There wasn't a word I said about Cooper that couldn't have been said about me as well. You need to grow up at your own pace. I shouldn't have stood in the way with the surfers or anyone else. You're going back to school in a few weeks and—"

I open my door and climb out while he's still talking, grabbing the backpack that sits at my feet.

"You're over it," I announce, cutting him off. "That's all you needed to say."

45

DAISY

After Harrison ended things, I sat in my car and wept for a full hour. We weren't supposed to be home for two more days. We were supposed to spend long hours surfing and hideously staining his couch and suddenly we would never do those things again, not together.

The way he ended things—as if I was a terrible mistake, something he was already leaving behind...God it hurt. It made it so much worse.

I found a cheap hotel. Though I could have made up some reason that I ended my supposed surf trip early, I knew I wouldn't be able to hold it together for five minutes.

Harrison would have been appalled by the room—by the stained carpet, by the long black hair on the bathroom floor. He'd have swept me out of there and taken care of everything, and that thought made me weep too. I never gave a shit about his money, but I loved feeling as if someone had my back. I loved, most of all, that it was him.

～

AFTER TWO DAYS spent crying in a disgusting hotel room, I drive home.

I sit while my mom places everything on the table, telling me an absolutely grotesque story about a kid at Dr. Thomas's office who broke his arm.

She's made an effort tonight: the table is set with her best plates, lasagna from scratch.

I don't see how I'll eat a bite of it.

"So, where were you surfing again?" she asks, setting a massive slice in front of me. I haven't lifted my fork yet, but it already sits in my stomach like an anchor.

Jesus, why did I have to lie? I don't have the resilience to lie to her about this and hold my shit together at the same time. I blew four hundred dollars on a hotel just to avoid this, falsely believing I could cry it all out of my system. Those two days didn't make a dent.

"Asilomar," I reply. "Near Monterey."

I close my eyes and picture an overcast day, Harrison grinning at me, the water too fucking crowded and neither of us caring—shivering as we stripped out of wetsuits in the parking lot, me claiming I'd blow anyone who could get me hot cocoa in the next five minutes.

He'd laughed. He'd thought it was charming then, but my charm never lasts, does it?

"Isn't that called the Ghost Wave or something?"

My mom doesn't care about surfing. I've never understood how she *couldn't* care about surfing, growing up here, but she doesn't, and I want to weep at the fact that she's trying so hard right now to feign interest in the trip I didn't actually take.

"The Ghost Wave is off Pebble Beach. Asilomar is cool but nothing special." I shrug and answer the question before she can pose it. "Just wanted to say I'd been."

Which is sort of a lie. Asilomar isn't anything special, but it's special to me. It was a favorite memory and now it's piercing and painful. I hate that the end with Harrison makes every fucking thing hurt.

She says she'd like to go back to Big Sur. That she and Scott went once after they started dating and that it was so romantic. I nod, but inside my chest, there's a cry that's about to turn into a wail.

Yes, I know it's romantic. It's so romantic you could convince yourself the thing you had might last forever if you were young and stupid enough. And when he knows all the lyrics to a Jack Harlow song, *filthy* lyrics, and buys you eight avocados you don't need, you'll feel as if it's all meant to be. Despite the amazing scenery, when he looks at you, it's as if *you're* now his favorite sight—and he has *always* been yours.

"Sweetie, why aren't you eating?" my mom asks.

I glance at the table, at my hand in the exact same position it was in five minutes ago, ready to lift a fork I don't want to hold, to scoop lasagna I don't want to eat.

I force a smile. "Sorry. Just thinking."

My lips are numb. My stomach turns as the first bite hits my throat.

If you'd told me two months ago that I'd be back in school, that they were refunding the money, it would have seemed like magic beyond my wildest dreams. Now I only want to wrap myself in a comforter and stay there until the pain goes away, just like I did last winter.

Except what really crushed me when it ended with Christian was that I was lost—he'd taken things away from me, and I'd taken some things away from myself too—while what crushes me about the end with Harrison is that he felt like home, a home I'd always sensed but never quite found. And I'm not sure how I'll live without getting it back.

"Are you coming down with something?" my mother asks, and I say *maybe* simply because I'm not sure I can keep pretending to be well for her sake or my own.

I go to bed. My mother holds a hand to my forehead and brings me ginger ale and promises I'll feel better by morning. I don't think I will.

I miss the sight of his head on my pillow, the way his hands would tug at his tie, the slow half-grin on his face when I'd paddle toward him at the break. I miss him because there was nothing I loved in the world that I didn't love even more when he was doing it with me. I miss Harrison because he made me feel safe, and lucky, and worshipped, but most of all, because he made me more *me*. The more irreverent, barefoot, sunburned, naked and sandy I was, the more he liked me...and the more I liked myself.

I don't know what I'm even thinking. I just miss him.

When my mother arrives home from work the next day, she frowns at the sight of me curled up under a blanket on the couch. I should have brought the LSAT study guide out here just so she wouldn't worry I'd been wasting time.

"If you're still sick in the morning, I'm taking you to see Doctor Thomas."

"I'm too old to see a pediatrician, Mom."

She clicks her tongue. "We see kids older than you," she says. "She won't care."

Jesus. A hundred bucks says Dr. Thomas asks me, just like my mother still does, if I've been brushing my teeth and eating vegetables at school. Maybe it's normal when your kid is twenty-one, but I felt like I was twenty-one when Scott came into the picture, and I feel thirty now. The past seven years were long ones, but no one gets that but me.

The next morning, I force myself out of bed and open the LSAT study guide just to tell her I did it but wind up asleep within five minutes. She makes a joke about me living up to my nickname, and I can barely force my laugh.

I don't think I've got it in me to keep faking so many things, to keep pretending I'm the daughter she wants. I rise from the couch and go into her yard, soaking in the sunlight. I'm still not happy, but I sense an answer here somewhere—in the bright light, in the slight breeze, the smell of freshly mowed grass. I'm not going to get better inside. I'm not going to get better by studying for a test I don't want to take.

On Thursday, I drive down to the farmer's market, and I sense an answer here as well in all the colorful displays. I'm still so broken, but there's something I love about the world, other than Harrison, and it's my job to fucking find it.

I buy impatiens and plant them in the flower beds Mom keeps along the side of the house. I let the soil crumble in my hands, and there's something here, too—something I'll be able to love again one day.

I'm still at it when Mom gets home from work. She stops in the driveway and rolls down the window. "You don't need to do that," she says.

I pat the soil down in front of me, surveying my work. It brought me such pleasure only seconds ago, all the velvety purple petals dancing in the breeze, and now the sight of them embarrasses me, as if it's shameful somehow, what I've done here.

And that's fucking ridiculous, isn't it? Yes. It's ridiculous. "I like gardening, Mom."

Her lips purse. "You're about to have a college degree. You need to keep your eyes on the prize."

What prize, though, Mom? What if this is the prize I want? Why are the things I love such a problem for you?

She walks inside and I swallow the retort down, putting the shovel and soil in the carport before I follow her in.

"I got some tomatoes at the farmer's market," I say, walking into the kitchen. "I was going to make Bolognese."

She waves me off. "You don't need to waste your time with that. Go study for the LSAT."

I grip the counter. *You don't need to waste your time with that.*

She's basically said it twice in the past five minutes. She's been saying it my entire life, except it's only ever been about the things I love.

Anything outside. Anything domestic. Those are worthless in her eyes.

"I like cooking, Mom. Why can't you just let me do the things I enjoy?"

She turns toward me as she pulls ground beef from the refrigerator. "Daisy, for God's sake. I'm just trying to help you focus on what's important."

My eyes squeeze shut. Yes, she's been trying to help me focus my entire life, telling me the things I love are wrong and guiding me toward the *correct* ones. By last winter, I'd switched majors four times. I'd taken the LSAT thinking I might go to law school and the GRE thinking I might get a PhD, and none of those plans ever made me want to get out of bed the next day.

Maybe it's because they weren't my plans at all.

Maybe I've been so lost because I can't live out her dreams for her life, the dreams she gave up for me, without giving up my own to make them happen.

And under normal circumstances, I'd keep all this to myself. I'd wait for a less emotional, more measured moment— one that would never actually come—except I've been happy. I've been so happy all summer, and I just can't go back to giving all of it up.

"I'm not going to law school," I tell her. "I'll finish my bachelor's, but I'm done after that."

Her brows pull together, a flash of confusion there before my words register. "You're being rash. You can't give up a plan you've had for years to—"

"It was never my plan!" I cry. "Name one time I ever said I wanted to be a lawyer, Mom. Name *one*. It was your plan. They're *all* your plans. And you can still live them. You're only thirty-nine. You can still go to law school. You can do whatever you want. But please stop trying to live vicariously through me."

Her eyes well, and the guilt hits the way I knew it would.

"I'm sorry," I say quietly. "I know you gave up everything for me, and Scott was like...this one good thing that came your way, and now you've given that up for me too. But I don't know how to make it up to you without killing myself to see it happen."

"God, Daisy," she says, her jaw agape, and just when I think she's going to scold me, she gathers me up in her arms and holds me tight. "Scott wasn't my one good thing. You were."

"You know what I mean," I tell her, my throat tight.

"No," she replies. "I really don't. And you've got it all wrong. You were the only magic my life ever needed to hold. The day you were born was the happiest day of my life, and the hundred happiest days after that were all yours too."

It's a nice moment, and we hold the embrace for a long time. By tomorrow, she'll have come up with a new plan for me, however—medical school, broadcast journalism, marine biology—but I'm not taking it back. Maybe I won't end up with Harrison, but I can build a life out of what's left. I can build a life that involves surfing, cooking, working in a garden.

I can build a life based on giving myself what I need, even if I'm never going to get the thing I need most.

46

HARRISON

I've spent my entire life smugly proud of how responsible and ethical I was. That I stayed at one job. That I didn't bounce from one woman to the next the way Liam and Beck did. That I didn't start one fight after another like Luke. I thought being responsible would keep me from becoming my parents, from getting left behind...which is what made the end with Audrey such a shock. I don't think I missed her when it ended. I just didn't know what direction to turn after discovering the entire philosophy I'd based my life upon was a lie.

And now I've done something so irresponsible, so much worse than anything my friends have done, and I want to do it all over again.

I want to call her. I want to hear her husky voice, her quiet laughter. I stare at her surfboard and mine every night when I pull into the garage and am sick with the desire for it.

I walk through The Hillside Market and stare for a long moment at the display of expensive honey. And then I buy one, like the sap I am, and I want to tell her this too, but I can't.

Your twenties are the years when you learn who you are, when you leave the safety of home and school and friends and really decide who you'll be in the world. You do a lot of fucking around, but there's value in that too. It's how you choose which parts are worth embracing and which parts can be written off.

Daisy needs to go through all that on her own. I've taken enough from her. And I shouldn't have taken any of it.

I HAVE to leave work early to meet the guys delivering the new couch. How fucking long will it be before I see that couch without thinking only of her?

Audrey calls again just as they're leaving. She's the last person I want to speak to right now, and I'd give anything to end the conversation before she's even said a word. Does she want the beach house? Fine, it's hers. Does she want our marriage annulled? Does she want me to put our wedding album in the shredder? As long as it means she'll leave me the fuck alone afterward, I'm willing to concede.

"What do you need?" I bark.

"That's an uncharacteristically rude way to say *hello*," she replies.

"You chose an uncharacteristically rude way to end our marriage," I counter. "What do you want? I'm busy."

"I just wanted to discuss some things, but if this is a bad time—"

My eyes fall shut. Fuck. I don't want to schedule a call for later. I don't want to talk. I just want her to go away. "Can't you just email me?"

"I take it things fell apart with the girlfriend."

Christ. It never occurred to me that she might still be in contact with my mother or my brothers, but anything's possible. I could see Oliver alluding to it just to needle her a little. "What are you talking about?"

She clicks her tongue. "Lucie implied you were seeing

someone, and I could tell by how preoccupied you were the last time we spoke. And I get it. I'm sure it seemed amazing and all-consuming until the infatuation wore off and you realized you were stuck with a real person, one who wasn't going to be the living embodiment of every dream and is as flawed as anyone else."

No, the infatuation hadn't worn off. And with Daisy, I saw the flaws first. I sought them out eagerly, because I was doing my level best not to acknowledge what I actually wanted from my friend's kid—or give in to it.

But this is nothing I care to discuss with Audrey.

"Like I said," I reply, "I've got a lot going on right now. I assume you had a reason for calling aside from discussing my romantic life?"

"I'm coming to California," she says. "I was hoping we could get dinner."

The old, responsible version of me would probably agree. It would be the polite thing to do. I don't hate Audrey and I could even see myself being friendly with her one day in the distant way I'm friendly with former employees or classmates. But I'm not in the mood to be polite.

"I bear you no ill will, Audrey, but I don't see any reason for us to get dinner together. Take whatever you want from the storage unit. I'll text you the—"

"Harrison, it's not working out here with Michael," she says abruptly. "I'm thinking about coming back."

I'm not sure what the hell is going on right now, but I'd prefer she stay in London. I don't want to make strained small talk with her every time we're both in the courthouse. I don't need years of her ingratiating herself with my friends or texting to ask about the whereabouts of some missing household item.

"Why? You hated California—at least this part of it. You hate the weather. You don't like the beach. You hate the attitude. You spent five years bitching about this state."

"I'd be willing to come back for you," she says. "You wanted kids and I wasn't ready, but I am now. I think maybe we just needed some time apart to see what we had."

I'm silent. Shocked. Time away from her didn't make me see anything but how much we lacked, but maybe that's because I had Daisy here. Every morning I woke with Daisy in my home, I was a little more alive, a little happier. I'd never been more at peace than I was when she'd fall asleep in my arms. It's something I never had with my wife. Not once. But I didn't know I was missing it.

"Audrey, we were never right for each other," I finally reply. "That hasn't changed."

"Harrison, you're thirty-two. You wanted to be a young dad. Sometimes you need to settle a little in one area to get the things you want in another."

Six months ago, I'd have agreed with her. Now I know there's not a fucking thing in the world I wouldn't give up for the right woman—one who turns everything into innuendo, who opens the doors wide and sings at the top of her lungs as she makes lunch, who surfs, who smiles with her heart in her eyes every time I walk in the door.

That person is Daisy. It will never be anyone else.

I end the call with Audrey and sit on my deck, staring blankly at the view while I think.

After I found out about Christian, I was so busy being consumed by the parallels that I didn't—or wouldn't allow myself—to consider the differences. But I want her for exactly who she is, while Christian wanted her to be someone else. And Christian was cheating on her the entire time and giving her nothing, while I'd give her my entire fucking world if she asked for it.

And doesn't that mean something? Doesn't it make me different from him and every other guy who tried to possess her?

Maybe I'm reconsidering it all now because I'm so fucking desperate to have her back, but I return, again and again, to a thought I wouldn't even allow myself last week: *What if I waited?*

What if I give her all the time she needs to finish college and live out her wild youth, and I just wait, hoping I'm still what she wants when it's through?

ON SATURDAY, I drive to Ocean Hills Country Club for Caleb and Lucie's wedding. I walk toward the venue, looking only for one face. It's the last time I'll see her for months, if not longer... a thought that makes me sick to my stomach, so I try not to think it.

I've got no idea what I'll say to her. It will probably be the wrong thing. I just need to hold it together. I need to get through the day without letting her know how fucked up I am over her, without letting her know I'm going to spend the next couple of years pining for her and praying she doesn't wind up with another guy.

I wave to Caleb, who's being photographed with Lucie's twins. I spy Liam, Beck, Emmy, and Bridget sitting at a table inside the tent, sipping champagne while a wedding coordinator fusses with the flowers at the altar and the string quartet begins tuning their instruments.

And then...Daisy, standing at the edge of the lawn in a strapless, pale yellow dress, so lovely she takes my breath away.

Her gaze, when it locks with mine, is a punch to the gut. I hate the despair in her eyes. *I* did that to her. I'd give up everything I have to explain it, except I'd just end up telling her things I can't say—that I am so in love with her that I'm sick with it. And that I'll be waiting. I'll wait for the rest of my fucking life if necessary.

I walk to the bar for a drink, trying to get a hold of myself. Fuck. If it was anyone else's wedding, I'd feign an emergency and walk out. Instead, I'll get through the ceremony and leave the reception as soon as possible. It's the only way I'm going to survive these hours watching Daisy, looking as destroyed as I feel.

I turn from the bar with a scotch in hand and seek her out again, though I just swore to myself I wouldn't.

Look at me, Daisy. Look at me and be okay this time. Smile and let me know you're not quite as broken as I am.

As if she's heard me, her head rises...just as a hand wraps around my arm. I turn to find Audrey beside me, looking just as she always did—not a hair out of place, wearing diamonds in her ears that could probably pay Daisy's tuition.

She couldn't possibly realize how bad her timing is, but there's a satisfied gleam in her eyes as if she does. "Hi. I was hoping I'd see you before the ceremony. Can we talk?"

My gaze jerks back to Daisy, who is staring at us in horror, the color draining from her face. I know exactly what she's thinking. Christian ended things with her, and she saw him with his fiancée weeks later. I ended things with her and here I am with my ex-wife, who has her hand on my arm as if I belong to her.

"Talk?" I ask. "I don't see that we have anything left to discuss. I don't even know why you're here."

"Lucie and I are friends, obviously," Audrey says. "Look, you're mad, and you have every right to be. I'd be furious in your position. But we were together a long time, and I think we should consider—"

I can't hear a word she's saying, because Daisy is walking off...and there were tears in her eyes before she turned away. I set my drink on a table. "You and I are done. Excuse me." I don't even glance Audrey's way as I break into a jog to catch Daisy, passing Liam and Bridget and knowing I'm grabbing everyone's attention but too worried to care.

Daisy's standing at the top of the hill, overlooking the ocean, with her arms wrapped around her.

She turns as I approach, her eyes wide and full of tears and it finally hits me in full, how badly I've fucked up. Even if seeing me with Audrey wasn't my fault, everything that led to it was.

She needs to know. She needs to know how I feel. She needs to know she's every fucking thing to me in the entire world.

This is the worst possible way to do this, but I don't care as long as Daisy leaves here with the truth. I don't think I could stay away for another minute anyhow. So I storm toward her and I don't stop until she's pressed against me, until I'm cradling her jaw in my hands, and my mouth is on hers in the same way she once showed me in a movie—with the sort of kiss that could get me brought up on assault charges, the kind that says *I want you, I want this, more than I want everything else I have, no matter the consequences.*

"I love you," I say against her mouth. "I love you so fucking much."

She steps back, blinking away tears. "I don't understand."

"I was wrong last week. Or maybe I was right, but I'm too goddamn selfish to give you up. I was so stupid to let you leave like that on Friday without telling you that I adore you, and that every single thing I did was because I love you so much."

A bit of the tension leaves her shoulders, but her eyes remain wary. "So...you're not back together with her?"

I was trying so hard not to make her feel tied down before she left for school, but I hate that she ever could have believed I'd get back with Audrey. My hand rests on her hip. "God, *of course* I'm not with her. I know you're leaving, and I want you to take all the time you need, but if you still want this after you've graduated or however long it takes, I'm—"

"Shit," she gasps, clutching my sleeve. "Harrison..."

I turn to find Liam charging up the hill, his eyes narrowed.

"What in the actual fuck was that?" he snarls, throwing his jacket in the grass. Bridget and Emerson are running up the hill behind him, both of them hampered by their dresses and heels. Emerson kicks hers off in the grass and hitches her dress when Liam starts rolling up his sleeves for a fight.

My jaw locks. He's got a right to be angry, but I'm not going to take it back, and I'm not going to apologize. "I'm in love with her. I didn't intend for it to—"

"Are you fucking kidding me?!" Liam demands. "No. *No*. This isn't fucking happening. You barely know her."

"Liam," Daisy says, stepping alongside me, "we've been together all summer."

He stares at her, his jaw open wide. "Together? You mean hanging out?"

"We were living together," I reply. God, it sounds bad. I fucking deserve whatever is coming. Daisy tries to step in front of me, and I pull her behind my back. "She needed a place to stay, and that's all it was at first."

Bridget rushes to one side of Liam, tugging at his arm, and Emmy's at the other.

"Liam, just calm down," Emmy says. "The wedding's about to begin."

"*At first*," Liam repeats, as if she hasn't spoken. "What the hell does that mean? Because it had better fucking have been platonic *the whole goddamn time*."

"I tried to stay away," I tell him. "I just couldn't do it."

Liam's spine goes ramrod straight. "You *tried* to stay away? You son of a bitch."

I brace myself as his fist flies out, landing square on my jaw.

It's been a while since I've been hit in the face. I'd forgotten how much it fucking hurts.

"Liam, stop!" Daisy screams, jumping in front of me while Caleb and Beck, who apparently sprinted up here, grab Liam from behind.

I rub my jaw. "It's okay. I deserved that. But in the interest of not fucking up Caleb's wedding any more than we already have, save the rest of the punches for later?"

Liam's nostrils flare. "This is insane. You know that, right?" He turns to Daisy. "And you. What the hell were you thinking?"

"Bro," says Beck, as he and Caleb slowly release him, "the fact that Daisy wants him is hardly news."

"I'm sorry," I say again, though it's mostly to Bridget. "I know this is a shock, and it's not what you'd ever want for Daisy. It's not what I'd want for her either, but I love her, and even if she's in DC for the next year and I'm here, that's not going to end things the way I'm sure you're hoping it will."

"Okay," says Bridget. "Everyone just needs to calm down. It's going to be okay."

Daisy and I exchange a look. While neither of us would have expected Bridget to be as violent as her brother, we sure weren't expecting this level of rationality from a woman who still reminds Daisy to brush her teeth.

Liam appears just as stunned as he rounds on his sister. "It's not going to be okay. He's *eleven* years older than she is. She's only been old enough to fucking drink for three months."

Bridget reaches into her purse and hands Daisy a tissue with a nod toward me. Daisy presses it to the lip I didn't even realize was bleeding.

"Daisy's not a kid, Liam," Bridget says with a sigh. "And yes, I'd have preferred that she date people her own age for a while, but she isn't seventeen and pregnant. She isn't dating a really reckless guy with a bunch of mental health issues. She chose the opposite for herself, and she's been in love with him her entire life. Can you honestly say there's anyone you'd rather see her with?"

I blink in surprise, quietly touched. Her vote of confidence was the last thing I'd have expected. Maybe, possibly, this won't turn out to be the disaster I assumed it would be.

Liam's arms fly out wildly in exasperation. "I'd rather see her with fucking anyone! I could go to the local middle school and find guys closer to her age. Fucking hell. Lucie's *son* is probably closer in age."

Lucie's son is seven. But when I do the math, a fourteen-year age difference doesn't sound a lot worse than an eleven-year one.

"Do you *want* to ruin Caleb and Lucie's wedding?" Emmy demands of him. "This is not the time or the place and you need to pull it together."

Liam scowls, but his shoulders drop as if he's a scolded child. If the situation wasn't so serious, I'd probably laugh at how thoroughly she's got him under her thumb when no woman had ever controlled Liam for a moment before her.

"Come on," she continues, tugging his arm to pull him back down the hill. "Anything you still have to say can wait until after."

"I might forgive Daisy," Liam says, as he shoots one more look at me, "but I'm never going to forgive you."

We've been friends since the first day of kindergarten. I hate that it might have ended here, yet I still wouldn't change what's happened.

Bridget rolls her eyes as he walks off with Emmy, Caleb and Beck. "He'll forgive you. But Daisy...God. You could have told me. You *should* have told me."

"You'd have just tried to change my mind, Mom," Daisy argues, "and you'd have told Liam. At some point, you need to trust that I know what makes me happy. And I promise you, it's this."

I wrap my arm around her and she leans against me. It feels so incredibly right that I can't imagine how anyone could see it differently. I can't imagine how I ever questioned it myself.

Bridget's shoulders sag as her gaze flickers between us. "Well, we can discuss it later. But good lord. You could have picked a better way to tell us."

She follows Liam down the hill, leaving Daisy and I alone again—or as alone as we can be with a hundred wedding guests still staring up at us as if we're the pregame show.

She wipes at her eyes. "I'd tell you I love you too, but several people just announced it on my behalf, so it seems redundant at this point."

I laugh as I cradle her face in my palms. "Say it anyway."

She goes onto her toes and kisses me. "I love you," she says. "I have always loved you, for as far back as I can remember and before then too."

I press my lips to her forehead and hold them there for one long, grateful moment before I nod at the crowd. "They're still staring. You'd think they'd have gotten tired of the show by now."

She laughs. "I hope you were ready to debut me as your girlfriend because it's gonna be an awkward reception otherwise."

I squeeze her hand tight. I've been ready for longer than even *I* realized.

I'm ready for her to be more than that, too.

One day, when the time is right, I'm going to give Daisy Doherty the entire world.

47

DAISY

We spend our final week together surfing.

Okay, that's a little inaccurate.

We spend our final week together doing a lot of things, and surfing is among them.

We also jog, bike, and break in the new couch. We break in the new couch *repeatedly*. Baker is livid that Harrison's taken most of the week off, and Harrison doesn't care in the least.

I'll fly back to school the weekend before class starts—my car isn't going to survive the trip, though I only talked Harrison out of buying me a new one by pointing out that DC, a relatively small city, currently averages eight carjackings a day. Now he's quietly fretting about me living there at all, though he tries to control himself. He'll see that it's not so scary once he visits —he already has a ticket booked to see me Labor Day weekend, and the weekend after that too.

I curl up beside him when I get out of the shower. He's on his laptop, looking at rentals in Costa Rica. "What do you think?" he asks, showing me the house. "I know you'll want to see your mom over winter break, but if you don't have to go back 'til the middle of January, we might be able to squeeze a trip in."

I take a deep breath, knowing he's going to argue with what I'm about to say. "Actually, I might be done by then. If I take twenty-one hours this semester, I can graduate in December. I only need a few classes in my major and a few electives, so if I choose easy electives, I can pull it off."

His brow furrows. "Twenty-one hours? It's too much. And I don't want you taking shitty classes and rushing through your degree."

I nestle my head into his chest. "I never wanted this degree. I'm finishing it for my mom's sake—not my own. If it had been left up to me, I think I'd have gone in another direction entirely."

He brushes the hair back from my face. "What direction would you have gone in?"

"I'm still working through it, but...I like to cook. I don't want to work in a restaurant, but I think there are other things I could do. Like some kind of healthy meal catering service or something."

It's not some atmospheric ambition. It's not being an interpreter for the UN or defending political prisoners or even getting an MFA. It's not going to suddenly prove to the world that the Dohertys are smart and ambitious and just as good as everyone else.

But it's something I'd feel good about, something I'd be proud of. I haven't quite gotten there yet, but I can picture a future in which I don't need to impress anyone but myself.

Maybe because I'm already enough for Harrison just as I am.

～

TWO NIGHTS before I leave for DC, I make dinner for us...as well as my mom, Liam, and Emmy.

My mom arrives first, and her eyes are wide as she takes in the house. "Good God," she says, awe in her eyes as she looks around. "No wonder you were so reluctant to come home."

"That wasn't because of the difference in your houses."

She smiles. "I have a feeling I know exactly why you wanted to stay here, but I'm still your mom, so let's pretend it was mostly about the house. And don't allude to any of this when Liam arrives."

He's coming under duress—because I begged him and my mom begged him and mostly because Emerson begged him, though I suspect she didn't actually *beg* but simply told him to grow the fuck up, because that seems like the kind of thing she'd say.

Harrison gets home from work. His smile is slightly forced and awkward as he greets my mom—the transition from being her friend to being her daughter's boyfriend is going to take us all a while. He doesn't kiss me or even touch me until she walks out to the deck, politely claiming she wants to look at the view, though I suspect she's just trying to give us a minute.

When I pull him to me by his tie and kiss him, he groans.

"Promise me you'll behave for the next few hours," he says. "No referencing sex in any way."

"I wasn't likely to reference sex in front of my *mom*, babe."

He laughs quietly, brushing his lips against my own one last time before he steps away. "Just listening to you describe the creaminess of Havarti cheese has gotten me hard, Daisy. The bar is set pretty low."

"I did taste a Gruyere today that—"

"Stop," he pleads. "Seriously. Liam's definitely going to walk in here ready to throw another punch, and I'll probably allow it. So if you want me standing when this is done, you've got to promise you'll be a good girl."

My mouth curves. I'm on the cusp of saying *I'll be such a good girl for you* in a filthy voice before I realize that's the exact kind of shit he's talking about. "I'll do my best."

I carry the pitcher of margaritas I made to the deck, and he follows. I'm just starting to pour the drinks when Liam and Emerson park in front of the house. She's smiling as they climb the stairs.

Liam is not.

Emmy hugs everyone while Liam looks around him with a scowl.

"I guess if you had to be seduced by a predatory old man," he finally says, "this was a decent house to allow it to happen in."

I laugh. "Fuck off."

He gives me the slightest smile. "I'm just saying...you've still got a room at my place, and it's always open. You don't *need* to stay here."

Harrison wraps his arm around me, staking his claim. "She wasn't being held hostage, Liam. And she's not going anywhere."

Liam's nostrils flare. Emmy slides her hand into his as if he's a child who's about to run into the street.

"You still haven't explained how this unfolded," he says, looking from me to Harrison.

I bite my lip as Harrison and I exchange a glance. Those months before I arrived are his to share, not mine. But it sort of feels like it's time.

"You might not be aware of this," Harrison begins, "but your niece is quite the little blackmailer."

Liam's still scowling...but then his mouth softens and an unwilling laugh escapes him. "Yeah. I guess that lines up."

The last of my guilt slips away. I knew their friendship would recover eventually. But that it only took about five minutes makes this feel more perfect than it already did.

48

DAISY

At the end of the week, Harrison drives me to the airport.

He parks and walks me all the way to security. I'm sick to my stomach as he holds me against him to say goodbye. I'll see him next weekend. It's ridiculous that I'm so sad.

"It's only six days," he says.

"Six days," I repeat.

It's still too long, and we both know it.

Late that afternoon, I land at Reagan. It's ninety-nine degrees and a hundred percent humidity. Traffic is snarled the whole way into the city. I don't know why the hell I'm here.

I get to my apartment at last, struggling with my suitcases. Claudia, my roommate, helps me get everything inside and then lowers the boom.

"We've got a bit of a problem," she says. "Helen's still here."

Helen is the girl I sublet my room to in June. She was supposed to have moved out earlier this week, but apparently the house she was renting with friends just got condemned. "She's a nice girl. I told her you and I could share a room until she finds something else since I've got a king-size bed."

"Which you usually share with your boyfriend."

She shrugs. "I'll tell him he can't sleep over."

"I'm not sure I want to sleep in a bed he's been in for *any* reason," I suggest. "Especially if he wasn't here to sleep."

She laughs. "We'll go to his place. It's only for a few weeks."

So I give in, while thinking that going from Harrison's house to *this* is quite the descent.

I already miss his deck. I already miss his bed. I'll miss surfing with him in the morning and the sounds of the ocean as we fall asleep, and thinking about it makes me want to cry because what I really miss is Harrison. The rest...it wasn't even the icing on the cake. He was the whole thing.

I take his call in the stairwell that night because it's the only place I've got any privacy. The ocean roars in the background on his side of the line. "You're sitting on the deck, aren't you?"

"I am. It's surprisingly dull without a scantily clad girl in a beige bra out here attracting attention."

"I miss it."

"I miss you," he replies. Ice crackles in my ear. He's drinking bourbon and probably didn't eat. I hate that, but I'm not much better. I didn't bother to make dinner because I just...hate it here. I hate being away from him. I hate that Helen blasts music whenever she's home. I hate that I'm going to sleep alone tonight, and that it's too muggy to open the windows, and if I *did* sleep with them open, I'd only hear cars honking and drunk guys getting into fights.

I want to go home, and home is California and the ocean, but mostly it's the outdoors and it's him and for the next four months, I'll have none of those things.

"This is making me sad," I whisper. "Tell me about your trip here. Tell me the first thing we'll do."

"I was trying really hard not to turn this conversation sexual, hon."

I laugh. "For once in my life I wasn't trying to turn the conversation sexual since I'm calling you from the stairwell."

"Why the fuck are you in the stairwell?" he demands.

"There's a situation and I don't have a bedroom for the next week or so."

"Go to a hotel," he says. "What's near you? I'll book it right now."

I laugh but I want to cry at the same time as I tell him he doesn't need to fix all my problems, that I'll be fine sleeping on the couch for a while.

We haven't even been apart for one full day, and I'm already not sure how I'm going to survive without him.

THE FIRST DAY of school feels endless by the time it's halfway through. I'm running from seven in the morning until lunch, with several classes to come in the afternoon so I rush home, planning to eat something and collapse on the couch for an hour.

But the relief I expected to feel when I near my building never comes.

Christian is here.

Standing on the sidewalk with his arm folded, obviously waiting for me...so someone gave him my schedule.

I stumble to a halt, more shocked than scared. I assumed he wouldn't stay in DC during his leave of absence—a leave of absence I set into motion.

He holds out a hand as if *I'm* the one who needs to be warded off. "I just want to talk."

I have no reason to be scared of him—it's not as if he was ever violent. But I also never thought he'd become a guy who'd wait outside my building to confront me. I grip the strap of my backpack as I look around. We're on a busy street, but that doesn't mean much. I've seen women getting harassed here and not a single person intervened.

"The time for talking was last fall," I tell him.

"Do you have no remorse whatsoever, Daisy?" he snaps. "Do you realize how bad you made me look?"

Christian is skilled at controlling the narrative—it's what he does for a living. And when he lashed out at me last winter—accusing me of being a gold digger, of being useless and *low rent*, I took every word he said as if it were canon.

But now I listen to him the way Harrison would. And Harrison would be fucking livid that Christian has the gall to demand remorse from me. That he has the gall to demand *anything*. "So…it made you look bad when I told the school that you, a *professor*, slept with his student and lied about his girlfriend? That part? Or the part where you found out I was pregnant and called me a gold digger?"

"It was consensual," he says. "I didn't have to talk you into a goddamn thing."

"I never said it wasn't." I look around me again. I can't reach my building without passing him. If I just went back to campus, would he follow? I'm shaking so badly I don't even trust that I can get the keycard out of my backpack to open the door anyway.

"So, if we're in agreement, why the fuck would you file a complaint?" he asks. "I seriously doubt they're even going to let me come back. My fiancée left me over this bullshit! Do you not care about that at all?"

I fold my arms across my chest and tuck my shaking hands beneath each elbow to control the motion. "Christian, did she leave you because I told, or did she leave you because you cheated?"

"They're the same thing."

"They're really not." I'm proud of the steel in my voice. Someone listening in might not realize I'm absolutely shitting myself here. "One of us lied to two different women—one of whom he had a great deal of power over—and cheated on *both* of them. That was you. One of us simply came forward and told the truth. Spin it however you want, but you're never going to convince me that I'm the guilty party."

"You stupid little bitch," he says. "I should have known you were too fucking dumb for an adult relationship."

I've heard enough. He's lashing out because yes, he's unlikely to get rehired, and his books don't sell enough to support him, and his fiancée left. But I didn't make those choices—he did.

I pull out my phone. "You need to leave. *Now*."

"Or what, Daisy? You'll tell on me? You'll ruin my career? You'll destroy my relationship? You already did all of that."

"I'll call my lawyer," I reply, my voice trembling. "He wanted me to sue for damages. And the first thing he'll do is tell me to call the cops, which will then become part of the university's record. Is that what you'd like?"

"Are you serious right now?" Christian shouts. "I'm not threatening you! I just wanted to have a conversation."

"You had your conversation, asshole," I reply. "Now start walking or I call."

"Fucking bitch," he mutters as he walks away. If the incident wasn't so upsetting, I'd probably love that I got to see him suffering his comeuppance firsthand.

I wait until he's gone before I turn toward the building. I'm so shaken that my hands won't work right, that my arms are barely capable of opening the door or hitting the elevator button.

I walk straight to the couch, unable to eat. And just as I stretch out, my phone buzzes.

Harrison is calling over video. I don't want him to see me the way I currently am, but he'll worry if I don't answer.

"Hey, hon," he says, crossing his office to shut the door,

tugging at his tie. "Is this a good time? You said you had a break between...wait, what's wrong?"

I force a smile. "Nothing."

I search for a joke I can make, a question I can ask.

But I burst into tears instead. "Christian was waiting outside when I walked up to the building. I don't even know why I'm crying. It just freaked me out."

"Call the cops, Daisy," he hisses.

I shake my head, brushing the tears away. "He wasn't threatening me. He just wanted to talk."

"He's under investigation in a case you brought forward, and showing up at your home is blatant intimidation. You need it documented."

I press a hand to my face, wishing I hadn't told him. Is he right? Undoubtedly. But it's all too much right now. With the course load I'm taking and the current living situation, it's just too much. And I'd planned to study late at the library but I'm going to be too scared to walk back alone in the dark after what happened. "Harrison, I see your point. I do. But I've got three more classes today and a ton of reading for tomorrow, and there just isn't even time right now, okay? I threatened to call my lawyer, so he walked away. I don't have time today. I really don't." I burst into tears again. What's really getting to me is being here, away from all the things I love. Mostly, it's being away from him.

"I'm sorry," I whisper. "I'm just exhausted. Not having my own room is a mess and I don't know how I'm going to study and..." I swallow to keep myself from saying "*I miss you.*"

His jaw grinds. He's going to argue, and I'll end up missing all my classes while I talk to the police.

He runs a hand over his weary face. "Okay."

I'm so surprised that I laugh, though it comes as a sob. "Wow, that was incredibly easy."

"I'm still going to push you on this, but we'll discuss it later, okay?" he says, his voice gentle. "Right now, you need to eat something and get back to class."

"I find it suspicious that you've suddenly become so reasonable."

"Don't get used to it. I'm only being reasonable because I want you home by December," he replies. "Go eat. I'll talk to you tonight."

We hang up, and I force myself to down some crackers and head back to campus, looking over my shoulder the whole time. It's not that I think Christian will do something to me. I'm just not ready to weather another round of accusations.

I somehow get through my next three classes and return to the apartment determined to get through my reading, though all I want to do is sleep. Except Helen is blasting death metal while she does some cardio workout on the TV and Claudia's got a scrunchie on the door, which means she's in there with her boyfriend so I *can't* study and I *can't* sleep. I'm too fucking nervous to even go for a walk. The only reason I don't call Harrison is because if he sees how despondent I am he'll probably try to come solve this for me. I don't want him to start feeling as if he's my parent rather than my boyfriend.

Eventually Helen goes to her room, but Claudia shows no sign of emerging from ours. I do my best to study and wonder why the hell Harrison hasn't called like he said he would.

> Hey, you've been quiet. Are you still at work?

HARRISON

> I'm going to call you. Give me thirty?

By ten, I'm exhausted. Harrison hasn't called, and Claudia and her boyfriend haven't opened the bedroom door, which means that I can't even pee or brush my teeth. I give up and shut out the lights, using my sweatshirt as a pillow.

Months after I went to Harrison's house intending to sleep on his deck, I'm back to feeling homeless.

> HARRISON
> Are you still up?

> Yes. Are you home?

Instead of texting me, he calls. "Hey," I whisper.

"Please tell me you're not sleeping on the couch," he growls.

If he realized that the alternative was sleeping in a bed my roommate just had sex in, he probably wouldn't be so appalled. Unless he was even more appalled. "The situation is a little fucked up at the moment. I'll figure it out."

"*We'll* figure it out," he says. "I'm outside. Let me up."

It takes me a very long second to understand what he's saying. And then I shriek so loudly that Claudia finally rouses and opens our door. I ignore her as I run out of the apartment, taking the stairs when the elevator doesn't arrive fast enough. I burst out the building's front door and leap at him, whole for the first time since I left California.

He laughs at my enthusiasm. And then he kisses me hard, and thoroughly, so it's a full minute before I can even ask him how this unfolded.

"You flew all the way out here to discuss this?" I finally manage to ask. "That's insane, even for you."

"No," he says, setting me down. "I flew all the way out here because I don't want to be where you're not."

Huh? "But...you're supposed to be coming over the weekend. Are you going to be able to take time off until—"

"I'm not going back," he says. "It's just not going to work, being away from you, even if it means living in DC for the next five months. But I'm not sleeping on a fucking couch."

I press my face to his chest. "You can't do that. What about your job?"

His hand runs over my back, and his laughter is quiet against my ear. "I must have forgotten to mention this, Daisy, but I'm pretty fucking rich. *Artisanal honey* rich, even."

"But—"

"I hated that job, and more importantly, I hated being away from you," he says. "You spent the whole summer taking care of me. Now it's my turn."

I throw my arms around him, and he's once again forced to support my weight while I press my lips to his neck, tears running freely down my face the entire time. It's not that he's going to take care of me. It's that he *wants* to. And there's no one I want to entrust that role to more than him.

We go upstairs. He has me pack an overnight bag, though Claudia sheepishly offers to let us have the room since her boyfriend is now leaving. The look on Harrison's face is exactly what you'd expect when a very wealthy adult is told he can sleep in a filthy bed someone just had sex in.

"We're staying in a hotel, thanks," he says, making no attempt to hide his disdain.

He ushers me into an Uber. "I'm going to talk to the police in the morning," he says, "and then I'm going to find us an apartment. Is that okay?"

I nod. It's better than okay. I nestle against his chest and breathe him in, grateful to be home at last.

EPILOGUE

JANUARY, 2024

The cottage we've rented in the south of Costa Rica sits right on the beach, under the shade of palm trees. The water is as warm as he promised. There's no need for wetsuits, no need to brace yourself before you venture out.

The tide came in a little late today, and we surfed for longer than we should have. The sand is brutally hot by the time we emerge, the sun so strong that it will melt the wax off our boards in minutes if we dump them on the beach. So we run—awkward with a seven-foot board under your arm—laughing at our own cries of pain.

Once we've showered, I'll experiment with smoothie bowls, and he'll do some work for Emerson's boss, who's dying for him to come aboard full-time. And then we'll surf again and eat dinner on our deck before we retire for the night. With the ocean breeze whipping in through the windows, we'll talk about our future the way we once spoke about the trip we're currently on, as if we're simply daydreaming, though we're not.

It's in no way what my mother hoped to see me doing at this stage in my life. Even at my graduation dinner, she was still trying to talk us out of this trip—there's some company in San Francisco that will pay for you to get your MBA at night, apparently, and she thought it was perfect for me.

Even though I've got no interest in an MBA *or* an office job *or* San Francisco.

Harrison squeezed my hand beneath the table as my mom talked, and though I appreciated the moral support, I no longer needed it. We'd lived together for the better part of eight months by then, which meant I'd had eight full months of someone I respected saying it was okay for me to be exactly who I am: a woman who loves to cook and surf, who needs sunlight and the outdoors the way someone else needs oxygen and sleep.

I could wind up with a big life or a small life, but the important thing is that it'll be a life *I* choose. And for now, we've chosen this: a year away from it all. A year for us both to stop leading the kind of lives that didn't make us happy while we figure out what we want instead.

When we leave here in a month, we'll head to Cabo for the late March swell, with stops in El Salvador and Panama on the way. From there, we'll go to the North Shore, renting a house next to Harrison's friend Luke—Liam's planning to join us for a week—after which we'll meet his brothers in Portugal to surf in Nazaré before moving onto the final leg of our trip: two months in Bali.

I'm looking forward to it all. I'm looking forward to what happens after we get home just as much, though I'm not sure what or where that will be. He talks about opening his own firm. I talk about opening a smoothie bowl place, though it's possible the things I want will be simpler.

I want Harrison. I want to surf for as long as I'm able to. I want to rinse our sandy babies off at the end of a long day, and I want those days to consist of the best parts of his childhood and mine: fresh air, sunshine, freedom, a surfboard stable underfoot for the first time.

He's insisting we wait for that, though he wants it even more than I do. *Years*, he said a few months ago. "Enjoy your twenties. We have all the time in the world."

But I don't want to wait. The future he wants so badly for himself is the precise one I want too, once this year of travel is over.

I lazily lean my surfboard against the side of the house and head to the outdoor shower. He dutifully remains behind to rinse the sand from his board and mine. I guess some habits—my laziness, his responsibility—can't be changed overnight.

"Hon?" I call over the spray of the shower.

He cuts the hose and opens the shower door. "Did you need something?"

I pull the tie to my bikini loose and swing it off my index finger. "I do, actually. I just thought we should conserve water. To keep the bills down. I'm trying to be responsible."

He grins as he steps inside the shower and pulls me against him. Wet skin to wet skin. He's already hard. "The day I see you worried about saving money is the day I start to question everything."

I reach between us, pushing his trunks down, fisting him. "You've got loads of it. And you never tell me no."

He kisses me, his lips soft, still flecked with sand. "Everything I have is yours, Daisy," he says, his fingers tugging at the ties on my bikini bottoms. "Every fucking thing."

I already know this. Except all I actually want is him, and I already have that.

He lifts one of my thighs around his waist and pushes inside me with a hiss of pleasure.

"You should probably propose one of these days." My voice is breathless as he moves in and out. "Just to make it official."

He already has the ring. Oliver told me it's hidden somewhere in the house, and that Harrison is refusing to propose yet because he wants me to have my youth. I've looked for it everywhere to no avail.

"*Fuck*," he says, his body coiling tight. He is possibly the only man alive for whom talk of marriage is *foreplay*. If I told him I've already looked at churches in Portugal, he'd definitely blow his load.

"You'd want that?" he demands, holding me against the shower wall for leverage, pushing hard inside me. "You really think you're ready?"

His breath is short. He's already close.

"I do. I'm ready." I gasp as he pinches my nipple. His free hand slides between us and circles my clit. "Just like that. Don't stop."

His jaw clenches. "We should give it a year or two, until you know what you want."

He hits something inside me and the world explodes. My eyes are still closed as he jerks inside me, his teeth in that favorite spot of his, right on my shoulder.

"I've known what I wanted since I was three years old," I whisper. "Everything else is icing."

He gave me this life. He made me realize that it's okay to want the things I want, that I don't need to live anyone's dream but my own. He gave me *him*.

But that ring he's got hidden? Those babies he wants me to carry?

I'm more than happy for him to give me those too. The sooner the better.

ACKNOWLEDGMENTS

Sometimes you struggle with a book and want a bunch of people to help you figure out what's wrong with it. And sometimes you love a book and know that you'll fly into a sociopathic rage if anyone suggests you change a single word. This book was the latter—I loved Daisy and Harrison and their story just as it was, and I guarded it like nuclear launch codes for half a year, showing it to very few people.

Thanks to my editing team: Sali Benbow-Powers, Lauren McKellar, Christine Estevez and Michelle Chen, as well as a small handful of beta readers—Maren Channer, Katie Friend, Katie Meyer and Jen Owens—pretty much all the people who read Liam's story and said "OMG is the next one going to be age gap?!" Thank you all for loving my babies as much as I did. I couldn't have lived with any other outcome.

Thanks to everyone who takes care of stuff I would be terrible at: my agent, Kimberly Brower; my assistant Christine Estevez and the teams at Piatkus and Valentine PR.

Thanks to my author buds for keeping me sane...Laura Pavlov in particular for stepping in to blow dry my hair :-). And finally, a shout-out to the whole crew at Kalon Surf and the amazing people I met there. My board hit each of you in the head at least once, but it inspired a book so I think we can all agree it was worth it.

Can't get enough of the Summer Series?

Go back to the beginning and meet Luke and Juliet.

Turn the page for the first chapter of *The Summer We Fell*.

He might not be the devil, but working under him for six weeks is my idea of hell.

Meet the temp assistant and the British boss she loves to hate ...

Available now.

PIATKUS

Do you love contemporary romance?

Want the chance to hear news about your favourite authors (and the chance to win free books)?

Kristen Ashley
Ashley Herring Blake
Meg Cabot
Olivia Dade
Rosie Danan
J. Daniels
Farah Heron
Talia Hibbert
Sarah Hogle
Helena Hunting
Abby Jimenez
Elle Kennedy
Christina Lauren
Alisha Rai
Sally Thorne
Lacie Waldon
Denise Williams
Meryl Wilsner
Samantha Young

Then visit the Piatkus website
www.yourswithlove.co.uk

And follow us on Facebook and Instagram
www.facebook.com/yourswithlovex | @yourswithlovex

PIATKUS